PLANET OF DINOSAURS

PLANET OF DINOSAURS

K.H. KOEHLER

The Monster Factory

CONTENTS

Author's Note — xv

I
PLANET OF DINOSAURS

1	2
2	9
3	11
4	18
5	21
6	30
7	36

8	41
9	49
10	52
11	56
12	65
13	71
14	74
15	79
16	84
17	86
18	90
19	93

20	97
21	101
22	104

II
SEA OF SERPENTS

23	108
24	111
25	113
26	116
27	123
28	125
29	132
30	135

31	141
32	147
33	152
34	156
35	161
36	167
37	174
38	178
39	180
40	183
41	185
42	189

43	194
44	196
45	201
46	204
47	208
48	213
49	218

III
VALLEY OF DRAGONS

50	222
51	226
52	230
53	236

XII - CONTENTS

54	244
55	254
56	258
57	262
58	267
59	271
60	273
61	275
62	279
63	282
64	287
65	289

66	291
67	293
68	297
69	299
70	305
71	307
72	309
73	311
74	317
75	321
76	323
77	325

| 78 | 331 |

About the Author 339

AUTHOR'S NOTE

This story is fiction, but the paleontology I've written into the story is real. For instance, the Ceratosaurus was considered an apex predator of its day, during earth's late Jurassic Period. Closely related to the more well known Allosaurus, the creature's fossil record was first discovered in Utah and Colorado in 1884, so Sasha Strange's extensive dinosaur knowledge isn't just a quirk of plot. She really would have known these things, since dinosaurs were exciting and fashionable scientific finds during the late Victorian Period when Sasha lived. It's entirely possible that she would have been exposed to all kinds of information if she read science periodicals, which I made sure she did.

At the time, the Ceratosaurus was a new discovery and a very interesting dinosaur in its own right. I can easily see Sasha learning about these "Colonial" dinosaurs and discussing them with Dr. Ulysses in their letters. Of course, the Victorians' idea of dinosaur body structure was vastly different from our more accurate modern findings. For one thing, Victorians believed that most or all dinosaurs walked on four legs regardless of species, like modern-day crocodiles and lizards. This concept was eventually corrected to depict predators and certain species of herbivores walking in the upright bipedal manner that we know today.

I've loved, and will always love, dinosaur movies, everything from *The Lost World* from 1925 up to the modern *Jurassic Park* movies and beyond. But for the most part, the writers of these books and films were out to create fantasy and entertainment, not to educate on real dinosaur science, and although they're fun to watch, most of the dinosaurs depicted in popular films did not live on the same continent together or, indeed, even in the same eras. I've attempted to create a menagerie of dinosaur species that might conceivably have existed in the same ecology together. Indeed, Sasha's World is not Earth, but rather a place much younger than our Earth, but similar environments bring about similar species. If you were somehow able to visit the late Jurassic Period, about

XVI - AUTHOR'S NOTE

forty million years ago, you would have seen such ship-sized land-walkers as Brachiosaurus and Diplodocus, armored tank-like animals like Stegosaurus, and, of course, the many species and subspecies of Allosaurus, of which Ceratosaurus is a distant cousin. Other animals, like the crocodile and the early forms of birds, also began to appear during this period, as well as small mammals, all poised to take over Planet Earth when the Great Extinction began.

A creature like Newton might also have existed, though Newton is no specific species of mammal. I simply chose several properties that I thought would make Newton interesting and well adapted to life on the Planet of Dinosaurs. The Sen, of course, are completely fictitious.

The only times I intentionally threw scientific fact to the wind was in depicting the sea scorpion that Quinn catches, a creature that died out during the Triassic period, and the herd of aggressive Styracosaurus that Sasha and Quinn witness on their journey back to the Sen's mountain. These spiky herbivores lived during the Cretaceous Period, and yes, I should know better and do. But I love sea scorpions and Styracosaurus, and though I knew better, like so many filmmakers, I simply didn't care!

Join Sasha, her men, and me as they encounter different dinosaurs, terrifying marine reptiles, and even some proto-humans. Love will be tested, won, and lost, and a beloved companion lost to the Planet of Dinosaurs.

I promise it will be amazing.

—K.H. Koehler
6/16/2011
revised
5/24/2020

I

PLANET OF DINOSAURS

In which our heroes are swept away.

| 1 |

London, 1889

"Sasha, I really must insist that you come out at once and stop acting like a child!" Lord Albertus Strange stated in a severe voice—or as severe as he was capable of, with regards to his only child.

"I am not acting like a child. And I am *not* coming out!" Sasha Strange insisted from behind the closed door of her bedchamber.

She paced across the vast expanse of hardwood floor in her fine white debutante dress and white satin slippers, turned on her heel when she reached her equally white, four-poster bed, then started back across the room, trying to find a way out of her predicament. She had to think fast. Only one hour ago, during supper, her father had stood up amidst the diners at their table, tapped his water glass with a silver knife for silence, and announced his daughter's engagement to the odious Lord Sirius Quinn. Everyone at dinner had been shocked at the news, including Sasha herself. Like them, this had been the first she was hearing of the engagement.

"Sasha!"

Sasha stopped at the locked door, facing it soundly. She clenched her little white-gloved fists at her sides, took a deep, trembling breath, and said, "Father, I will not be marrying Lord Quinn! He drinks, he gambles...and...and he's a terrible boor!"

"Sasha, be reasonable, girl! You are *nineteen* years old. Do you want to become an old spinster like your Aunt Margaret?"

"Aunt Margaret raises horses and is quite happy in the country."

"Aunt Margaret is a scandal. And I will *not* have my daughter lollygagging about with horse manure on her boots. Now open the bloody door!"

Sasha gasped. It was the first time she'd heard her father use such foul language! She took a deep breath, steeled herself, and opened the door. Maybe, she thought, she could make her father see reason if he realized how this arrangement distressed her. Sasha was not above a little manipulation, especially when it was her future on the line.

But the moment she cracked the door open, Lord Strange saw his chance. He stuck his foot into it and nudged it all the way open, glaring down at his daughter with disapproval. Sasha was not moved by her father's bluster, though he was a large, robust man and could easily swing her over his shoulder and carry her downstairs if he was so inclined. He stood an inch shy of six feet and filled out his suits very well. He was deeply tanned despite the sunless London weather and his ears were bright red. He had steely hair, long sideburns, and a well-trimmed mustache. He liked riding and hunting. In his time, he had made many a young lass blush, including her mother. Back then, he'd had a reputation as something of a rake, though Sasha found that very difficult to believe, considering how stern he was.

Sasha, on the other hand, was willowy and pale, small for her age, though very strong. Many summers riding horses at Aunt Margaret's stables had seen to that. Her mother had often said she resembled a little Dresden doll, her ceramic white skin made whiter still by the dark ringlets that framed it, her slightly upslanted eyes huge and dark and contemplative. When Sasha was seven years old, she'd caught the consumption. Her mother and father, understandably concerned for her health, had sent her to a sanatorium in the South of Wales. The doctors there had been very talented, and the air good, and within a year she had made a full recovery and had returned home. By that time, however, her mother had fallen ill to the same sickness and passed on. Sasha had left home ill and returned fit but motherless.

Her father had seen to it that Sasha's childhood from then on had been sheltered and rigorously controlled. He hadn't allowed her to attend finishing school or academy like other girls for fear she might strain herself unnecessarily. Instead, he'd given her tutors and trainers and his vast library of books. For many years, she'd been locked away in the Strange Manor like some princess in a tower in a fairy story, with only a once-yearly retreat to her Aunt Margaret's horse farm in Lancashire for physical activity.

She'd had her books, but little else in the way of human contact. And as she grew from a willowy child into a sturdy young woman, she most certainly had no suitors. Yet despite these things, it had not been a bad childhood. Her father was protective but loving, his books her best friends and playmates. Sasha had read all of them at least twice. She liked books by Charlotte Bronte and Jane Austen, of course, as other young women her age did, but she adored books of science and romance—Jules Verne and H. G. Wells, in particular.

Her curiosity grew, and she began wondering about the viability of the machines theorized in fiction by Mr. Verne and Mr. Wells. Her father indulged her, of course, and this Sasha took full advantage of. Armed with her father's extensive coffers, she began designing several curious devices in the conservatory, the only room in the house large enough to contain the steam machines necessary to carry out her experiments in sound waves and electricity. Once, she'd managed to light the entire manor house on electric lights for one whole day, though that was the exception, rather than the rule. For the most part, Sasha's experiments had not been very successful.

There were few people at the house that she could discuss her interests with, but many science journals available, and it was through one such magazine advertising for pen pals that she became acquainted with an American scientist named Dr. John Ulysses of the University at Cornell, a new and very excitingly academy in the United States. Unlike so many others who dismissed her wild theories, John took an interest in her admittedly amateurish work in sound waves and mechanics. He was trying to invent a practical power generator. Together, via letters sent overseas, they both slowly began work on what John called a Tuning Machine—she at Strange Manor, he had University. John hoped that he might one day create an unlimited source of energy using high-frequency oscillations.

By this time, Sasha had turned eighteen years old, and her father was becoming increasingly worried that she was too cloistered for her own good. He admitted to making a grave error in isolating his headstrong daydreamer of a daughter and made a great effort in throwing debutante parties in the hopes that Sasha might find a viable suitor. Unfortunately, most of the young gentry who attended these lavish parties found her much too...well, strange to be of interest. They did not understand her talk of Tesla coils and Electromagnetic motors or her admiration for such things as deep-sea submarines and time machines. They were appalled by her demands for a full library of books and a laboratory to experiment in. One curious young suitor played with her steam-powered electric machine and was shocked nearly to death, coming out of it with a full head of white hair. All and sundry slipped quietly out the door and scurried to their carriages, never to be seen again.

A desperate Lord Strange began looking toward older gentlemen for a decent match for his daughter. He knew a small number of available lords who, if not young and virile, were at least steadfast, strong-willed, and of a proper status for Sasha. But each of these Sasha stalwartly rejected. Lord Pemberton was much too old (fifty, at least!), Marquis Bonnevet was French and did not bathe at all, and Count Drogo of Romania couldn't speak a lick of English.

Finally, at wit's end, Lord Strange invited his old friend Lord Sirius Quinn to the latest in the long line of what was becoming colloquially known in polite society as "Sasha Parties"—a term many unmarried English and European men of status regarded with fear and dread. Sasha anticipated the usual farce, of course. Her father would introduce the two of them, highlight Sasha's beauty and finer talents, and see what interest the middle-aged Lord Quinn might take in his daughter. Sasha, for her own part, would remain polite but aloof. They would dine, speak of trivial things, and Lord Quinn would leave scorched like the others.

She had not anticipated a wedding announcement over roast beef and red potatoes!

"I simply *cannot* marry Lord Quinn," Sasha stated, then turned to march across the room to her bed. She dropped down, her skirts mushrooming out about her, and took her favorite doll Elizabeth into her arms. Newton stirred on her pillow, stretched, and bumped his head against her hand. She petted the orange tomcat, holding him and Elizabeth against her like shields that might protect her from her father's ridiculous machinations.

Lord Strange sighed wearily. He stood with his hands braced against the casting of Sasha's door as if he might rip the whole house down upon them like Sampson pulling down the temple in the Bible story. "I assure you the stories you've heard about Quinn are *greatly* exaggerated by the press."

Sasha raised an eyebrow at that. "Papa, ever since you announced his imminent arrival, I've been reading the *Times quite* studiously. Lord Quinn has been taken into custody by the police at least twice for drunken behavior and once for assault! What kind of husband is that for your daughter?"

Lord Strange looked uncomfortable. "Lord Quinn is a very…complicated man."

"I'll say!"

Lord Sirius Quinn was tall and as thin as a snake, with terrible reddish eyes and even redder hair and a perpetually unsmiling face. He looked like Lucifer himself! According to the paper, his fortune was in jeopardy due to his drunken behavior and bad gambling habits. He was nothing more than a gold-digger hoping to seize the Strange fortune for his own dubious needs! She thought about bringing this up as well, but her father looked so hurt and desperate, Sasha felt her throat close up and her heartbreak at the sight of him. For once, he didn't look very strong or robust, and she realized he was a hunched old man deeply afraid for her future.

"Sasha, my darling," he said, stepping toward her and pitching his voice as reasonable as possible, "you must realize I won't live forever." He took her tiny hand in his much larger one. "If something were to befall me, what then would become of you, my darling?"

Sasha thought about that. Her Aunt Margaret was old and not in good health these days, so the farm was no refuge, should she find herself alone. And she had no other family. Well, there was her Uncle Mycroft, her father's brother, whom she hadn't seen since she was a child. But her father and Uncle Mycroft were estranged. According to her father, Uncle Mycroft had an unnatural predilection for indecently young women. Her father's death would spur Uncle Mycroft to seize Strange Manor, and as a young, unmarried woman, Sasha would have little holdings on it. In fact, she'd likely become his ward, and she shuddered at the idea of sharing a house with such a lecherous old man.

    She held Elizabeth close for a moment before standing up. She made a decision then, something reasonable, something to placate her well-meaning father, if not her own heart, which would forever belong to Mr. Verne and Mr. Wells. "I will spend half an hour in the drawing room with Lord Quinn, but no more," she announced. "After that, he absolutely *must* leave. I shall do my best to consider him a viable candidate for a husband. But if he proves himself unsuitable, you absolutely must break the engagement."

    "But if you reject him like all the others, my darling, will you consider further candidates of my choosing?" He stroked her hand.

    Sasha bowed her head and hugged her doll close. "All I can promise is that I shall do my best to be fair to Lord Quinn."

| 2 |

Sasha went cautiously down to the drawing room where Lord Sirius Quinn waited to court her. She opened the great oaken double doors, stepped inside...and struggled to suppress a shudder.

Quinn was tall and rangy, nothing like the dashing suitors in the books she had read. He slouched in his chair, face pale and freckly and remote as he stared into the hearth, a glass of her father's finest whiskey in one hand. His unfashionably ginger hair was mussed as if he'd been running his hands through it, and he was dressed in a black mourning suit that suited him rather well. *Villains always wear black,* she thought to herself as she stepped into the room and curtseyed properly to the lord. Even his name was appropriate, Sirius from Osiris, the Egyptian god of the underworld. She forced a smile.

Lord Quinn looked up, regarding her with watery blue eyes rimmed by dull crimson haloes before forcing himself to stand. He gave her a courtly, if empty, nod. "Sasha." He sounded bored to pieces.

"Lord Quinn," she said and extended her gloved hand.

He looked at it as if it were a snake that might bite him, dutifully took it, kissed it, and led her to the opposing wing chairs by the hearth. Her father joined them after a few moments and they all sat together in a civilized manner and took refreshments. Her father had his nightly brandy, Lord Quinn had his whiskey, and Sasha took tea. They sat in unbroken silence while the drawing room clock ticked solemn ticks and solemn tocks. Her father lit a cigar. Lord Quinn took more whiskey. Sasha shifted uncomfortably in her seat, picked up her petit point from the basket next to her chair, and did a few stitches, not very well. Lord Quinn politely inquired about her interests, and Sasha explained about the Tuning Machine that she had built in the conservatory, making her father cringe back in his seat as if blows were falling upon him. Lord Quinn seemed unperturbed, disinterested. He did not ask to see it.

Finally, her father could take no more of this. "I think you'll be very happy together," he announced. "I think you will make a fine couple and will be good for each other."

"I'm sure we shall," Sasha agreed, not very enthusiastically, and snapped the thread she was sewing with her teeth, making her father cringe even more. She might have pointed out that he had nothing to fear; Lord Quinn had long since passed out in his seat. Newton took that moment to wend his way into the drawing room. Sasha jumped up. "I should take Newton into the kitchen and see if Cook has any scraps for him. It was good meeting you, Lord Quinn." She curtseyed respectfully.

Lord Quinn snored rather dramatically.

Sasha carried the cat away, Newton hanging over her shoulder and hissing at the sleeping lord.

| 3 |

How bad could marriage to Lord Quinn be?

Sasha sat at the table in the pantry where Cook normally prepared their meals and watched Newton lick up his milk from a bowl on the floor. She would marry Lord Quinn to please her father and protect herself from Uncle Mycroft, and she'd likely never have to see him. He'd be too busy cavorting every night at gambling halls and pubs. It might even work to her advantage. She could work on her experiments and never experience a distraction. She could read her beloved books all night and never see her husband. Except...well...

"I don't *want* to marry Lord Quinn, Newton. I don't want to marry anyone."

Well, that wasn't *strictly* true. When she thought of marriage—not practical marriage, but fairy-tale marriage, the kinds of marriages that really *ought* to happen to young women—the image of the husband that came to mind was Toby Hallowman, their stableman.

They'd practically grown up together, Toby having come to them as a boy of seven from a nearby workhouse. He'd been thin and sallow back then. Now he was twenty-one, and tall and lean and muscular, with brown hair that fell in a froth over his brow and a permanent summer tan and the most amazing brown eyes.

What's more, he was good to the horses, always making certain the mares she rode in the frosty early morning were in good spirits before lacing his fingers together and bumping her up into her saddle. Her father's carriage horses never bore whip marks like so many other lords' horses, and every resident of their stable was properly shoed and groomed every day, even when it rained. Toby loved the horses.

Galvanized by such thoughts, Sasha jumped up and ran for the courtyard door. The lights in the stables were still burning, which meant Toby was still there. He hadn't gone into London for the night, thank goodness. She needed to see him, needed to talk to someone she understood. Lifting her skirts, she scuffled across the pavilion to the stables and ducked inside, where he'd thoughtfully hung a long line of lanterns on hooks. Toby always kept the stables properly lit in the event she came visiting unexpectedly.

Toby sat on an overturned bucket with his broad back to her, carefully oiling a harness.

"Toby," she said, "the most horrible man is here. Have you seen?"

Toby immediately stood up and turned to face her. His entire face lit up with a lopsided smile. "You mean Lord Quinn."

"Yes," she said, wrinkling up her nose. "He's as pale as a Morlock and as heartless as Captain Nemo."

"You and your books." Toby shook his head and grinned as his eyes took in the full sight of her still dressed in her debutante dress. He had read many of the same books as Sasha. In fact, Jules Verne had brought them together in the first place. One of the first things Sasha did was teach him to read, starting with *Twenty-thousand Leagues Under the Sea*. Since then, she'd shared book after book with Toby. Right now, they were sharing *Moby Dick*. Toby was smart, understood the concepts and devices in the books they read and was always happy to help her with an invention. If she could have chosen anyone to marry, she would have chosen Toby in a heartbeat, though of course she knew her father would never approve such an arrangement. Toby had no status.

"I wish I was more like you, Toby," she mused, watching him hang the shining harness on a hook near the ceiling among the other tack.

Toby shrugged his broad shoulders. "No, you don't."

"I do! If my Papa wasn't a lord, I could marry anyone I wanted." She didn't know if that was strictly true, but there had to be more freedom away from the gentry. "We could even marry, and then you could be my assistant in the laboratory."

Toby laughed at the fantasy and turned around. "I'll be your assistant, even after you marry. You know I'm forever at your service, Sasha." He said it solemnly, with a deep bow, a kiss of her hand, and a big grin that was so infectious it had her smiling in return, even though she was in a positively *un*smiling mood.

She thought about his offer. "Will you come now? I'd like to show you the Tuning Machine."

Toby glanced at the oil lamps on the walls. He could always tell what time it was by how much oil remained in them. "It's rather late, Sasha."

"Just for a few minutes! After this terrible day, I'll never get to sleep. And it's already done. I want you to be the first to see it!"

"I can't resist you, Sasha," he said as she took his hand.

They raced each other back inside and up the stairs to the third floor of the manor where her father's conservatory was located. It was a huge space with a glass ceiling, set up long ago with an array of telescopes. Her mother had once had an intense interest in astronomy. But now a great deal of the space was filled with Sasha's notebooks, workbench, and experimental devices, many of which stood dusty in dark corners, a testament to Sasha's learning curve when she first embarked on becoming an inventor.

In the center of the room squatted the enormous Tuning Machine, which she had finished only a few short days ago. Much of it had been constructed with a combination of organ parts, a printing press, a typewriting machine, plus several odds and ends mostly borrowed from the manor. Attached to the machine via wires were two great Tesla coils that Sasha had redesigned to emit not electricity but sound. Once the Tuning Machine was cranked up and running, it was possible to encourage the two orbs atop the Tesla coils to produce songs and images by running one's fingers over them. The idea of high-frequency sound waves to generate power had been John's theory, though much of the design of the machine belonged to Sasha. John had a similarly constructed machine in America, and Sasha wondered if it was possible for John's machine could generate such a wide variety of images.

She had no idea where the images came from. She was still exploring the mystery of it, but she hoped to share her findings with John in her next letter.

Sasha explained the function of the machine to Toby as he circled it, touching the chimerical design on all sides. With Toby as her audience, Sasha began cranking the giant clockwork wheel. Once she had it at a sufficient speed, it would run on centrifugal force for more than an hour. She positioned herself before the two Tesla coils and extended her hands, her fingertips just touching the orbs. As always, she felt a rush of excitement as the machine powered up, its gears clicking and clacking along with an almost hypnotic speed.

Newton, always up for an adventure, raced into the room and jumped up onto the embroidered seat of a nearby chair to watch the proceedings, his tail switching cautiously.

Sasha felt a tickle of electricity from the orbs, a sensation like a hum throughout her entire body. The serene humming quickly deepened and soon she could feel it deep inside her bones like an ache.

Toby smiled, his face full of light and wonder.

Sasha played her fingers across the orbs. The music that came out of them was not music in the traditional sense; rather, it was like bird call, or the sound of a rushing stream—natural, elemental. Sasha moved her fingers to make the pitch change, and it wasn't long before the Tuning Machine was at full power, the gaslights of the old mansion flickering, and the space between the two coils growing foggy and shimmery with pinpricks of light.

The first moving image that appeared was of a deep emerald green forest, not perfectly illustrated, but like a broken painting seen through a fuzzy dream. Figures moved in the picture, men darting through the trees on horseback, archers with bows and men with broadswords. A war was being fought in some other place. A warrior raised a blood-slathered sword over his head and emitted a silent battle cry as he charged toward his enemies.

Toby was left speechless by the sight, but Sasha felt the image was much too grim. She moved her fingers and the tune and image changed. Now she saw the surface of some grey, pocked foreign world, with a tiny glass city cradled in a giant-sized crater. Large airships darted overhead, as fast as wasps. This picture was much more pleasant if a bit dull. She moved her fingers again. Now she saw a primordial jungle with large creatures slithering beneath the undergrowth. Start-bright eyes glowered out at her, hungry eyes...

"Sasha?"

Sasha lifted her hands off the orbs and turned to find Lord Quinn slumped in the doorway. His sudden appearance surprised her. He was the absolute *last* person she'd expected to see standing in her father's conservatory. He'd obviously been drinking heavily because he was weaving dangerously on his feet. He took an unsteady step forward, then stopped to grasp the back of a settee to orient himself. "Sasha, I need to speak with you at once," he said, before venturing another drunken step. "Your father said you'd likely be here." He looked about the conservatory populated with its many bizarre devices with some dismay. "It's terribly important."

"Lord Quinn," Sasha began, eyeing him angrily, "Because of my father, we will be seeing *quite* a lot of each other in the near future. So I really don't see what we have to talk about now…"

"It's important, I assure you. It's about the wedding…I…" He'd reached the chair that Newton was crouched on. The cat, understandably upset about the strange man grasping at the air around him, screeched and jumped at him. Lord Quinn jerked his hand back. The cat jumped down and arched his back fearsomely. "Bloody beast…" Quinn began, trying to kick the cat away, but the motion only unbalanced him. Before Sasha could give warning, Quinn, standing within easy reach of Toby, had gotten hold of the boy's arm in a desperate attempt to regain his balance. The motion offset Toby, who tried to jerk his arm back, and the two pitched forward…straight into the moving picture of the jungle.

Before Sasha's very eyes, both men vanished.

She experienced a moment of disbelief, followed by panic. She rushed forward but stopped abruptly inches away from the Tesla coils. Her first instinct was to utter a cry for help, except that the conservatory was on the third floor of the mansion, and almost no one was up here at this hour. There were no servants, and her father was likely preparing for bed. She might have very little time, she realized. The two men could be in terrible danger…wherever they'd gone. Her invention had caused this anomaly. She needed to help them immediately. Taking a deep breath, she dropped to her knees and reached into the shifty, dreamlike field of the picture. "Toby!" she cried, hoping to feel the familiar warmth of his hand.

A sudden, powerful gust of wind ripped her hair right out of its coiffeur. It was like being sucked into a swirling vortex. Before she could even scream for help, the darkness beyond the picture had its claws in her. Her long dark hair was dragged relentlessly forward and the rest of her followed, her skirts flying up around her face, obscuring her vision. The vortex swallowed her whole...

Sasha screamed. And screamed again...

| 4 |

When next Sasha opened her eyes, she saw a clear, summery blue sky burning high overhead. It reminded her of the meadow behind the manor house, and, at first glance, she thought perhaps she'd fallen asleep while lying on a blanket, reading a book. She'd done so often enough in the past. Except there was something peculiar about the trees overhead. They didn't look like the alders, silver birches and grand oaks she was used to. These looked frilly and exotic, like something from the South Seas, or something she'd seen in drawings in her archeology books. She sat up slowly and looked around. Strange birds she didn't recognize were cackling overhead and unseen creatures were hooting busily to each other in the trees. She knew there were no queer cackling birds or hooting tree creatures on the manor estate.

Jungle growth closed in on all sides of her, thick thorny bushes, tall, upright frond-trees, and low, ground-clutching bushes with great red and orange orchids she had never in her life seen growing on the shores of England. It had to be a dream; there was no other logical explanation. She closed her eyes and lay back down on the leaf-littered forest floor. She was just dreaming. If she closed her eyes and waited long enough, she'd wake up. And then everything would be normal again.

She waited. And waited.

But nothing happened. Nothing changed.

"Bloody hell, get it off of me!" a panicked voice shouted.

The sound galvanized Sasha. She jumped to her feet amid the possibly-not-a-dream-jungle and turned her attention on some furious bushwhacking going on not ten paces away from her. Leaning forward, she started parting the undergrowth when Lord Quinn jumped out of the bushes with what looked like a giant beetle attached to his back, its carapace a slick oily black, its antenna flickering over Quinn's head of disheveled red hair. It was making the most frightening clicking noises! Sasha squeaked and jumped back at the sight.

Quinn swung around, his blue eyes wild and unfocused. "Get...it...off, girl!" he commanded.

So Sasha bent down, picked up a half-rotted log lying at her feet, and when Quinn turned his back, she used both hands to hit the beetle just as hard as she could. It made a wet, crunching noise that made Sasha flinch. Lord Quinn and his beetle landed face-first on the jungle floor and lay still.

"Oh dear." Sasha dropped the log that was dripping with black beetle juices and stared at Quinn lying there unconscious. The squashed beetle was roughly the size and shape of one of her father's silver serving trays, and it was *that* fact—more than anything—that convinced Sasha that she was probably not in England anymore. In fact, she didn't think she was *anywhere* anymore.

"Sasha? Sasha, are you all right? I heard you screaming," said Toby, emerging unharmed from a copse of the peculiar jungle trees, palm fronds brushing his cheeks. With his work shirt open at the throat and the sleeves rolled up, he looked rugged, bronzed, and relaxed—and much more at home in the jungle than Lord Quinn in his sunless white skin and dark, severe suit. Long hours of work with the horses had turned Toby's face a burnished golden-brown, and his sun-streaked brown hair was wild from their sudden trip through...well, whatever portal she had opened. He stopped when he saw Lord Quinn lying so still on the jungle floor. "What happened to him?"

Sasha gestured at the fallen man. "He wanted me to squash a bug. So I did."

| 5 |

Together, Sasha and Toby got Lord Quinn up and propped against one of the exotic tree trunks. He was still out cold, and there seemed to be a nice-sized goose egg growing on the back of his head, but at least Sasha hadn't killed him. Toby joked that that was either good or bad, depending on how one was looking at things, but Sasha didn't laugh. She was starting to feel bad about Quinn.

Toby bent low and slapped Quinn across the face, using more force than was necessary, in Sasha's opinion. Almost immediately, the bright blue, bloodshot eyes flared open and Quinn let out his breath and exclaimed, "Dear God!" Then he started panicking all over again. "Is it off? Is…it…?"

"It's dead," Sasha told him, indicating the bug parts scattered all over the jungle floor and, presumably, on the back of Lord Quinn's suit as well. She nearly rolled her eyes in exasperation. She'd never seen a grown man react so nervously to a tiny bug. Well, maybe a not so tiny bug, but still…

Lord Quinn took one look at the remnants of the beetle, turned his head, and vomited all over Sasha's slippers, making her leap back in alarm. His breath wasn't roses, that much was obvious. He smelled like the inside of a cheap tavern. "Bloody hell," he said when he'd recovered. "I hate bugs!" He ran his hands over his face and hair, mussing it further. "I swear I shall never again drink your father's whiskey, Sasha."

"You shouldn't be drinking so heavily in the first place!" Sasha exclaimed, attempting to stay downwind as she contemplated her ruined shoes. Toby looked surprised; he'd never expected her to speak so plainly, and neither had she, but Sasha had a feeling that the normal rules of polite society no longer applied here…wherever they were. And if she was going to be stuck in this…whatever this place was…she was bloody well going to speak her mind! She patted at her loose, mussed hair, attempting to fix her coiffure, then realized the futility of the gesture. Her combs were gone, her hair too heavy to manage, and now her shoes were ruined beyond repair!

Sighing, she sat down on a log and waited for Quinn to recover. "Why do you drink so much, Lord Quinn?" she asked. It was not that she much cared, but she was curious nonetheless.

He eyed her savagely. "It helps me deal with…things."

"What things?"

"Loose-tongued, opinionated women, for starters."

"Lord Quinn!"

Toby gestured at their surroundings. "Could we discuss this at a later time?" he pleaded. "In case you haven't noticed, we're in the bleeding jungle! What are we going to do about this situation? Where *are* we?"

Sasha sighed and clapped her gloved hands around her cheeks. "I've no idea."

"You made the picture, girl!" Quinn shouted. "You said nothing about it being a…a doorway to some godforsaken jungle!"

"That's all it was!" Sasha insisted, clenching both hands into fists in her lap as her mind whirled to try and make sense of their predicament. "It was only a picture!"

"Obviously not," Lord Quinn sneered, glaring up at them both.

Oh, she wished she could discuss all this with John! Maybe he would know how they had gotten here, and how they might get back.

"What jungle is this?" asked Toby, using a stick to prod at the remnants of the giant beetle. "Do such things as these live in Africa, or South America?" At least he'd read enough of her books to know where they *might* be.

"There are no insects like these in Africa," Quinn insisted.

"How the bloody hell would you know what lives in Africa?" Toby shouted, which set both men off into a new round of arguments.

Sasha felt like screaming and insisting that it was indeed only a picture she'd been making, not some…portal into an unknown jungle world. But Quinn was right. It was obviously more than a picture. People did not fall into pictures. They were not *pulled* through pictures. But how could this be? She and John had never even postulated such a ridiculous thing! She sniffed. She knew crying would fix nothing, so instead she stood up and stamped her foot for silence. Toby and Quinn, presently involved in a shouting match, barely heard. "Please, stop, both of you!" she cried. "I don't know where we are, or how we got here. But it's obvious we're very far removed from *any* kind of civilization. And arguing about it won't help!"

The two men stopped shouting at each other and turned to look at her.

"We're not in South America," said Sasha in a softer voice, venturing a few steps into the jungle before stopping. "And I don't think this is Africa, either." Palm fronds seemed to embrace her and insects buzzed about her ears. Fecund life was everywhere, but not the type of life she had read about, even in the most exotic places on earth. She touched a flowering vine with blooms of a glowing green color she wasn't sure even existed on earth. A dragonfly with a wingspan as wide as a bird's buzzed up to her, then away. "We may not even be in our own world anymore."

"Is that even *possible?*" Quinn demanded to know.

"I don't know!"

"Don't yell at Sasha, you pompous lout!" Toby interrupted Quinn.

"How dare you..."

They started arguing again, but Sasha hushed them. "Hear that?" she said, raising a hand.

"I hear nothing," said Toby.

"Yes, exactly." The bird twitters had ceased abruptly, and the hooters had vanished, leaving the jungle eerily still, with only the irritating, tepid buzz of insects to fill the silence. Sasha waited, holding her breath.

And then, out of the jungle, she heard it for the first time, a sound that would change her life, and the lives of her friends, forever: a deep, nasal trumpeting, like the sound of a child blowing through a conch shell, only much, much louder. It froze all three of them in their tracks and sent a quivering, primal fright crawling down Sasha's back. She had never heard such a sound before, and, she realized after a moment, she never wanted to hear it again.

She turned slowly to Lord Quinn. "Can you stand?"

"I think so," Quinn said softly, sounding as cowed by the noise as she felt. Slowly he shimmied up the tree until he was standing in a semi-upright position. His hand went to the back of his head, wincing when he encountered the lump there. "What *is* that sound?" he said in a hushed tone.

Sasha was trembling all the way down to her slippers. "I think it would be in our best interest to move on."

"Move on where?" Toby asked, his eyes darting around the jungle with alarm. "Where is there to go?"

"Anywhere."

The unfamiliar jungle stretched out around them in every direction, as frightening and alien as a dream. But not as frightening as *that sound*. They started following what looked like a rough animal path cut through the undergrowth. Behind them, the trumpeting sounded again, making their hair stand literally on end. It sounded much closer this time.

"I really don't care much for that noise *at all*," Quinn admitted as the thin limb of a tree whipped him in the face, leaving a red mark.

Sasha struggled as some thorny bushes caught the hem of her gown, for once in full agreement with Quinn.

They instinctively started picking up their pace. Foliage whipped them as they tunneled through it. Something snaked under Sasha's foot and she jumped, then forged on regardless. She did not like snakes, but she wanted to put distance between herself and that terrible echoing noise. She *had* to get away from that sound. Toby and Lord Quinn started pulling at the foliage hanging before them like ragged curtains, being less careful about snakes or other creatures, and a lot less quiet. Excited insects buzzed into their faces, then away, some gigantic. At first, they noticed them, then they all started concentrating on making more headway and worrying less about things flying into their eyes and ears.

The trumpeting noise sounded again. This time it was almost deafeningly loud and the vibration made the trees shake and the earth tremble under their feet.

"I *really* don't like that noise," said Quinn.

Around them the forest buzzed, birds took sudden flight, and foliage crackled alarmingly as large bodies tunneled through it at panicked speeds. Some large creature like a saber-toothed crocodile broke through the undergrowth to their left and dashed down the animal path, so intent on escape that it didn't notice them at all.

Sasha nearly screamed, only cupping her hands over her mouth at the last moment, which resulted in a mouth full of flies that she quickly spat out. A pair of creatures that looked like reptilian forms of gazelles galloped past them. She saw them only for a moment before they disappeared into the trees.

Again with the trumpet. The sound was on their very heels now, blasting down their necks.

Quinn said something she didn't catch. "What?" she cried.

"*Stop!*" He grabbed her by the wrist, pulling her up short so she nearly stumbled. "It's herding us!" he shouted, and Toby, hearing, slid to a stop beside her.

"What are you doing?" she cried.

"It's herding us," he repeated. "That creature is herding us!"

"How can you know?"

"I know."

The trumpeting was almost upon them, the sound followed by a low, trembling growl that sounded like a thunderstorm was moving upon them, though no cloud was visible in the achingly bright blue sky. "Follow me," he said and started back the way they had come. "Follow me if you want to live."

She let Quinn steer her away. She didn't know why, except he seemed to know what he was doing. Toby followed, but only because he was following her, she knew. Quinn hurried them back down the rough little path they had made. The alcoholic stupor seemed to be lifting and his eyes were suddenly fierce and wary. Before long, he stopped them before a tree with low-hanging branches. "Can you climb?" he asked.

"Yes." She was slight, and she'd spent a long childhood climbing trees at her Aunt Margaret's, so it was no trouble at all. Quinn made a saddle of his two hands. "Up you go," and he bumped Sasha up to the first branch. Toby, who was tall and young, with long arms, swung himself up onto the limb beside Sasha with the dexterity of a monkey.

Quinn had some difficulty. He was wiry but middle-aged, and not as sober as he could have been. He grabbed the limb and slid off. Sasha leaned down and grabbed his sweaty hand. Toby took his other. "Hurry," he said. "Hurry, please." Together, they pulled and wriggled him up the tree, no small task; he was heavier than he looked. The three of them took a moment to catch their breath, then went to work on the next limb, scrambling up the tree and into the higher bows as quickly as they could. It was terrible, sweating, grunt-worthy work, but they managed it, Sasha making it almost to the top first.

And good thing too, because within minutes something enormous barreled out of the trees like a huge, living, breathing locomotive, though it was larger than any locomotive that Sasha had ever seen. Its wake was enough to rock their whole tree side to side, and all three of them clung madly to the swaying branches as the monstrous...*thing*...charged through the jungle in pursuit of the various creatures fleeing through the underbrush.

Sasha started scrambling higher, kicking at branches and snagging her long skirts, tearing them mercilessly as she grappled the branches over her head. She didn't mind in the least; she had to see what creature had inspired such dread in the whole forest.

"Sasha, be careful!" Toby cried in warning from below, but she ignored his cries. She'd been climbing trees since she was a little girl. She considered herself an expert tree-climber.

After some leg work, she found herself above the tree line where she was finally able to get a good look at the creature dashing through the jungle only twenty or thirty meters away. It was a bipedal creature of over twenty feet in length, in her estimation. It looked robust, with powerful hind legs and an enormous head that swung side to side like a heavy pendulum as it made those ragged trumpeting noises. Its head was broad, bony and almost skull-like, the dark, mottled, reptilian skin pulled taught. Two long, bony ridges topped its eye sockets, with another, longer, bony horn riding over its snout. Its teeth were almost ridiculously large, and armor-like spikes ran the length of its spine and down the long, whip-like tail. Despite its enormous size and considerable girth, it ran with astonishing grace and speed, driving a small herd of smaller animals ahead of it. It reminded Sasha of how lions hunted on the Savannah, according to her zoology books. The big male lions herded prey animals into groups of waiting females, which did the killing almost exclusively. She wondered if Quinn had read the same books.

The smaller animals—they were a mixed lot of tall, thin-legged bipedal reptiles with long necks and ground-hugging, almost mammalian beasts—topped a tall ridge...and there was the second predator she thought might be waiting in ambush. It resembled the first creature, which she finally recognized as a form of predatory theropod called a Ceratosaurus, discovered as fossil remnants in the Americas only a few years prior—her science magazines were certainly useful now!—but it differed in size. This creature, the female, was least ten feet longer, bulkier than the sleek male, with an enormous horned head that looked capable of swallowing a third of her mate in one bite.

Sasha scurried out onto a thick branch to see what the pair of hunters was up to.

The male drove the prey animals on, making those startling trumpeting noises that shook the whole jungle, while the female lunged, opening her enormous, slavering jaws and crunching up at least half of the onrushing animals whole before pouncing on those trying to escape. Her speed and dexterity were amazing for her size.

This was nothing like the lumbering prehistoric creatures she had read about in the periodicals.

Sasha shivered, realizing how easily they could have been like those poor animals, gone in one gulp, had Quinn not encouraged them to climb this tree. She wondered how he had known what was to come; he didn't strike her as the kind of man who followed science journals. Shielding her eyes from the sun, she leaned out further on the branch and watched as the two creatures picked off the escapees, their jaws snapping like giant, bloody animal traps.

Too late, she heard a sharp snap as the tree limb gave way beneath her. Then she was in freefall.

| 6 |

Claws snatched her, digging deep into her shoulders and halting her downward momentum seconds before she would have hit the ground. Sasha screamed. She watched the ground rush up to meet her...then away as she was dragged through the sun-streaked, squalling forest and over the treetops at a tremendously sickening pace. The wind ripped at her hair and clothes, and tree limbs raked her cheeks like cat claws. She glanced up and saw a huge shadow and thick, knobby black claws wrapped tightly about her shoulders. She screamed again, punctuating it with a few useless kicks as she was carried away, her abductor angling toward the sky. Then she screamed some more when she realized they were headed straight toward a tall, black volcanic mountain looming just ahead, not that it did much good. The creature that had her simply winged on, oblivious to her terror.

Sasha stopped screaming and closed her eyes as the mountain rushed toward them. She couldn't bear to see them crash into the side. But after a few tense moments, she felt them angle downward and felt the climate change from hot and wild to cool and enclosed. She chanced a peek and realized they were now traveling down a dark, shadowy tunnel of some kind. Her captor must have flown them right down the chimney of the volcano. The realization didn't make her feel much better.

The creature carrying her slowed down, making a series of high-pitched squeals that were answered by a cacophony of noises as other dark shapes joined them in an enormous, almost pitch-black cavern. Sasha screamed anew and jerked in the thing's embrace, trying to un-wedge herself from its grasp. It released her at last and Sasha dropped to the dusty cavern floor, so dizzy she couldn't stand for some moments.

More squealing surrounded her, so loud she felt like her skull was being cleaved in two. Shadows flitted about her, as fast as lightning. She rose unsteadily to her feet, aware that her debutante dress was in tatters, her hair snarled around her face, her face and lips windburned from her flight. She felt weary and sore in a thousand places, like a rag doll all pieced together. Dark shadows wheeled in and out of the spare light, man-shaped creatures with shining white eyes and star-bright teeth. She realized there was a very good possibility that she would die now, torn apart by monstrous *things* she couldn't see, things that had no name. She might have despaired had she not been so frightened.

Human screams broke her sickening reverie. She turned at the sound and watched two more of the giant flying things skirt by. One dropped a disheveled Toby to the floor, another Lord Quinn. Quinn could not possibly look any worse than he did now, with his suit tattered on his ragged form and his face full of scratches. Sasha felt her heart sink. It was bad enough she was going to die here, in this cavern on this unknown world. But, somehow, it was worse now that she knew the others had been captured as well. None of them would make it out alive to tell of the things they had seen.

"Sasha?" said Toby, rising shakily to his feet and reaching for her. His face and arms were full of scratches, a testament to the fight he had put up as he was carried away by his captor. "Are you all right?"

"Oh Toby." She hugged him, clutching him tight as he buried his face in the side of her neck. She took some small comfort in the fact that at least she would not die alone.

Lord Quinn swayed to his feet and joined them, his eyes very sober. Together they formed a little circle of protection, their eyes going everywhere around the ancient cavern, watching the tiny, flame-like eyes that watched them all with a primitive hunger that sent shivers down their spines. "What are those *things?*" Quinn asked.

Sasha bit back her tears, struggling to be brave for Toby. There was nothing in any of her father's books or in any of the periodicals to describe the creatures that fluttered around them now, their strange, alien forms passing in and out of the spare light leaking into the cavern from the opening far above. They stood as large as men, but that was where the similarities ended. They had dark, befurred bodies, rat-like faces with huge, upright ears, and large, membranous wings that beat chillingly cold air at them all as they fluttered excitedly about the circle of frightened humans. They made low clicking noises, not human, not even animal, but almost like Morse code. Sasha knelt to pick up a large rock from the ground. The others followed suit. She struggled to keep her terror in check. She had survived the Ceratosauruses. She was a Strange, her father's daughter. Her father was a huntsman and had been to war, no idyll lord with soft hands and a wilting spirit was he. If she was going to die tonight, she would die a Strange, and she would not make it easy for her murderers.

Not necessary.

The thought made Sasha pause. It wasn't *her* thought.

One of the odd creatures settled down in front of her. It was larger than the others and streaked with silvery fur around the face and head. It tilted its head with interest. *Throw no stones. Please.*

"What?" she said.

We will not harm you.

Sasha sucked in a quick breath when she realized the thoughts she was hearing were coming *from* the creature in front of her, projected right into her head. "Are you reading my mind?" she asked, though she didn't loosen her hold on the big stone in her hand for one moment.

No. It considered, making low chirping noises, its wet black nose twitching. *We are reading only the thoughts you project to us. We can read those and respond appropriately.*

"Like telepathy."

It thought about that. *Yes. In a way.*

She turned to glance at the others. "Can you hear what he's saying?"

Toby frowned. "I think so. He doesn't want us to fight him or his people. Or something to that effect. He doesn't want a war."

"*I* don't want a bloody war," Quinn added, looking especially peevish. He stood taller and pulled at his tattered frock coat, straightened his cravat, trying desperately to put himself to rights while still keeping a hold of the stone in his hand. "Do you know who I am, sir?" he said with an air of authority that made Sasha consider hitting him with the rock in her hand. Before she could stop him, he'd lunged at what she could only think of as the leader.

The creature raised its wing and struck Quinn across the side of the head, knocking him to the floor. *Muk,* he told Sasha. *I am the leader, yes.*

"Bloody *hell*, why is it always the head?" Quinn said, sitting up and rubbing his skull.

She ignored Quinn and examined the leader, wondering if she ought to thank him or be upset with him. "Muk?" she said with caution. "Is that your name? Or is it the name of your people?"

The others in the cavern started making excitable clicks, but the leader flicked his wing irritably and the others quickly settled down. *My name is Muk. My people are the Sen.*

If Muk could speak and was willing to communicate with strangers, it was likely that he was civilized, Sasha thought. He certainly wasn't anything like the animals they had seen in the jungle. Maybe the Sen weren't as fearsome as they looked. Maybe the three of them would find their way out of this yet. Her heart lifting with optimism, she took a step toward the Sen leader, her hand outstretched in a universal sign of friendship. She smiled, hoping she looked friendly and unthreatening. "Thank you for saving us from those giant creatures, Muk. We are very grateful for your assistance."

Muk narrowed his wise, dark eyes. *You need give us no thanks.*

"I disagree. In my world, it's a sign of goodwill to thank someone for a great act of kindness. You have been kind."

Muk leaned down and sniffed her hand. Both Toby and Quinn inched forward as if to intervene, but Sasha shook her head, warning them back. Muk might be a queer creature to look upon, but she was beginning to like him. And after all, perhaps this was just their way of saying hello in their world, the way the Chinese bowed to each other.

"I don't like this," Quinn complained. "I don't bloody like this one bit!"

Sasha ignored Quinn's dramatics. "Is it customary for you to rescue complete strangers, Muk?" she teased.

You are not strangers, Muk answered with gleaming cold eyes that seemed to pierce right through her flesh and into her bones. He grinned, showing razor-sharp eyeteeth. *You are food.*

| 7 |

"You cannot eat me! I'm British!" Quinn shouted to the roof of the cavern.

Sasha cringed, sitting with her back to the bars of the crude, narrow wooden cage where she and the others waited to see what would become of them. There were three cages in a small semicircle at the back of the Sen's volcano. She, Toby, and Quinn occupied one, one was empty, and a third held a small group of proto-humans who looked more like apes than people, though they stood upright and seemed to have a crude sort of communication that involved hand signals and soft groans. She'd tried multiple times to communicate with them, even going so far as to use basic hand signals—she had seen apes use Sign Language in zoos in London—but so far, the four primates stayed huddled together, eyeing the darkness around them with big, glassy eyes.

Sasha thought she knew what they were feeling. Terror of the unknown. She felt it herself.

They were in trouble. *Really* in trouble. The kind of trouble that Mr. Verne and Mr. Wells had written about but always seemed to have a way out of. She reminded herself that that was fiction, and this was reality. There would be no clever escapes, no last-minute rescues. They were going to die tonight, and it was all her fault. She had to stifle the desire to cry.

Toby slid down beside her and offered her a lopsided grin. "Hey..." he began.

Sasha put a hand upon his chest, stopping him. He felt warm through his clothes, a vast contrast to the coolness of the cavern. She wanted to bury her face against his shirt. But she had to be strong. This was all about their survival. "Don't say it, Toby," she whispered.

Toby put his arm about her shoulders, pulling her close. "I was only going to ask if you were all right."

"I'm not all right. None of us are all right."

"You certainly have that right, girl," said Quinn from the opposite side of the cage.

Toby glanced over with a hostile frown. "You, sir, are exceptionally rude."

Quinn offered the boy a nasty little laugh that rode Sasha's spine like a knife-edge. He had long since given up trying to salvage his clothes. Instead, he let them hang off his lanky frame in dirty tatters, but he had resorted to smoothing his unruly hair as if he might somehow recapture his pride.

"I beg to differ. I'm only speaking the truth. We're in a fine mess because of your girl there." He shot Sasha an even nastier look. "What now, Sasha? I don't see you *inventing* a way out of this mess you've gotten us into."

Toby climbed to his feet. Forgetting his status—or lack thereof—he marched forward and took Quinn by the remnants of his frock coat, hauling him to his feet. "How *dare* you speak to Sasha like that?"

Quinn smiled grimly. "What a sad, love-struck little stable boy you are. Your girl there has doomed us all and you don't even see it." His eyes simmered with rage. "Now unhand me, you toerag, before I...."

"Stop it, just stop!" Sasha cried, burying her face in her hands. It was all she could do to keep from panicking. They were all going to die tonight, and there was nothing she could do about it...that is *if* they didn't tear each other apart first like animals. To her utmost surprise, both men backed down and returned to their respective corners like boxers who'd had second thoughts about going a round in the ring. Toby rolled his shoulders and clenched his fists, eyeing Quinn like he was looking for the soft spots. Lord Quinn yanked fretfully on his clothes, pulled loose his pocket watch, and clicked the clamshell open, then cursed loudly when all the broken clock parts fell out into his lap. It must have been smashed when the Sen dropped him in the cavern.

She had to do something, bring them together somehow. She didn't want to die like this, with all of them *hating* each other. Wiping her tear-clogged nose on the dirty sleeve of her dress, she turned her positively red-eyed attention on Quinn. "How did you know about the Ceratosauruses' hunting pattern?" she asked. It was an odd thing to have such intricate knowledge about. She doubted Quinn was into archeology or the study of extinct animals.

"An animal is an animal. They follow the same patterns everywhere, regardless of species or size," he answered simply, flatly, his shoulders sagging against the bars of the cage. He put his pocket watch away, clearly disappointed. She waited. There was nothing else to do but fight or talk, and all the fight had gone out of him. "I have a tobacco plantation in Rhodesia. I know Africa, and this place very much reminds me of it."

"Tell me about Africa."

He looked on her warily, like a man unused to kindness. "Africa is only about teeth and meat. That's all there is. You hunt and eat or are hunted and eaten by something bigger and more sophisticated than yourself."

"Very clever."

"Those creatures follow the same patterns as lions in our world. There's nothing very clever about it."

"So this world is no different from our own," Toby guessed.

"It seems to be millions of years younger," Sasha explained, glancing at both men. "If you'd lived about forty million years ago, you would have seen creatures like those beasts roaming everywhere."

"Then I'm glad I didn't live forty million years ago," Quinn quipped, and Sasha had to suppress a smile. She hadn't known that Quinn lived in Africa, that he had a plantation there. Africa had always seemed so foreign and exciting to her, hardly a place that a boor like Quinn would call home. His words made her curious, and sad.

"Is that all there is in Africa, Quinn?" she asked. "Death?"

Quinn looked on her finally with something that wasn't contempt. She saw his eyes soften just a bit at the memory of the Dark Continent. "No, of course not. There is great beauty in Africa. The skies taste like rain. The earth itself seems to breathe beneath your feet. But it's a primitive place, Sasha. Survival depends on not making even one mistake."

"I see." She watched him carefully. "Did you love Africa?"

Quinn frowned. "One does not 'love Africa.' Africa loves you. That or it destroys you."

Sasha waited for him to say more—his notions were incredibly romantic for such an angry man—but he'd fallen into a contemplative silence, his chin resting on his chest as if he were seeing other places, other times. Better times, presumably.

Sasha felt terrible all over again. "You're right, of course. All this *is* my fault. I don't know what to say except that I'm sorry." Toby started to say something in her defense, but she raised her hand, cutting him off. "Don't. Quinn's right. This is my mistake. *I* invented the Tuning Machine. *I* sent us here. I was naïve, and if the two of you die here tonight, it's entirely on my head, I realize that."

"Sasha, it was a mistake," Toby insisted.

"Still a mistake," she said, watching Quinn's drawn face as he stared off into space. She finally understood what he'd been telling her. She had made the error, but all of them would pay for it. She had thought Quinn an angry, boring old man without a single thought in his head. She hadn't known he'd lived in Africa. She wondered what his life had been like back then, what he'd seen and experienced. She wondered what had brought him back to London.

She was about to ask when they were interrupted.

Muk had returned. And he wasn't alone.

| 8 |

The Sen leader and a small circle of fellow tribesmen moved about the cages, speaking low to each other in chirps and clicks. Sasha wished she knew what they were saying, what their fate would be.

Muk was dressed grandly in a kilt made of elaborate palm fronds and spiky yellow flowers. Around his neck, he wore a heavy mantle of bone decorated with trinkets and baubles. It looked heavy, which was probably the reason he didn't wear it while flying or hunting prey. It would only weigh him down.

As he drew nearer, Sasha's two companions edged back. Sasha stayed close to the bars. If they were going to die, it was only fair that she go first, seeing how all this was her fault. She swallowed, wondering how brave she could possibly be. She stared at the necklace. Small skulls, tusks, teeth, and bones hung from it, some of them bronzed. She thought they were probably hunting trophies or good luck charms. She was sure Quinn could have educated her in tribal customs in Africa…had they lived. But among the trinkets was something very unusual, something especially un-Sen-like.

One of Muk's hunting trophies was a gold pocket watch with a hunter case and fob.

Five little Sen the size of children flitted around Muk, squawking excitedly and reminding Sasha of baby birds begging for food.

Muk indicated the apelike creatures in the cage beside them. They became even more excited, evidently more accustomed to such creatures. The young Sen flapped their wings and took off into the air, attaching themselves to the cage where the ape creatures were stirring. There was nowhere for them to run so they started pulling at the bars of their cage, whimpering in terror. Pushing their faces between the bars, the Sen opened their squashed up little faces and unrolled long, bright red tongues that acted like barbs, sticking into the backs of the ape's skulls and holding fast. The apes' cries turned to shrieks, the sounds thankfully short-lived as they dropped to the floor one after another as the young Sen began to feed right through their tongues.

Sasha dropped to her knees, a hand clapped over her mouth to keep her vomit down. A cold sweat made her shiver like a victim of fever. Someone moved to kneel beside her. At first, she thought it must be Toby, but the smell of spirits on clothing made her turn. Quinn leaned close to her, observing the feeding with an almost scientific detachment.

"How horrible," she said.

"Is it? I think it's rather interesting, actually."

"Quinn, please..."

"This is just their way. The only way they can feed, Sasha."

"How can you be so cold?"

Quinn looked at her then. His once bloodshot eyes had cleared and he looked keen and focused. He still looked rough, his hair mussed and a light shadow at his chin and throat, but somehow that improved his appearance. She couldn't explain it. He seemed more alive now than he ever did in London. He touched her shoulder and, for once, she didn't want to run screaming from him. "I don't know that you would survive Africa, Sasha."

"This isn't Africa, Quinn."

"Perhaps," he answered, watching the Sen draw the last nutrients from the ape creatures lying in a heap on the floor of the cage. "But it's close. There are tribes in Africa that still engage in a form of cannibalism. They eat the hearts and brains of respected enemies to absorb their bravery and knowledge. It's considered an honor."

Sasha looked away. They were going to end up the same way. She had no idea what they were going to do.

Quinn watched the display before them, his eyes steady. He was made of stouter stuff than she was. "Perhaps we can negotiate our way out of this. I've dealt with primitive tribes in the past."

"Were they planning on eating you?"

"Well, no," Quinn admitted. "We had disputes about hunting grounds and water rights. But it's the same thing, in a way."

"Dear God, we're going to die." Toby leaned his head against the bars of the cage and closed his eyes.

Quinn narrowed his eyes. "We just need something to negotiate with. Something we can give the Sen that they don't have, but want."

"Like our blood?" Toby asked sarcastically.

"I was thinking of something more practical. Something we wouldn't miss. Do you have anything in your pockets?" He looked at them both. "Something that Muk might find of interest?" He too had noticed Muk's preference for shiny trinkets.

Sasha and Toby began ransacking their pockets. All she had were her gloves and a small emerald ring her father had given her when she turned sixteen; these she gave to Quinn. Toby came up with a few pence, a handkerchief, and a three shoeing nails. Quinn added his broken pocket watch to their collection and spread their coffers out on the handkerchief. After a moment, he added his cufflinks, which were small but made of real gold-plated elephant teeth, he said. It wasn't much, but hopefully the items were novel enough—and *shiny* enough—to interest the Sen.

Muk flitted up to their cage, eyeing the objects that Quinn had laid out in plain sight. He studied them carefully, tilting his head.

"I hate it when he does the head thing," Toby whispered. "It means he's up to no good."

"Shh," said Quinn, presenting the items to Muk with a flourish, like a magician performing a trick.

Muk leaned close and sniffed the items. The trinkets on his mantel flashed, the pocket watch again catching Sasha's eye. It was obvious that someone had come before them, someone from their world. There was no way a pocket watch would have come into Muk's possession otherwise. As Muk examined their offerings, Sasha said, "Who was the man who came before us?"

Muk looked up. His eyes were cold, mechanical. Sasha had to remind herself that he wasn't really a monster, and that this was just the way of the Sen, as Quinn put it. It proved difficult. *His name was John Ulysses,* Muk said.

Sasha felt her heart seize up in her chest and she feared she might start hyperventilating. "John?" She gripped the bars of the cage and leaning against them. "Dr. John Ulysses was here?" She thought maybe Muk was lying, that he had somehow plucked the name out of her head to frighten her. Then she rethought that. In his last letter, John had talked about the pictures he'd made on his Tuning Machine in the States. Was it such a stretch of the imagination to assume he'd created the same portal as she and that he, too, could step through it? Among the "pictures" of the worlds she'd seen, this one was among the most beautiful. She could easily picture an insatiably curious John Ulysses stepping too close to the vortex to examine an exotic flower or a bizarre animal.

And that brought another important thought to mind. She hadn't received a letter from John in over three months, which was very unusual. She hadn't given it much thought until now, what with her father's mad dash to see her engaged. She looked again at John's pocket watch around Muk's neck and felt her heart sink within her. "John's dead, isn't he?" she said. She didn't want to say it. If she didn't and never made it back to her own world, she might be able to pretend that John was still alive in New York, still inventing devices. But she had to know. She couldn't shield herself from the truth.

He is dead, probably, said Muk.

"What do you mean…probably?"

He went to fight She. He has not been seen since.

The actual name Muk used for whatever John had fought had no direct translation. It was like a goddess's name in some foreign language, but no name a human mouth could form. Her mind had automatically filled in the blank. "She?"

Muk seemed to search for a name she would understand. The great one. The one who consumes. She is a warrior and, yes, a goddess. She has stripped our land of prey.

Sasha could think of only one creature. "You mean the Ceratosaurus?"

Muk wagged his head from side to side. Of course, he did not know the word. English words—even those from Latin and Greek —held no meaning for the Sen. So Sasha formed the picture of the vast creature in her mind, scooping up prey in her bloodied jaws.

She! Muk's answer was immediate, full of fear and awe.

Sasha glanced at Quinn, wondering if they'd found an even greater bargaining chip. Quinn nodded her on. She turned back to Muk. "What you're saying is that John went to fight…She, but never returned?"

Muk blinked once, slowly. *Yes.*

"Why would he do that?"

Muk narrowed his eyes. To earn his freedom, of course.

Of course. John would have promised almost anything to escape the Sen, as any sane man would. It made sense. Yet Sasha despaired. John must be dead. That or John had used the opportunity to escape from Muk's territory and travel on to other lands.

Muk's eyes hardened as he reached for the pocket watch around his neck, fingering it with his clumsy set of claws. He told us that this object was of great importance to his world, a mighty weapon he must not be parted from and that he would return for it after he had slain She. But he did not return. He lied.

Sasha nearly bit back a smile at John's deception, which was just like him. "Or he died fighting She."

Muk tilted his head. *Perhaps.* He did not sound convinced.

She took Quinn's pocket watch in her hands. "As you can see, we too have a weapon of great importance."

Muk made a warbling noise that Sasha immediately identified as a chuckle. It didn't help that the pieces kept falling out of Quinn's pocket watch. The young ones gathered around, licking their wet, teethy little snouts and eyeing them like they were the next course in a great feast. *We are not fools,* Muk informed her. *We know these objects are of limited value. We will not be deceived again.*

Quinn pushed to the front of the cage. "I understand you have trouble with...She?"

Muk narrowed his cold black eyes. She is stripping the land. The hunting is bad since She and her mate have come.

Sasha turned to glance at Quinn. "Is this like tribes in Africa?"

Quinn shrugged. Yes, no, maybe. "More like the British Colonies."

"I don't understand."

"Once the colonization of Africa began, it drove the game further inland. It made prey scarcer for the indigenous tribes who live there. As a result, some have declared war on all Englishmen."

"Hence the cannibalism," she guessed.

"The cannibalism has been used as a scare tactic to hold back the Colonies. But Muk and his people genuinely need blood to survive. There's precious little of that since She's come." Quinn narrowed his eyes slyly on Muk. "If we killed She for you, would you allow us safe passage out of your lands?"

Muk returned Quinn's gaze with one just as sly. You would not kill She. You would only run away, as the man before you did.

"I give you my word as an Englishman."

Muk looked unimpressed.

"My word as a lord among my people," Quinn corrected himself. "If you release us, we *will* kill She for you."

Toby swore under his breath. "Do you *know* what you're saying, Quinn?"

"I'm trying to get us out of his mess, boy," he answered neutrally, his eyes never leaving Muk's face. "If you have a better idea, you might let me know about it."

Muk considered him carefully.

Quinn gathered up the handkerchief containing their motley collection of items and deposited it outside the cage. "You have everything we own. Let us go and we'll kill the creature and bring you its claw. You can wear it as a trophy. You will be powerful among your people."

Muk considered the bundle of trinkets. Then he turned his ice-cold gaze on them.

Sasha felt her heart lurch. She wondered if it was enough. She prayed it was.

Muk seemed to smile. Or maybe it was a snarl on his face. It was difficult to tell the difference. *You will not return for these small things. We know. We learn. You will return for your own kind.*

Muk nodded, once, satisfied. *You and the female may leave the mountain to kill She, and you will bring me the claw of She as proof.* He turned his ferocious gaze on Toby. *But the boy stays with us.*

| 9 |

"You do know you can never marry Toby?" Quinn said after the two of them had been deposited at the foot of the Sen's mountain. He glanced up at the brutal red morning sun riding high above the peak of the volcano. "Your father simply won't allow it."

Sasha ignored his statement and started trudging out into the endless jungle that stretched green and fecund in every direction. She knew it was best to pay absolute attention to her surroundings, but she couldn't help but see Toby's face in her mind as she'd left him alone in that despondent little cage. His last act had been to give her a long look of concern, not for himself but her, and the memory of it haunted her. It made her want to call the Sen back, to beg them to fly her back to him, even though she knew they were his best chance for freedom.

She stopped to watch Quinn break a long, sharp branch off a tree. It was almost perfectly straight. He hefted it, testing its weight. In this primordial world, she doubted a long stick would offer much protection, but she couldn't bring herself to say as much.

Quinn tested it as if it was a javelin, hurtling it at the trunk of the tree he had taken it from. He hit it dead center and watched it clatter down. "Toby has no station," Quinn added, helpfully pointing out the obvious. "The arrangement would be ridiculous and inappropriate."

Now he had crossed the line. "My father isn't here, Quinn," she said, impressed with how steady her voice was. "In lieu of a guardian, I shall have to make my own decisions from now on."

Quinn picked up his homemade javelin and turned to look at her, lifting an eyebrow with something like admiration. "Well said, little Sasha." He reached out to take her hand, to help her over some rocky bits of ground. "We should be off now."

"I can take care of myself!" she said angrily, shaking off his touch. Quinn had no right to speak to her so forthrightly! And he needn't help her; she was more than capable of taking care of herself. All she needed was a stick. How difficult could it be to learn to throw it? She rooted around the ground, coming up with a much smaller one than Quinn sported. It wasn't much protection, but it was all she had. She took a step without aid and stumbled in her heeled slippers, almost falling on her face.

Quinn caught her at the shoulders, steadying her on her feet. She looked up into his face. It wasn't a handsome young face like Toby, tanned and classical. Quinn could never be described as handsome. He was too gaunt and strained and unhappy for that. But he had a striking, unforgettable face. A determined face. And there was a lean strength in his arms, she decided. When he wasn't dead drunk, he was very strong. And he seemed to have a good eye for the javelin. He eased her back, then dropped to one knee before her like a man about to propose in a romance.

"What are you doing?" she asked in dismay.

Quinn took her debutante dress in both hands and ripped it soundly up the middle. Sasha flinched. Without saying a word, he gathered each half of the dress around her ankles and started tying it, making improvised harem trousers for her. "This will be more practical for the journey ahead. And will protect you from insect bites in the jungle. Your legs are already covered in bites."

Sasha felt her ears burned. She'd no idea that Quinn had seen her legs, or that he was looking.

When he finished, he stood up and gave her his arm and an unexpected smirk. "We need to work together, Sasha or your young man may never be free. We need to trust each other. If we don't work together, we'll never survive this world." He took her arm, looping it through his own. "There's no shame in requesting help."

"It's not that."

He waited patiently for her to explain.

But she couldn't. It felt odd to be relying on Quinn…Quinn, of all people! It should be Toby here with her, Toby she was relying on. How had she wound up with the odious man her father had chosen for her future husband? All right, perhaps Quinn wasn't exactly *odious*…but he certainly wasn't dashing, handsome, or even witty. He was nothing like the suitors she had read about in books. He seemed the antithesis of that in every way.

Quinn offered her that brief, insouciant smirk of his. "You're not afraid of me, are you, little Sasha?"

"No!" This time she clutched his arm, feeling his warmth through his sleeve. "I'm not a child!"

"No, Sasha," said Quinn, looking her up and down. "You are most certainly *not* a child."

| 10 |

"Which way do you think She went?" Sasha asked once they were in the thick of the jungle and surrounded by birdcall and giant flying insects. She brushed a low flying dragonfly away, hoping Quinn knew which direction they were walking. It all looked the same to her.

"She was going west, thus I suggest we go west too." He stopped to examine an animal print stamped into the mud, much too small to be She, but perhaps one of her victims. "I'm sure we'll pick up her trail soon."

Sasha nearly shuddered at the thought. "Can you tell which way is west?"

Quinn glanced up, shielding his eyes from the sun. "We're lucky, Sasha, in that your world only appears to have one sun. Assuming the dynamics of astronomy are the same here as in our world, then we're walking west, into the setting sun. Of course, a compass would be of great assistance now."

"It's not *my* world," Sasha protested.

"You discovered it. It's Sasha's World."

"Don't tease."

"I'm sorry. I do apologize."

They started walking again, following the animal tracks, the long grasses and shrubs flattened by the weight of its passage. The path was as wide as a coach path—probably made by something coach-wide, she reflected with another shiver—and made traveling much easier. The jungle licked at them on all sides, ferns and flowers brushing their faces, strange bird calls echoing like a cacophony far above. The entire jungle was redolent with flowers she had never seen before, and insects she did not recognize. She kept reflexively grabbing at Quinn's arm, terrified that he might disappear right in front of her, leaving her utterly alone on this strange primordial world. Sasha's World, as he called it.

"Any idea as to how we'll kill She when we find her?" she asked.

"We'll think of something." He didn't seem to mind her walking close to him, clutching his hand. He didn't shoo her away or make any disparaging comments. After some time, he said, "You're very worried about Toby, aren't you?"

"Of course I'm worried. We've no idea if Muk will keep his promise. His people might hurt Toby while we're gone." She thought of what the young Sen had done to those ape-men and shivered again, despite the heat soaking through the back of her dress and making her corset painfully tight about her ribs. It was so hot it hurt to breathe.

"Muk seems honorable enough, and his people respect him. I don't think he would betray a trust. He seems keen on folks keeping their word."

"Muk is a monster."

"Is he?" Quinn tilted his head as if sniffing the air. "I find him a rather extreme chap, but not entirely unlikable."

"Are you mad?"

Quinn turned and looked at her. "At least he was willing to negotiate. If he was a monster, he and his brood would have disposed of us by now."

"I expect you're right."

He patted her hand reassuringly where it rested on his arm, his touch lingering perhaps a few seconds longer than was appropriate. "Sasha?"

"Yes, Quinn?"

"I'm sorry about what I said. About all this being your fault. Of course, you could not have foreseen any of this."

That surprised her. "You were right," she said, feeling a lump form in her throat. "It is my fault. My folly. I was naïve."

"When I was your age, I felt much the same way."

"What happened?"

He stopped to check the alignment of the sun. "Africa happened." And that was all he said.

They started down the animal path again. "You were very young when you went to Africa," she said, making it not quite a statement.

"My father took me there to help him work the tobacco plantation. He did not want a lay about for a son. He felt it would be good for my education."

"Why didn't you stay?"

Quinn hesitated, resettling his improvised javelin on his shoulder. He seemed to calculate a response. "I grew tired of it? Yes...perhaps. After all, London was my home."

He was lying, but she didn't understand why. "So Sasha's World is like Africa."

"Nothing is like Africa."

They moved on. The sun sank lower against the horizon. The air grew heavier, cooler, with the onrushing evening. A few miles into the jungle, as the shadows began to lengthen and the sound of chittering day creatures gave way to the lowing of night predators on the prowl, Quinn steered them off the animal path and into the jungle proper, the tall underbrush switching their faces.

"Is this a very good idea?" she asked, brushing away a spider clinging to her dress.

"It's better than staying on that path near nightfall when whatever made it comes up out of the river to feed."

He had a point. "I didn't think of that," she said in admiration.

Quinn smirked. He never smiled, but his smirk made his face seem younger, however briefly. "If we're stuck here for some time, you will." Without waiting for a response, he released her arm to reach into his boot and withdraw a large-bladed knife, not a machete, but something like a Bowie knife like they had in the Americas, with a worn and scarred ivory handle. She thought of his cufflinks, which had been made of elephant teeth. The Bowie was likely real ivory. Quinn started cutting down the tall, dry yellow grass in their way, using a swinging motion that he seemed to be very much at home with. Sasha noticed that the landscape was slowly transforming from jungle to more of a primordial grassland dotted with tall horsehair conifers that were long extinct in their own world. Dark, rocky formations rose in the far distance as they approached what seemed to be a dormant volcanic range.

"Did you clear your father's lands as well?" she asked as she watched Quinn work up a good sweat under his dirty white dress shirt and waistcoat.

"My father didn't own many slaves, so yes. After he was gone, Gabrielle forced me to release the rest."

"Gabrielle?" she asked.

He hesitated mid-swing, then continued downward, cutting a swath through the dry grass with renewed vigor. "There's a mountain range only a half-mile or so away. We can find a cave and set up a camp there. It'll be good shelter for the coming night."

He said no more after that.

| 11 |

The sun went down and the temperature dropped so dramatically that Sasha was shivering by the time they reached what seemed to be a serviceable cave entrance. Quinn offered her his coat, then ducked inside to search for any potential dangers.

Under the cover of darkness, the landscape changed, becoming even more alien. The night seemed to come alive with a million eyes. As she waited, Sasha pushed herself against the side of the cave, trying to make herself small, her eyes straining to track any small motion in the livid night. It seemed forever when Quinn finally returned, and she had to force herself not to throw herself into his arms.

"It looks safe enough," he announced.

They set up camp at the back of the cavern where Quinn said the mountain formed a natural flue to keep the fire he struck from dry kindling and flint from choking them out while they slept. He thought the fire would keep most of the animals away. Sasha moved closer to the warmth of the flames, and closer to Quinn, licking her parched lips.

"Thirsty?" Quinn asked, his voice echoing too loudly in the cavern.

"I'm perfectly all right," she answered, watching the firelight flit across his face. She wanted to move closer still and clutch him like she might fall off the edge of the world otherwise, but that would be childlike. And inappropriate.

He stood up.

Sasha felt her heart catch. "Where are you going?"

Quinn indicated the darkness of the cavern with the tip of his javelin. "While I was exploring earlier I heard water splashing. I think there may be a natural underground lake. A lake means food and water. No worries, I'll be back soon."

Sasha stood up, too. "I'll come with you."

"You look tired, Sasha."

"I'm not. I'm coming with you." Clutching his coat, she put her hand on his arm as she had earlier. But now, in the dark, it seemed a much more intimate gesture. But she couldn't pry herself off him, it seemed. Quinn was safety, and home, and sanity. She couldn't let that go.

She waited for him to protest, to shake off her touch, but instead, he drew her near, so near she could feel the warmth of the fire in his clothes. "Come along, then," he said. Together they moved deeper into the cavern.

Half-seen creatures flitted far above their heads, and the strong reek of ammonia assaulted them, testifying to the presence of bats —real bats, not bat people. Quinn seemed unperturbed. "What if they're vampire bats?" she asked. "Won't they bite us?"

"That's a distinct possibility."

She was getting tired of Quinn teasing her. "They could attack us. They could have rabies."

"I think I'd rather take my chances with the vampire bats than with the things out there."

He was right, of course. And that made her want to kick him. But she just clutched his arm tighter as lights flickered across the rock walls from a pool of water further on. She could smell the pungent aroma of the underground lake long before she could see it, and her dry mouth was suddenly pooling with saliva. Water. After hours of being dehydrated under a relentless alien sun, water was the most delicious idea in the world to her.

They both had the same idea when they finally reached the underground lake. They got down on their hands and knees and began palming water into their parched mouths and over their dirty faces. It was shockingly cold, but good, so good. After a moment, Quinn stripped off his shirt and waistcoat and began splashing water down his bare chest. He had a stronger physique that she'd expected; his alcoholism had only just begun nipping around the edges of his body. Sasha stood up and moved back a step. "Don't splash me!" she said, laughing to cover her embarrassment. From behind, she could see his back bore a thin spiderwebbing of old pinkish scar tissue. Had he been in some war in Africa? Now she was even more embarrassed...and curious.

Quinn stood up, seemed to recall he was naked to the waist, and quickly grabbed up his shirt, slipping his arms into it and pulling it over his head even though he was still dripping wet. He too looked embarrassed, as if he had forgotten himself. "Did you want to bathe? I'd be happy to give you the privacy necessary."

Sasha thought about that. The idea of swimming in the icy water made her shiver. "No, I think I'll wait until tomorrow."

"Very well." He stepped onto some rocks and, balancing precariously, set the javelin on his shoulder.

"What are you doing?" she asked.

"Are you hungry?"

"Yes!"

"Good. Fish is on the menu tonight." He narrowed his eyes and waited.

Time passed. Sasha slowly sank down on the dirt floor of the cavern, clutching Quinn's coat about her shoulders. Quinn stayed perched on his rock, moving not a muscle.

Together, they waited for dinner to arrive.

Sometime later, a ripple broke the surface of the water for the first time. Quinn crouched low, his javelin, now a fish-killing weapon, at the ready. Another ripple. Quinn smirked.

An amphibious creature that looked like an overgrown toad leaped out at him, its long, black tongue snapping out. The tongue opened like a miniature mouth, snapping at him with ragged proto-teeth. Sasha squeaked and nearly jumped out of her skin at the sight. Quinn leaped backward, landing with remarkable grace and balance at the edge of the water. The toad-thing, which was as big as a pony, glared at him with shiny black onyx eyes, then smoothly ducked back under the water, leaving almost no ripple behind.

Quinn started, then laughed unexpectedly. "I expect we're not eating *that.*"

Sasha shivered. "How can you joke?"

"What else am I to do?"

"It's not funny!" Sasha insisted. "You could have been hurt. And…and you act like you're enjoying this! Like you *like* this world!"

Quinn thought about that. "I suppose I do." He raised the javelin, preparing for round two. "On Sasha's World, there are no debt collectors, no moneylenders. No one I know, no one who knows me." He repositioned himself on the rocks and stared keenly down into the pool of dark water. "In a way, it's like being reborn, starting all over again."

He was right, in a way. There were no laws here, no rules. No one to tell you what to do. No people, so far as she knew. And if there was a civilization somewhere, surely they had their own rules of conduct. For the first time in her life, Sasha realized she was free. Free to live by her own code, free to make her own decisions. It should have thrilled her, she supposed; instead, she was only afraid. She'd had a beautiful little ruddy chaffinch like that. She'd found him injured one summer in the garden and kept him for months in a cage, nursing his broken wing. Then one day she let him go. The following day, she found him dead outside the back door of the manor house. He'd battered himself to death in an attempt to get back inside. Back to captivity.

Sasha stared at the water, huddling in Quinn's coat. "All the fish have been chased away again," she said, depressed by her inner thoughts. "We'll never catch anything now."

"Do you always do that?" Quinn asked.

"Do what?"

"Talk like a little girl?"

"I'm not a little girl!" she shouted, then instantly regretted it because that's exactly what was happening. She was sounding like a little girl, a petulant child kept up far beyond her bedtime…and without a single parent in sight! She had to remind herself that she was nineteen, a woman. That on Sasha's World, she could make her own decisions.

As if to read her mind, Quinn quoted, "'When I was a child, I spake as a child, I understood as a child, I thought as a child: but when I became a man, I put away childish things.'"

She glared at him. "What's that supposed to mean?"

"Poor old Albertus. He's no idea what damage he's done to his precious little Sasha." He was laughing at her again, not outwardly, but within, that smirk back on his face.

She jumped to her feet and glared at Quinn. Suddenly it was too much, all of this. She was tired and hungry and cold and *finished*. She didn't feel like a woman, quite the opposite. And she did not care. She wanted to go home now, sleep in her own bed. She wanted to see her room, her dolls lined up in a neat row against her pillows. She wanted Toby. She wanted her Papa. She wanted her mother, over ten years dead. It was simply too much to bear. "How dare you speak to me like this?" she shouted, clenching the fabric of the coat in her fists. She had to force herself to keep from sobbing. "How dare you speak of my father this way? You're so mean and horrible! You're a horrible old man, Quinn!" Her words reverberated around the cavern, sounding childish even to her own ears. She stopped and sank to her knees and just stared at him as hot tears welled up in her eyes. She didn't like this world the way Quinn did. She didn't like *him*. She didn't like *any* of this!

Quinn watched her, his eyes dark and pitiless in the spare light shining off the underground lake.

Sasha gave in finally. She started to cry, great heaving sobs that racked her body and made her tremble. Quinn waited, saying nothing. He let her cry and cry. Toby *never* would have let her cry herself dry, and neither would her Papa. Her father would have comforted her, held her, and made things right. But nothing was right. And Papa wasn't here. And neither was Toby. And from Quinn—who was a horrible old man—there was no comfort. There was just cold and fear and loneliness and silence. He stood there, one eye on her, one on the water, waiting until she was finished, all cried out.

"Are you finished, little Sasha?" he asked in a mocking tone.

"I hate you," she told him, patting at her sodden face with the ripped sleeve of her dress. "I hate you, Quinn."

"No, you don't."

"You don't care about anyone but yourself! You enjoy hurting people."

He gave her a bored look as if her words meant nothing to him as if he didn't believe them at all. He said in a whisper, "Have I hurt you, Sasha?"

She pulled at her hair, then let it go. It was as snarled a mess as leaves on a bush, full of leaf litter and jungle debris. She sniffed as her sobs subsided and her anger cooled. The cry had helped. She felt all washed out. "No." She looked up at him, studying him more carefully. He watched her now, intently. She realized after a moment that he was always watching her, studying her. He looked at her as no one had ever looked at her before, as if he were stripping her down to her soul, and it made something deep and primal in her belly move. She looked away, embarrassed. "I'm sorry. I shouldn't have said that."

"No, you shouldn't have."

"I was thoughtless."

"You were."

She looked back. "But you're not like Toby, Quinn."

He raised his eyebrows at that. "Why should I want to be like Toby?"

She didn't know what to say to that, what was appropriate. Or true.

"Ah," said Quinn, and went back to watching the water.

"What?"

"Nothing, nothing."

"What do you mean 'ah?'" Slowly, she climbed to her feet. "Explain yourself, Quinn! Please."

Again, with the little smirk. She sensed it more than she saw it in the dark. "Little Sasha, I think I understand you now."

"What do you mean?"

"You've known Toby a long time, yes?"

"We practically grew up together."

"I see. So Toby is your playmate. Your friend. Toby is…safe."

"I don't understand."

She watched him tense as he spotted something. But after a moment, he relaxed his shoulders as his prey swam away. He held the javelin perfectly still, like he was stone, like he could hold it that way all night long. "You love Toby because he's *safe*. You can never marry him because of his station, therefore, he's safe to you. He's no threat to you, or to your…innocence."

"You're being ridiculous."

"Am I?"

"I love Toby because he's Toby." She raised her chin, pinning Quinn with a determined look. "And I'm not afraid of *you*, Quinn. You can bluster all you please. You don't frighten me at all."

"I'm very happy to hear that," he said. He was quiet a long moment as if he were considering something. Then his voice changed, becoming softer, more intimate. He did not look at her. "So if I were to tell you that you were a very desirable young woman, you would appreciate my words for the compliment they're intended to be. Is that true?"

Suddenly she was afraid again, but for an entirely different reason. She realized she was more afraid of Quinn than the toad-creature that had nearly eaten them. She had to try twice before she found her voice. "Were you to feel that way, I would say you were not honorable, and certainly no gentleman." She tried to make her voice strong, but it came out a whisper instead.

"Because a gentleman would never desire a woman? Or because a gentleman never speaks his mind?"

Sasha stared at the water. Fish were swarming around the rocks, but Quinn paid them no mind. He simply gazed at the water, or maybe at her rippling reflection in it, wholly concentrated on that. She looked too. In the torn debutante dress, with her hair fallen down, she didn't look like Sasha Strange anymore; she looked a great deal more like her mother, a grown woman. She wished she were anywhere but here, with Quinn. She didn't know what to say to him. For all her classes, tutors, and books, she did not know what was appropriate, or what was true. She didn't know anything anymore. "I'm going back to the camp."

And so she did.

| 12 |

Quinn returned with what looked like two small, armored shark-like fish on the end of his javelin. The fish didn't seem to have traditional scales, which made them that much easier to clean. Using his knife, Quinn sliced off long pieces of pale pink flesh and secured them to a long stick that he then held over the fire. The moist flesh cooked quickly, giving off a pungent, salty aroma that had Sasha nearly whimpering in anticipation. Quinn even found some wild berries outside the cave that Sasha believed were related to gooseberries on Earth. She was so hungry by the time the fish came her way that she shoveled the still boiling hot meat right into her mouth, burning her tongue and fingers in the process.

"Careful," said Quinn, laughing, and Sasha endeavored to eat more ladylike in his presence. She did not respond to him, but Quinn seemed unperturbed by her silence. After the fish had been eaten, and the remains and berries rolled up in a piece of fabric to be taken with them, he went about hunting down different flints, gathering some for his pockets, and examining other, larger pieces as potential weapons. After an hour or so of flint hunting, he'd chosen a large, serrated piece and secured it to the end of his javelin with strips of cloth, cursing his lack of catgut, which would have made things much easier. The javelin was now, truly, dangerous.

Sasha watched him work from across the fire, following his example in making her own javelin. She was an amateur engineer, so she found ways of securing the flint better than he, which made him then follow *her* example. It was good work. She didn't have to talk to him, and she didn't want to, not after the lascivious way he had spoken to her. But the angry silence was oppressive, making her feel alone even in his presence. "I'm not a child, Quinn," she finally said. "I learned to hunt fox with my father. I can ride horses. I can shoot a gun." She felt stupid after saying it. They were not hunting fox. There were no horses in this world. And she didn't have a gun.

Quinn finished securing the flint to his homemade spear.

"I can learn to fish. And to fight," she insisted.

Quinn stood up, testing the weight and balance of his weapon.

Sasha stood up too. "I can learn to use that."

He glanced at her, finally. His eyes looked dark, foreign to her. She would have called it anger, but it didn't have that edge. She suppressed a shiver. She stood up straighter and showed him her own, smaller, javelin. "Show me how to throw," she said in a softer tone. "I'll learn. I'm not afraid."

Quinn thought about that, then wordlessly moved to encircle her. He stood very close, so close she could smell the vague, damp smell of the long-dried alcohol still on his clothing. But the smell was fading; he smelled more like jungle than anything else. His heat engulfed her. He took her hand, which held her javelin, and drew it back until it was just past her ear; then, with his other hand, he straightened her arm. He said, in the shivery cup of her ear, "You throw from your shoulder, using your arm, but never putting your whole body into the throw. You must keep your center of gravity at all times." He extended her arm into the throw. He put a heavy hand on her back to keep it straight.

He let her throw the javelin a few times. Mostly, she missed the target, a wet spot on the cavern wall some ten feet up. He said she was trying too hard, throwing too soon, or not turning with the throw. She threw the javelin a few more times. She was getting closer to the target. By that time, Quinn was very close, pressed against her back, a hand holding her straight at the waist. She had never been this close to a man before. She had hugged her father on many occasions, of course, and even Toby when they were both children, but this was the first time a man's body was pressed against her, tense and expectant. His warmth seeped into her, and his touch made her feel safe....which was something of an oxymoron, she supposed because she didn't feel safe with Quinn at all.

She was never so acutely aware of a man's scent, the feel of his body. She stopped trying to throw the javelin and just held very still while Quinn's arm tightened about her waist and his hand went to the side of her face, to brush the long, tangled curtain of her hair away from her cheek. She probably smelled very bad, she thought. Like the jungle. But it wasn't an unpleasant odor on Quinn, wild and flowering. It smelled primal, like life itself. Gently, he turned her about-face in his arms and gave her one of his intense looks. Her thudding heart seemed to lurch from her chest into her throat. He held her securely in his arms and bowed his head to lay a rather chaste kiss on the corner of her mouth. She had never been kissed before, and the tenderness of it surprised her; she'd always assumed that Toby would be the first boy to kiss her.

Quinn's mouth tasted sweet and wild from the berries they had eaten; it didn't feel like a boy's mouth at all. He cupped the side of her face in his big, roughened hand. He turned his head to find her mouth more fully, and the coarseness of his unshaven cheek grazed her as he kissed her much less chastely. Sasha closed her eyes. She felt him press himself tightly against her as he kissed her, his warmth soaking into her dress. The tip of his tongue brushed the roof of her mouth, then darted over her teeth and tongue. Somehow, they had stumbled backward, until Sasha's back was to the wall, with Quinn holding her up, cradling her, keeping her warm and secure in his arms. He kissed her with his lips but also his tongue. She had to work to keep up. She wasn't a child and she would show him. She had a moment to think, *This is how adults kiss*, and then Quinn drew back and eyed her as if he might very much like to eat her for dessert.

She shivered under the weight of that look. "I'm not very good at this," she complained, lowering her eyes shyly. "There's nothing in the books about—"

He kissed her again, silencing her. He kissed her until she was breathless and made a small kitten-like noise in the back of her throat. Then he drew back. "You are very good at this," he said, the first real compliment he had paid her. But then his expression changed, his eyes darkened, and rather than kiss her again, he released her and stepped back. She felt a dull, frustrating loss as the distance between them grew.

He was watching her carefully—with desire, yes, but also regret. He swallowed, and his throat clicked. "There's something you ought to know, Sasha. The reason I was in the conservatory in the first place when the accident happened."

She waited expectantly. Her heart was ticking very loudly in her throat. She wished he would just keep kissing her. If he kept kissing her, she knew she'd get so much better at it. Then he'd see she was no child, that she was useful to him. "What is it, Quinn?" she asked.

He looked reluctant.

"Tell me," she said. But she was afraid. He was going to say something terrible, something that would dash everything to pieces.

"Sasha," he began, "I had plans to release you from any obligation. From marrying me, I mean." He swallowed again, his Adam's apple bobbing. He looked piqued, but she didn't know if it was embarrassment or the result of their kiss. She wanted to believe it was their kiss. "I'd planned on returning to Africa. In fact, I was there at your father's house to tell Albertus that evening when he made his ridiculous announcement."

"You mean…"

"The wedding is off, yes."

She waited to feel a great wave of relief, but all that came out of her mouth was, "Oh."

He smiled at her, a little. "So you see, you had nothing to fear from me, after all."

"I see," she said. She didn't have to marry Quinn. She was free to marry whomever she wanted—or no one, if that was what she desired. She should have been happy, ecstatic. Instead, she wondered if any of this had to do with Gabrielle, whoever she was. Was Gabrielle Quinn's woman, waiting forlornly back in Africa for his return? Gabrielle for Gabriel, an archangel. She must be very beautiful to have such a beautiful name. Was that why he was so eager to return to the Dark Continent? It couldn't be his debts he was running from; the Crown ruled there, as well. Quinn wouldn't be getting away from anything. It must be Gabrielle, then.

She felt a sting of outrage. "So this was all some *ruse*?" she said, sounding angrier than she'd intended. Quinn's hands still held her tightly. The idea hadn't disturbed her until that moment. She put her hands up between them and pushed him away. "You're just playing with me? Entertaining yourself until you return to Africa?"

Quinn scowled. "I am trying to set things straight between us, revealing my intentions toward you, or lack thereof, before things get too…out of hand." He removed his hands from her. "That is the honorable thing a gentleman does, isn't it? And you prefer gentlemen."

"Yes," she said.

"Well then."

She gave him a hard shove and a harder look. Quinn stumbled back before catching himself. "Do you kiss a lot of women that you have no intentions toward, Quinn?"

He looked surprised by her vitriol. "I've had my share of women in the past, yes. I'm not perfect, Sasha."

"So you're a roué as well as a drunk and a gambler?"

"Now, hang on. I'm attempting to be honest here…"

"I'm not one of your loose women, Quinn!" she shouted angrily, balling up her fists.

"No, I can see that." Suddenly he bit back a smile. "Are you angry, little Sasha?"

"No!" she stated, angrily. "I simply don't appreciate being played with!"

His face suddenly grew serious, like carven stone. His eyes pinned her. They were not a child's eyes, Toby's eyes. They were Quinn's eyes. And Quinn was a hunter. "I'm not playing," he growled. He leaned toward her. His body brushed hers, and Sasha learned that a man's body was nothing at all like a woman's. He caught her face in his big hands; he kissed her, hard, a bruising kiss.

She pushed him away. "Who is Gabrielle?" she demanded to know.

Now he looked angry, his vivid blue eyes clouding up. He drew back, a small snarl on his face. "*She* is no concern of yours."

"I hate you, Quinn!" she shouted, and struck his chest hard, though it did almost nothing to stagger Quinn, much to her disappointment. He wasn't nearly as fragile-looking as he seemed.

"I'll never speak to you again!" With a cry of frustration, she returned to the comfortless fire. Alone.

| 13 |

*C*hirp.

Sasha opened her eyes to the sound so close to her ear. A wet nose probed her ear and she nearly screamed as she sat up in the dim firelight, throwing off the coat that Quinn had laid over her shoulders. The something by her ear darted away and scrabbled up a nearby rock, but in the chancy light, she couldn't see it clearly. She started to scream again, but Quinn's big hand suddenly clamped over her mouth.

"Shh," he said in her ear. She held very still as he rooted around, taking a burning branch from the edge of the fire and bringing it close to the rock where the chirping was loudest. Something squealed in alarm and leaped away.

Sasha shivered, even with Quinn pressed securely against her. What if it was a vampire bat come to feed on them? Her mind wanted to make up all kinds of monsters in the phantom dark.

Chirp...chiiiirp.

Quinn moved the homemade torch to follow the sound, and Sasha saw something small and quick dart to the top of a boulder and just stare at them with lemur-large eyes. It looked like a cross between a squirrel and a small monkey, with orange and white fur and huge, owl-yellow eyes. Its nose was longer than it ought to be, wriggling like a short elephant's trunk, and its back legs were long like a kangaroo, easily helping the small creature dart from rock to rock.

"What is that?" Sasha breathed, watching the little beastie dance in and out of the firelight.

Slowly Quinn wrapped both hands around the torch. "It's called dessert. And catgut." He started moving slyly toward it.

"What?" Sasha stopped him, a hand on his arm, touching him even though she was still quite cross with him and absolutely *not* speaking to him. "Don't, Quinn! Don't kill it."

"Why in hell not?"

"It's a mammal."

"So?"

"John and many of his friends at university believe that we evolved from just such small creatures."

"Sounds like rubbish to me."

"But what if it's true? You could be killing what might one day evolve into millions of people. A whole civilization on this planet." She waited, her heart thudding and her hand gripping his sleeve. She couldn't see Quinn's face in the dark, so she didn't know if she'd gotten through to him or not. She tightened her grip and added, "Besides, he's cute."

"I'm sure he'll make a cute dish."

"*Quinn!*" She made it a command. "If you kill that mammal, I shall never speak to you again!"

"You said that last night, yet here you are, speaking to me."

She shook his arm. "I *mean* it, Quinn."

Finally, he relaxed. Sasha released him and withdrew a few berries from her pocket and started crawling toward the small creature.

"I cannot believe you're feeding it!"

Sasha ignored him. When she was close enough to see the creature's twitching whiskers, she held a bright green berry out to it. It sniffed at her hand with its trunk-like nose; it didn't seem overly concerned with their presence; then again, it had probably never seen a human being before so had no reason to fear one. It took the berry from her with tiny, claw-like hands and nibbled it down quickly until it was gone. Sasha offered it another berry. This time it jumped boldly to her shoulder, startling her. It sniffed her hair. She fed it another berry. "I'll call it Newton the Second," she said with delight, its nose tickling her ear.

"Saints preserve me!" Quinn grumbled, turned over, and immediately went back to sleep.

| 14 |

The following morning, they made two very useful discoveries. The first happened when Quinn and Sasha returned to the pool of water to drink and wash. With dull sunlight filtering through the chimney of the cavern, Quinn spotted an abandoned reptile's nest with three large rotting eggs in it. They were too large and awkward for the toad monster to wrap his mouth around, so they just sat there amidst the rocks. Sasha didn't understand why this was of interest to Quinn until he used his knife to carve small holes in the tops of the leathery eggs and pour out the rotting contents. Then he washed the eggs thoroughly in the underground lake and refilled them almost to the top, plugging the holes with scraps of fabric. He handed their three homemade waterskins to Sasha to carry, explaining that such survival techniques were common among African tribes—though in Africa they used ostrich eggs, not dinosaur eggs.

Since carrying the eggs and her javelin was going to prove problematic, and Quinn couldn't carry the waterskins and cut down the tall grasses in their path at the same time, something had to be done. Sasha ducked behind some stalactites and shimmied out of the remnants of her corset and petticoat, fashioning from the fabric and whalebones a secure homemade rucksack to carry their water-eggs and remaining food stores. If Quinn could be clever, so could she.

Quinn said she was *very* clever indeed, though not very practical where Newton was concerned. The last thing they needed coming along was a *pet*. Sasha ignored him. Newton was extremely alert and she knew that could only be useful to them in their travels. Besides, she was still angry with him. Quinn was no gentleman to have kissed her like that. In fact, he was positively beastly, and she had no idea why she'd let it happen. She vowed to be more vigilant next time.

Sasha made the second discovery as they were preparing to leave the cave. She was carrying the waterskins and her javelin, Newton riding on her shoulder, when she spotted something she'd overlooked the night before when the light had been bad. The inside of the cavern wall was covered in small, cramped markings. At first glance, they looked like primitive cuneiform, something the ape-men might have made, but as Sasha drew closer, she realized the markings were letters. *English* letters. She felt her heart catch and she forgot her anger with Quinn for the moment. "Come look at this."

DEAR FRIEND, read the small, precise script, PERHAPS ONE DAY SOMEONE WILL READ THIS AND UNDERSTAND. MY NAME IS DR JOHN ULYSSES OF CORNELL UNIVERSITY, USA, AND THE DATE, AS FAR AS I UNDERSTAND IT, IS THE 15TH OF FEBRUARY 1889.

I STUMBLED INTO THIS WORLD BY ACCIDENT THROUGH A PORTAL OF MY OWN DESIGN. SOON AFTER MY ARRIVAL, I WAS CAPTURED BY AN ANCIENT PREDATORY PEOPLE CALLED THE SEN, AND THEIR LEADER, MUK. MUK OFFERED ME MY FREEDOM IN EXCHANGE FOR AGREEING TO KILL THE CERATOSAURUS THAT IS RAVAGING HIS LAND.

I AM PRESENTLY ON THE TRAIL OF THE CREATURE AND PREDICT I SHALL CATCH UP TO HER WITHIN A FORTNIGHT, BUT I WON'T BE KILLING HER. MUK LET SLIP THAT THE CREATURE HAS A VAST TERRITORY THAT INCLUDES WHAT HE CALLS THE "VALLEY OF SONG," A SACRED LAND BY WHICH HE THOUGHT I HAD ARRIVED. WHEN I INQUIRED FURTHER ABOUT THIS "VALLEY," HE EXPLAINED THAT IT IS A NETWORK OF MOUNTAIN RANGES THAT PRODUCE ODD SONGS WHEN THE WING BLOWS. I SUSPECT THE VALLEY IS NOT UNLIKE THE GRAND CANYON, WHICH PRODUCES ITS OWN NATURAL WINDSONGS AT TIMES.

SINCE IT WAS A TUNING MACHINE THAT BROUGHT ME HERE, NATURALLY I BECAME VERY INTERESTED IN THIS VALLEY. I HAVE A THEORY THAT I MAY BE ABLE TO RECREATE THE TONES THAT OPENED THE DOOR TO THIS PREHISTORIC PLANET BY CHANNELING WIND THROUGH ROCK FORMATIONS. I ONLY WISH I HAD A COLLEAGUE TO ASSIST ME.

I AM EN ROUTE TO THE VALLEY NOW BUT WILL WRITE MORE IF I AM ABLE. GOD BE WITH YOU, MY FRIEND.

It was signed by John with a scrawl she recognized from his frequent letters.

"Dr. Ulysses is your friend, yes?" Quinn said. "The one Muk mentioned as the man who ran away."

Sasha touched the chalked writing with her fingertips. It was still so fresh. "Yes." She swallowed against what felt like a walnut stuck in her throat. "John wrote this in February, around the time he disappeared."

"Three months ago," Quinn calculated. "Do you think he made it to this 'Valley of Song'?"

Sasha shook her head. "It's been three months, Quinn. I think if he'd reached it, he would have made use of it by now if he could. Obviously, something went wrong." She took a deep breath that hurt, swallowed hard, and added, "Something happened. Something bad."

She.

Sasha felt the food in her stomach lurch at the thought. Newton chirped with concern and put his nose to her ear.

"Maybe the Valley of Song just didn't work out and he moved on," Quinn suggested in an obvious effort to cheer her up. "He wouldn't have stayed here in Muk's territory when Muk discovered that he had failed to kill She."

That sounded reasonable too. "Maybe you're right."

"We should move on as well, as soon as possible. See if we can find Dr. Ulysses. I'm sure between the two of you, you can find a way home."

"We have to kill She first, Quinn, and free Toby," she reminded him.

Quinn spoke softly. "Yes, of course. And if we kill She, then Muk will be in our debt. He may even grant us a guide to help find this Valley."

Sasha nodded. It was the only plan they had, as flimsy and ill conceived as it was. She took a deep breath. They couldn't go on being angry with each other, she knew. Without Quinn, she would die out here in the jungle. She turned around. Quinn was right there, standing over her, protective, possessive. It made her angry. It made her afraid. It made her stomach leap up in a funny way, like a stabbed fish. "I'm sorry, Quinn," she said. "For everything."

In answer, he leaned down as he had last night and laid a light kiss on her cheek, on her nose, and finally on her lips. She opened her mouth to him, despite her vow, despite everything. He kissed her, his tongue tracing her bottom lip.

Chittering, Newton reached out and clawed Quinn's cheek.

"Bloody hell!" he barked and drew back, letting out a long stream of curses as he clutched his face. Newton chattered angrily, admonishing him.

Sasha giggled, then reached into her pocket and withdrew her handkerchief, staunching the blood on Quinn's face. He looked angry, and then, after a while, he did not.

They went back out into the grasslands. Back into danger.

| 15 |

As they crossed an idyllic sea of swaying golden grass, they started seeing a greater variety of dinosaurs. Long-necked sauropods as vast as whales swayed by in trumpeting, ever-mobile herds, while smaller plated dinosaurs scampered between their enormous feet. The smaller ones were capable of feeding in the dense, sporadic woods that dotted the landscape, but the enormous herbivores could only knock down trees with their sheer bulk and feed on the fallen branches. The density of the underbrush forced them to keep to the open plains. The smaller ones followed, because moving with the sauropods was safer. No Ceratosaurus—or, indeed, any predator—was willing to take on such huge, ship-like beasts.

Sasha and Quinn, like the smaller dinosaurs, moved with the herd; unlike them, they kept a safer distance. Quinn commented that even though they were herbivorous, a frightened African elephant would still charge a man just for being in the way. Sasha fed Newton berries and talked about the different dinosaurs they encountered, the meaning behind their scientific names, and their behaviors. She was delighted to learn that Quinn knew almost nothing about paleontology, even if he was good at survival in the wild. That meant it was her turn to educate *him*. Around noon, when the herd stopped to deforest a small copse of trees, they stopped to rest and feed themselves from their store of water and food. When the herd moved on, Sasha and Quinn moved with it, always west, toward the distant territories of She.

"You like dinosaurs, don't you?" Quinn said at one point.

"I like the big herbivores," Sasha admitted as Quinn steered her away from a rambunctious young stegosaurus that had wandered away from its mother to explore them. It pranced up to them, the size of a draft horse, then bounced away with its spiky tail held high. "I'm not overly keen on the predators, though."

Quinn smirked, briefly. "Nor I. May I have some water, please?"

Sasha reached into her homemade rucksack and passed Quinn one of the water eggs. Quinn drank, then splashed a handful of water over his face and hair. It made his shirt stick to his back and shoulders and Sasha looked away, wondering if she'd have an opportunity to see Quinn shirtless again. It was an absurd thought, she told herself.

Yesterday, Quinn's sensitive redheaded skin had burned to the color of a Heritage rose. Now his skin was peeling and developing a bronze sheen, like something emerging from his African days. She imagined she was even worse off—she never so much as walked in her father's garden without a hat—but luckily for her, Quinn had harvested some oils from a strangely pointed-looking plant that he said would help with the redness and peeling. The salve helped cool her angry burns, though it felt uncomfortably like syrup coating her face.

Sasha picked absently at the insects sticking to the goo on her sunburned face. "Do you have any new idea as to how we'll kill She when we find her?"

Quinn thought about that. "In Africa, bushmen sometimes lever boulders off high cliffs to crush the backs of the large animals they're hunting, like elephants and water buffalo. Perhaps we could do something similar."

"But elephants and buffalo are much smaller compared to She. Will that work?"

Quinn hefted the spear over his shoulder and considered that. "Maybe we can start an avalanche. Bury her alive."

His idea seemed reasonable, though not foolproof. She had no idea how they would start an avalanche. And even if it was possible, what was to keep them from burying themselves along with the creature? Sasha stared up at the brutal midday sun and scratched at her face some more, wishing there was a safer way of killing the creature—preferably from a distance. "Did the bushmen teach you a lot in Africa? Is that how you know so many things?"

Quinn didn't look up, just marched onward, using the javelin like a walking stick. "They taught me everything. After years of living in Africa, I considered them the most civilized men in the world. Especially compared to my countrymen, and my father."

He said the last bit softly, bitterly, as if he already regretted saying it.

She looked at him, at his bowed head of windblown red hair. "What was your father like, Quinn?"

Quinn never broke his stride. "A devil. The devil."

"But he took you to Africa with him." Even her father didn't take her anywhere of importance with him when he traveled.

As if reading her thoughts, Quinn added, "He took me to Africa because I was his only child, Sasha, not because he liked me."

"That's a horrible thing to say about your father," she said softly. "You should honor your father as they say in the Good Book."

"I don't believe in God. Watch your step." He pulled her out of the path of a creaking, falling tree that a sauropod had bullied over only a few meters away. Branches crackled and leaves fluttered down like strange rain, but she just kept staring at him, unable to pull her eyes away.

Quinn stared back, his eyes dark and hooded in his sunburned face. "My father was an evil old git. He beat our servants, our slaves, even my mother almost from the beginning of their marriage. She had three miscarriages because of him. She finally died of her injuries when I was six years old. Then it was my turn." His smile grew, infinitely bitter, so he looked almost like a devil with his red hair and red face and dark, desperate eyes. Sasha flinched internally. In her mind's eye, she saw again the old scar tissue webbing Quinn's back.

"Quinn, please..."

"That's who the esteemed Lord Horace Quinn was. And *that* was the day my faith died. Do you understand, Sasha?"

She looked away. She marched on, putting more lift into her steps. She was too stunned to react. She had never heard of such horrors in a family before. Her father had never struck her in his life, no matter how petulant a child she'd been. He probably wouldn't have known how. He had loved her mother. He loved her. She concentrated on just walking and not tripping over her own feet. Finally, after the heat and silence had slipped in between them like a burning wall, she said in a soft, broken voice, "I'm sorry, Quinn. I'd no idea."

"Why are you sorry, Sasha? None of it was your fault."

His words stung. "I mean...I'm sorry. I don't know what to say, Quinn."

Quinn took mercy on her at last and said, "You don't know what to say because you're a good girl, Sasha. A pure woman."

She didn't feel pure. She felt naïve. A stupid girl who, for all her books and tutors and learning, knew absolutely nothing about life.

Quinn walked on, a small, evil smirk playing on his lips. "When my father finally died, and I became the new Lord Quinn, I threw a week-long party at the old house. We'd stay up all night drinking and carousing. I celebrated the death of that old bastard. For the first time in my life, I felt my mother was truly at rest. Am I an evil person, Sasha?" He turned to look at her directly, to demand her judgment. "Am I evil in that I rejoiced in my father's death?"

Sasha felt his burning gaze on her profile but kept her eyes down on her feet stomping through the tall grass and over the ragged rocks.

"Am I?" Quinn insisted. "Am I evil to have celebrated the passing of a monster?"

Sasha swallowed, her throat clicking. She hated Quinn, she decided. Before Quinn, her world had been whole and good and beautiful, populated with Godly people she understood. She did not like Quinn's ugly world of ugly, evil people. She swallowed again over the lump in her throat. She forced her voice out. "No. I don't think you're evil, Quinn." She licked her parched lips. She needed water. "Is that why you drink? To forget all that?"

"No," he answered flatly. "I was a very happy man after my father died. A free man."

"Then why?" She thought about the newspaper stories she'd read, his carousing at taverns, the trouble he was in with his creditors, and with the law.

Quinn's smile grew, ragged and demonic. "God cursed me. That's what happened." He moved ahead of her, using his javelin like a crutch to move along. He spoke no more on the subject after that.

| 16 |

Sasha knew they were nearing the sea long before they saw or heard it. She smelled it.

When she was only a wee thing, her Aunt Margaret had taken her to Boscastle on Cornwall on holiday, and the breezy little seaside village had had this odor, like air and salt and fish and storms. She thought about saying all this to Quinn, but he seemed lost in his own thoughts. He'd gone to some other place, a dark place she was unfamiliar with—a place she wasn't allowed to come. Only when Newton became agitated and started chirping on her shoulder and the herd of sauropods began turning back in clouds of dust and thunder did he seemed to awaken. He laid a hand on her arm, a now-familiar gesture that told her that something was wrong.

The grasslands were giving way to more rocky terrain. After another mile or so, Sasha spotted sand dunes and sparse grasses up ahead. They crested a rise and she heard the dull telltale roar of the sea for the first time. Together they stood at the top of a cliffside ridge and looked down on a rocky coast of glittering brown sand. Beyond lay the distant sea, dark and greenish and forbidding, with furious whitecaps snapping at the beach as if a summer storm were well on its way. Enormous creatures breached just offshore, creatures bigger than the sauropods, bigger than whales, the sun glinting on their sleek backs as they sliced bladelike through the water.

Sasha shielded her eyes from the angry glare of sun on water. "There is no Valley," she said aloud. She felt a pang of disappointment followed by a swell of relief. Muk must have made a mistake. Or he'd lied to John about the Valley of Songs. Either way, this was certainly no valley. Maybe John had discovered the lie and moved on. Maybe that was why he'd gone missing these past three months. Maybe he was still searching. Of course, that didn't mean that John hadn't encountered She or some other dangerous predator. It was only that now she could afford to be hopeful.

Quinn looked things over with narrow, analytical eyes. As if to read her mind, he said, "I don't see any evidence of John's having camped here. Of course, he might have moved on a long time ago and left no trace."

"You don't think he went out to sea?" John could certainly have made a raft if he put his mind to it.

"If he did, he wouldn't have survived long with those dinosaurs out there."

"They're marine reptiles, actually."

Quinn gave her a peevish look.

Sasha bit her lip. "You're probably right. I think John would have been smarter than that."

"There are sea caves down that way," he said, indicating some cliff heads further along the coast with his javelin. "John may have taken shelter there…"

"And if so," she finished, "maybe he left us another message."

Together, they started making their way down the beach.

| 17 |

They found John's note chalked on the wall of the fifth sea cave they explored. It read:

DEAR FRIEND, I HAVE REACHED THE OCEAN ONLY TO LEARN THAT MUK HAS LIED. THERE IS NO VALLEY, OR, AT LEAST, NO VALLEY HERE.

I SUSPECT HE KNEW I WOULD NOT FIGHT HIS BEAST FOR HIM. IN RETALIATION, HE SENT ME ON A WILD GOOSE CHASE. HOWEVER, I'M NOT REALLY VERY ANGRY. AFTER ALL, I HAD PLANNED ON BETRAYING MUK FIRST! HONOR AMONG THIEVES AND ALL THAT. HE HAS OBVIOUSLY ANTICIPATED THIS. PERHAPS IT IS A RESULT OF THE TELEPATHY HIS PEOPLE SEEM TO POSSESS.

I DON'T KNOW WHAT LANDS LIE BEYOND MUK'S TERRITORY, BUT I MUST MOVE ON BEFORE HIS PEOPLE RECAPTURE ME, AND BEFORE THE CREATURE WHO HAUNTS THESE LANDS RETURNS. MY PLANS ARE TO FOLLOW THE COASTLINE OF THIS INLAND SEA FULL OF STRANGE SEA SERPENTS. WHAT ELSE IS THERE TO DO? THE FISHING IS GOOD, AND THE LARGE LAND PREDATORS WILL NOT VENTURE DOWN TO THE BEACH.

I WILL WRITE MORE WHEN I AM ABLE. GOD BE WITH YOU AND HOPEFULLY, WE WILL "SPEAK" AGAIN.

John's name and a date approximately two months old followed. Sasha touched the chalk, which was faintly damp from the sea crashing only a hundred meters away. Quinn moved to stand close to her, as he liked to do. He did not touch her, but he did say, softly, "I'm sure he's fine. He seems like a smart chap, not like your young Toby."

Sasha swallowed, ignoring his ribbing. "You're just saying that. He's probably dead by now."

"Together the two of you invented an amazing machine that can send men to other Earths, Sasha. Like you, I'm sure your John is very clever and very resourceful. I look forward to meeting him one day."

She looked at the chalk on her fingertips. Maybe in forty or fifty million years, a human civilization will have evolved on this planet. Explorers would one day find these caves long buried in the earth and wonder what the chalk marks meant. "She might have killed him, Quinn. A hundred things could have killed him. Hunger, an injury, just a single mistake…"

"Don't think that way, Sasha."

"How else shall I think?" she shouted. This was all his fault! Quinn himself had torn the veil away from her eyes. Quinn made her see the world for the grim, unhappy place it was.

"I don't think She ever caught him," he said softly, with authority. "The sand here is extraordinarily soft. I doubt She, or even her husband, would have chanced being trapped in it. It's almost like quicksand."

Sasha bit her lip and considered his words. Was he only being overly optimistic for her sake, or did he believe that? She turned around. She was trembling. Quinn put his arms around her, held her, and rested his chin on the top of her head. It felt good to be pressed into all his sun-baked warmth, into the damp, male scent of him. She felt protected. "You're shaking," he said.

"I'm tired, Quinn. And scared. And worried about Toby. And worried about John. And, oh...hungry and cold, and I really want a slice of steak and oyster pie."

Quinn laughed then, the rumbling sound coming from deep inside his chest. "I'd be partial to some Yorkshire pudding right about now."

"Sunday roast, lamb with mint sauce."

"You are making me very hungry, little Sasha," he complained, though his voice had changed, grown airy and husky at the same time. He looked at her the way a man looks at a woman, ran his hands over her mussed hair, and ducked his head to kiss her lightly...cautiously, mindful of Newton, who, at the first opportunity, had leaped to some nearby rocks to chase down a spider.

She meant to stop Quinn, to tell him it was inappropriate, that they needed to make camp and prepare for their hunt tomorrow, but the moment Quinn's mouth found hers, she felt a spill of heat deep inside, like she was full of sun-warmed honey. It didn't help that the dried goo on their faces made them stick together. Or maybe it did.

She kissed him back, slipped her hands around his sunburned neck, and pulled him down so she could deepen the kiss and run her tongue across his teeth. The motion seemed to weaken him—or maybe it was the long journey—but he simply spilled down on top of her so he was kneeling over her, pinning her to the floor of the cave. The cool rock felt good against her sunburned neck and shoulders, and his heavy warm hands on her made her feel better still.

For once, she didn't feel like an ignorant little girl. She felt like a woman. She wriggled around a bit, and Quinn used the opportunity to anchor himself down on top of her and bury his face in her hair and the side of her neck. It raised shivers all along her skin. He traced the edge of her collarbone with his lips. She traced his back with the palms of her hands, feeling the roughened, raised scar tissue there. It brought her back to resounding reality for a moment, and she feared where this might lead. She'd read about such things in romance novels, these complications, and it never ended well for the heroine who'd been compromised.

"Quinn," she said, her shoulders grinding into the stones of the floor as he buried his face in the warm, sweating cleft between her breasts. She was acutely aware of her lack of a corset. "Quinn...stop..."

He kissed the sensitive flesh over her rapidly beating heart and then looked up at her with such a longing it was a labor just to breathe. No one had ever looked at her that way before. "Don't..." she began, her chest rising and falling so rapidly she saw sparkles of light in the corners of her vision. She felt a blush start somewhere near her toes and work its way up her body before settling into the apples of her cheeks. "Don't...compromise me, please."

Quinn drew himself up on his elbows and watched her carefully. "You're right, of course. This is all very awkward." He sounded disappointed, breathless, not himself. Slowly, he climbed to his feet, dusted himself off, and went off to explore the cave they would be using for their camp.

Sasha remained where she was for the moment, her face turned away so he couldn't see the tears welling up in her eyes. She'd never been so close, so intimate, with a man before. She could have hoped for more. She could have wished for...so many things. She wondered what it would feel like to lie every night in Quinn's arms, to kiss him, to be with him, together, in their marriage bed.

But Quinn didn't love her. Quinn loved Africa.

| 18 |

The light was turning rosy orange outside the cave and reflecting off the ocean like a spill of blood on the waves. The sea air was growing heavier, cooler. Sasha finished tending the cooking fire and climbed to her feet, gathering Quinn's frock coat more securely about her shoulders. The coat smelled like him, and she buried her face in it for a moment. Quinn had gone down the beach to fish just over an hour ago, and still he hadn't returned. That worried her. But she swallowed the lump of childish panic in her throat, and, wrapped in his coat, she ventured down the beach in search of him.

The sand was incredibly soft under her feet, almost springy like a horsehair mattress. Now she knew what Quinn meant about it being unsafe for the Ceratosauruses to venture down the beach. Such large creatures were much too heavy to find any kind of support in the sand. They'd likely sink right to their knees.

She stopped to watch the foamy evening tide washing in. Quinn stood perched on some large rocks in the shallows, his javelin stabbing deep into the little pools of water formed by the rocks and into the bodies of fishes and crustaceans trapped in the shallows. As she watched, he dragged out yet another one of those queer, bony fish. He flicked it to the beach, where it writhed in the sand for a bit before falling still, then returned to watching the shallows with keen eyes. John had been right about the fishing; Quinn had quite a catch—three or four different kinds of fish, some crabs, and what looked like a sea scorpion the size of a hound dog.

"We have enough for a banquet!" she observed, clapping her hands.

Quinn turned and offered her a smirk and a dramatic bow. He was sunburned and shirtless, and the sight of him so touchably bare made Sasha's cheeks burn. "This isn't for us," he explained. "Not all of it, anyway."

"What do you mean?"

He climbed off the rocks and reached for his dirty white shirt lying on the sand. "I've been trying to determine how to trap that beast." He slid his arms into the shirtsleeves and slid it over his head as he spoke. "Another method the bushmen use is to trap a large animal in quicksand. And the sand here is certainly quick." He turned to indicate a steep cliff head that loomed just over their heads. "I think if we could lure She down the beach using our catch, we might just have her. Many large creatures are opportunists; they'll eat carrion in a pinch. If I can get She over that cliff, I think it likely she'll become mired in the beach sand. Then I can finish her off." He stabbed at the open air with the javelin to indicate what he meant.

It sounded reasonable—and, more importantly, less dangerous than their avalanche idea. Sasha smiled, satisfied. "It's a sound plan, Quinn. I'll get my javelin then."

"That won't be necessary."

She blinked. "What do you mean?"

"There's no reason to put yourself in danger," he stated—rather imperiously, she thought. "I must insist that you remain at the cave whilst I work at trapping the creature."

She looked at him. "You *insist?*" Then she laughed. "Quinn, you're not my husband, nor my father. You cannot *insist* on anything. We work together, understand?" She started walking back toward the cave, but Quinn stopped her, his hand on her arm.

"Now see here, I won't have you running about, getting yourself in danger. I'm *responsible* for you..."

"No, you're not," she said.

"Yes," he insisted, getting angry now, "I am. Albertus will be expecting me to return you in one piece. And besides, you're my..." He hesitated, and Sasha lifted an eyebrow, wondering how he would complete that sentence. "...a woman. I cannot allow you to put yourself in peril."

Maybe, just maybe, had he said *my* woman, she would have listened. But he did not. Again, Sasha laughed, this time bitterly. "There's no need to put me in peril, Quinn. You should realize by now that I'm perfectly capable of putting *myself* in peril." Pulling her arm free, she marched back to the cave.

| 19 |

Near morning, they heard She's hunting cry for the first time echoing across the distant plains, the sound almost drowned out by the dim roar of a sudden rainstorm. The storm had Quinn worried; he couldn't decide if the wet sand was going to work to the creature's disadvantage or their own. Distantly, something alive screamed piteously until it was dead. Consumed.

Sasha, sitting just inside the mouth of the cave, the javelin across her lap, breathed in, out, in, out, trying not to panic, trying not to let the terror show in her face and eyes. Newton chattered excitedly, jumped off her shoulder, and started clambering up some rocks to a higher, safer, perch.

Quinn was already on his feet. "She's coming."

Sasha let out a long, ragged breath even as her heart tried to beat its way right out of her chest. She gripped her javelin with aching white fingers. "Yes," she agreed.

"Sasha…"

"No, Quinn."

They'd had this conversation a thousand times during the course of the night. She was *not* staying behind, and that was all there was to it. Quinn, not happy, but grimly resolved, focused his attention on the beach and the sea beyond, where some gigantic, porpoise-like creatures with long jaws and razor-sharp teeth were breaching in the rain and waves.

She and Quinn had spent the night close to the fire, speaking, but not touching. She didn't want to touch Quinn, be with Quinn, *be* Quinn's when she knew nothing could come of it. If they ever did make it back home, Quinn would only return to his beloved Africa. To Gabrielle. Sasha was resolved. In the real world, things did not always go according to fairy tales. The knight didn't always slay the dragon and win the maiden fair—sometimes he did not even want her. And sometimes the dragon won and ate the knight *and* the maiden.

Quinn stepped out of the sea cave and into the downpour, Sasha right on his heels. They were instantly drenched and the sour smell of the slowly rotting fish hit them in a head-spinning miasma. It was no surprise that She was here, considering the stench, which could probably be detected for miles. Another roar sounded across the plains like a clarion, the sound closer this time. It caused some small Rhamphorhynchus to flutter bat-like up and away from their lure on the beach only a short distance away.

They hurried under the overhang of the cliff, their backs flat to the rock wall. Sasha waited, her heart ticking so rapidly in her throat she thought she could swallow it. Quinn gripped his javelin in both hands, listening, waiting, tense—fully prepared to drive the flint point into She's soft underbelly as she reached for the lure that was set just out of reach. In theory, the cliff head would offer them the protection they so desperately needed. The wounded animal would tumble over the edge and into a sucking pit of soft, wet sand. And there they would finish her off.

Reality proved much different. The creature that lumbered out onto the cliff was smaller and lighter than She. It moved like lightning. Suddenly it was right there, huge and fecund and overhanging them both like a deadly, breathing cloud. The sight turned Sasha's blood to cold sludge and simultaneously made the sweat break out all over her body. Quinn cursed violently at the sight of She's "husband"—as he liked to call the male Ceratosaurus—and prepared to ram the javelin home.

He wasn't quick enough. The male, balanced on the edge of the cliff with its heavy head fully extended and jaws snapping wildly at the carrion on the beach, suddenly jerked backward and swung his head down as if sensing they were there. Quinn jammed the javelin upward between his massive teeth but hit no soft spots. The javelin just bounced off, and Quinn pushed Sasha down and out of the way of those swinging, open jaws.

They landed in a heap under the cliff head.

Sasha screamed, clutching Quinn.

"Sasha, let go!" Quinn snarled, gripping the javelin and preparing for a second strike.

She held tight to his arm, hoping to keep him out of the line of the monster's jaws. "It isn't She!" she insisted. There was no reason to continue this insanity!

"But it'll destroy her if I kill him!" He shook off her hold, gripped the javelin, and stepped out from under the shelter of the cliff. Dear God, Sasha thought, sitting up in the sand, he's insane!

She's husband immediately lunged, and Quinn stabbed at the creature's massive head with the flint tip, gouging a hole under its eye socket. The beast bellowed and reared back, its jaws clacking together like some weapon. Thunder crackled overhead in time with the beast's angry cries. Sasha gasped as the cliff began to crumble, dirt and rocks raining down upon her as the massive creature stomped and screamed. It was going to bring the whole thing down!

Quinn saw, and knew. His face set in a determined grimace of pain and rage, he stabbed at the beast again, this time nicking its nasal horn. Something had snapped inside Quinn's head, she realized. It was as if he had lost all reason. She had to act before he killed himself! She didn't think; she just launched herself at Quinn, hitting him full on in the chest. The two of them tumbled down the beach, missing the flashing jaws by inches, the squishy sand deadening their impact at the bottom of the hill. "Quinn!" she screamed from atop him, hoping he'd wake up and return to his senses. "Stop, Quinn, stop!"

He did. He saw her, took her face in his big trembling hands, his eyes pained...then moved her off him. She tried to hold him down, but he scrambled up, his eye set on his prey, and there was no stopping him now. Quinn fully extended his arm, took aim, and launched the javelin at the creature's head. His shot was spot on. The javelin punctured one of the beast's vapid yellow eyes, black fluid bursting forth and making the creature jerk wildly with hellish screams.

Quinn grinned in triumph.

Then the unexpected happened. The twenty-foot, screaming reptile launched itself off the cliff, jaws fully agape and aiming for them both.

| 20 |

Quinn pushed Sasha out of the way, a hard push that sent her spinning down the slope of the beach. The sand broke her fall but she lost her javelin halfway down. The moment she came to a halt, she started scrambling to her feet.

She was just in time to see the worst sight imaginable. The male Ceratosaurus was trapped knee-deep in the sand, its body fully extended in Quinn's direction and the cuff of Quinn's trousers in its teeth. It grunted and whipped its head from side to side like a gigantic demonic terrier, thrashing Quinn in the sand. Were the sand not so soft, he would have been dashed to death in seconds. As it was, Quinn was trying desperately to find some purchase by clawing at the sand. It just slid away from him, offering him no traction whatsoever. The Ceratosaurus seemed to understand that it was sinking, that it was going to die because it was determined to take Quinn with it. It stopped thrashing Quinn and started methodically dragging him forward, inch by slow inch. Its one remaining eye was cool, dark, and evil. Triumphant.

"Quinn!" Sasha started running uphill toward him but was like trying to run through molasses, each step a labor in the wet, heavy sand that sucked at her ankles.

Grunting with the effort, the irate creature dragged Quinn another inch along. Its jaws were as wide around as Quinn's whole body. It could swallow him whole in just one bite, and Quinn well knew it. He grabbed a handful of sand and flung it into the beast's face, cursing it. As it snorted and shook its head, Quinn tried to worm backward. Man and beast just sank further into the sand.

Sasha stopped to yank her javelin out of the sand, then raced headlong toward the beast. Each of her legs felt as heavy as lead like she was stuck in a nightmare, unable to move toward her intended target. She was so frightened her mind was numb, a blank slate upon which nothing readable was written. All she could concentrate on was Quinn. Quinn needed her. Quinn was dying. She had to help him. She was gasping, almost blind with panic, when she finally reached the creature's blindside. She uttered an exhausted battle cry and raised her javelin over her head, using both hands to ram it into the side of the beast's neck. Blood burst forth, spilling brilliant scarlet ideograms across her face and over the remnants of her gown. She tasted the beast's cool blood in her mouth. It screamed so piercingly it made Sasha's ears ring, and Sasha realized she was screaming with it, at it.

The beast twisted its head and knocked her down in the sand. Sasha sat up, bruised and battered in a dozen places. The creature clawed at its throat with its underdeveloped talons, knocking the spear into the sand in front of Quinn. Then all Sasha could see through the silvery sheets of rain was one black mechanical eye turning to her, the glistening, leathery grey head, the flash of starbright teeth. All she felt was a blast of hot, fetid air from its stinking gullet. She had no time to scream, no way to prepare for the end.

Its jaws surrounded her and Sasha closed her eyes.

She waited...but nothing happened.

Letting out a sob, she opened her eyes and saw Quinn had her much shorter javelin in his hands, which was a blessing because it allowed him to land a final thrust at a much closer range...right into the creature's soft throat. It made gagging noises, its jaws froze around her, its teeth just denting her flesh. It extended its long, blood-red tongue, the tip brushing wet and viscous across the bodice of Sasha's dress. Sasha screamed as the rain lashed them all. Quinn cursed the beast and drove the javelin all the way in. The beast gasped, and blood foamed out of its massive jaws. Then it fell still, dead, looking like some great stony statue.

The creature began to sink more rapidly. Quinn climbed over the beast's head and wrapped his arms about her middle, extraditing her from its jaws seconds before the massive bulk started the long descent down the beach. It knocked them both over in the sand. Then it slid over hills of sand and rocks, finally coming to a splashing rest in the shallows.

"Sasha?" Quinn said, sounding panicked. He sat up with Sasha sitting in his lap.

She was shaking too badly to speak. All she could do was cling to Quinn and cry.

"Oh, Sasha...my girl," Quinn said. He clutched her and stroked her hair while she trembled and wept against the comforting wall of his chest, now decorated with sand, dirt, and dinosaur blood. "Sasha," he said, "that was very brave...and very stupid."

Hiccupping, she raised her head and looked into his pale, somber blue eyes. She could have said the same about him. He'd looked like a madman, like nothing would have stopped him from killing the creature trying to kill her. She wrapped her arms about his neck. In the rain, he looked like a drowned, red-haired rat...and the most beautiful man she had ever seen. "I told you I wasn't afraid," she said as a river of unladylike snot ran from her nose.

"You're not, are you, my dear?"

She shook her head.

A sound made them turn and glanced down where the beast lay dead in the rain. Or not so dead. She'd expected a corpse, but the male was making little distressed noises and trying to crawl awkwardly back up the slope of the beach, struggling against the sand and its terrible injuries, its remaining eye set on them with something like hateful determination, its jaws clacking together like a machine that would not stop, would never die.

"Dear God," said Sasha, clutching Quinn even tighter. He tried to rise with her in his arms, but his legs gave out and he fell back down into the wet sand.

The Ceratosaurus was a quarter of the way up the beach when one of the giant porpoise-like creatures breached and flung itself onto the beach. It clamped its hungry jaws onto the creature's back end and bit down, dragging half the creature out to sea and leaving half a dinosaur floundering on the beach.

Sitting there in a daze, being pelted by rain and dead fish smell, they watched the light go out of its one good eye until, finally, it lay still forever.

| 21 |

Their last act before returning to Muk's people was to take the claw of the monster lying shredded down on the beach. During the walk back, Quinn carved a small hole through the claw with his knife and threaded it with a thick black vine, creating what he called a trophy necklace for Sasha. It was beautiful, the most wonderful gift anyone had ever given her. It was just a shame that she had to present it to Muk.

The journey seemed much shorter going back. They did not encounter She, or anything more ferocious than a small pod of Styracosaurus grazing in an open plain and occasionally clacking their armored heads together as they competed for mates. Quinn and Sasha moved steadily east with the herd, using them as a shield; the predators of the plain seemed much too reluctant to tangle with them. On the morning of the third day, they finally sighted the jagged mountain that Muk and his clan called home. Sasha felt a swell of dread and excitement as they drew near the dormant volcano.

They were less than half a mile away when two of Muk's couriers appeared to transport them inside the volcano. The moment Sasha touched down and saw that Toby was all right, was alive, she forgot all about the pain and terror they had experienced in their little adventure and stumbled forward, nearly falling against the cage where he waited with bright, tear-struck eyes. He clutched her in his big hands, dragging her as close to him as the bars of the cage would allow, and without saying a word, kissed her. It was so unexpected that Sasha never had a chance to respond. Toby's kiss was warm and gentle and wanting. It tasted like tears. She thought of Quinn standing nearby, watching them both. Her cheeks flushed and she pulled away abruptly.

"You're alive," she said, to cover her embarrassment.

"You too," Toby answered, running his hands over her tangled hair and down the sides of her scratched and dirty face like he couldn't believe she was there, that she wasn't a dream. "I was so afraid you'd been hurt, Sasha, or that you'd left me, or that Quinn had taken you away with him."

"No, of course not." How could he even think such a thing? They were in this together, all three of them.

He must have sensed her unease, because he added, "I'm sorry, Sasha, it's just...the last few days have been difficult. I've missed you." He smiled that familiar, lopsided smile.

She smiled back. "And I you." It felt good to see Toby, to feel his warm hands, to know he was alive. But at the same time, she couldn't shake the feeling that Quinn was watching them coolly, in that calculating way he had.

Toby's smile grew. "I have something important to tell you, Sasha. Something I should have said long ago."

She got a very bad feeling then. "Tell me later, Toby," she said as carefully as possible. "When we get out of here." She rocked back on her heels and looked up at Muk. He was as ugly as she had remembered, but at least he had kept his word. He hadn't harmed Toby, as he'd promised he would not. He seemed, as Quinn put it, an honorable bloke. She showed him the heavy black claw around her neck. He approached her, tilting his head to one side as he examined it, making low clicks in his throat as if he were deliberating.

Sasha held her breath.

He narrowed his eyes. Finally, he spoke. This is not the claw of She, he said. Now all three of you will die

| 22 |

In one smooth motion, Quinn grabbed one of the young Sen standing nearby, drew his Bowie knife from his boot, and raised the razor-sharp edge so it sat just under the creature's chin, making it chirp excitedly. Quinn's eyes were blue and pale and deadly, like fired steel. "I'm not dying today, Muk. Not after everything I've gone through to earn my freedom."

Muk's eyes flared. *Release that boy*, he said.

Quinn grinned, evilly. "Why? Is he yours, old boy? That's just too bloody bad. Now show me the door!" He jabbed the edge of the knife in deeper, cutting the boy enough that a thin trickle of blood dribbled down his hairy chest. The young Sen began making panicked shrills in his throat. Quinn ignored him.

Muk bared his impressive set of saber teeth. *What about your people?* He glanced at Sasha and Toby. *Don't you care at all about their safety?*

Quinn looked the two of them over. His eyes were cold, dead. "Why should I care about that lot? The boy despises me and the girl only used me to get back to her childhood lover. I've no time for those two fools, and no love lost in their deaths."

Each of his words was like a nail to Sasha's heart. Each one pounded a little more love right out of her. The resulting space was quickly filled with pity and fear...and bitterness. "Quinn," she began, biting back the awful tears clogging up her throat. All she could think about was the last kiss they had shared, the way Quinn had held her like she was precious to him. *Like he loved her.* "You're lying. You're just making all this up, aren't you?" A small part of her hoped, wanted to believe that Quinn was merely trying to escape so he could free them later. But was that too much to hope for in Quinn? She feared so when she looked into the soulless chambers of his eyes.

"Quinn," she insisted, "I *know* you're lying."

"He's not lying," Toby said, face darkening, voice dropping in pitch and timbre. "He's a drunk and a coward. He really does hate us. You hate *everyone*, don't you, Quinn?"

Quinn smirked emptily on them. He raised the knife a hair and more blood flowed from the young Sen. "I hate only when someone betrays me. When they *lie*. When they *use me*."

Toby looked to Sasha, but Sasha had no answers for him. She took a step toward Quinn, then stopped when she saw it was hopeless, that she would never be able to convince him otherwise. She wanted to plead, to rage, but she couldn't pull her eyes away from him, his twisted mask of despair…disappointment.

"That escort, Muk," Quinn said, his knife hand dead steady at the throat of the young creature. "*Now.*"

Sasha continued to stare long after Quinn and his hostage were whisked away from her. She continued to stare even after she'd crumpled to her knees and the hungry, shadowy shapes of the Sen closed in around her, chirping excitedly.

"Quinn!" she cried.

And then the Sen were upon her.

II

SEA OF SERPENTS

In which our heroes must escape a deadly threat.

| 23 |

Sasha Strange screamed.

The looming, bat-like Sen clutched the bars of her cage and stuck out its long, barbed tongue, teasing her. The tongue slithered across the floor like a snake, but it could easily penetrate her flesh like a spear, Sasha knew. She had seen it done. She screamed again, grabbed up a sharp stone lying on the floor of the cave, and smashed it down atop the encroaching tongue. The Sen roared and retreated from her cage.

She clutched the stone, a solid, reassuring weight in her hand, her only weapon. She wished she still had the javelin she'd used to help kill She's mate, but that was long since gone, lost when she and Quinn had brought the great male Ceratosaurus down on the beach. Now all she had was this stone. She gritted her teeth and boldly took a step forward, much to the astonishment of Toby crouched on the floor nearby. "Next?" she asked.

She was proud of herself. And amazed. A short time ago, she would have been happy to stand by and let the men in her life handle this. No more. If she had learned anything from her journey with Quinn, it was that she had an indelible appetite for survival. She wanted to survive—*needed* to—to spite Quinn. She would find him and spit in his face for leaving them all to die this way. She clutched the rock in her trembling hand, imagined lobbing it at his head. Or at his chest, where no heart beat.

The Sen flew into a frenzy. The one with the bruised tongue turned and chattered excitedly with Muk, their leader. Muk looked to his clansman, then her. He nodded, and the clansman unlatched the door of the cage and climbed inside with her and Toby, moving awkwardly with his big, unwieldy wings. Sasha shuffled back a step, keeping herself between the creature and Toby, so weak from days without nourishment he could not even crawl. She clutched the stone in both hands, prepared to pitch it at the monster the way they pitched balls in cricket games at home in London. The creature hissed at her.

Sasha wound up and threw the rock. It bounced harmlessly off the chest of the creature in front of her. The creature emitted an ear-splitting cry and bared it long saber teeth. Then it lunged, driving her to the floor under its weight.

"Sasha!" Toby cried. But he so weak from days without food or water; there was nothing he could do.

Sasha began to fight, scratching and kicking and even biting at the tough fur and tougher skin of the beast pinning her to the floor. If she must die, if there was no other way, it would not be easy for the Sen, she vowed. She was punching at its sides and kicking at its legs when she smelled damp wood smoke for the first time. The creature must have sensed it too. It immediately leaped off her and turned to face Muk, seeking instruction from its leader.

Muk tilted his big shaggy head and scented the air. It smelled like a bonfire out of control, something that the Sen probably knew very little about, seeing how they did not utilize fire. Muk turned and pointed to the ceiling of the cave where a natural chimney acted as their exit, making a high screeching noise of emergency, directing his clansmen to escape.

At that moment, a puff of wood smoke began crawling into the room.

| 24 |

The Sen's home was nothing more elaborate than a maze of caverns carved into a dormant volcano, so they filled up fast with smoke. Within minutes, the Sen had cleared out through the chimney exit in the ceiling and Sasha and Toby were alone. Sasha coughed and tried to get Toby to his feet. Smoke stung her eyes and hung like heavy, torn veils in the air all around them. The formerly cool cavern was quickly heating up; the fire was eating its way through the mountain passages and rising as any good fire would.

"Toby!" Sasha cried as she worked at levering his weight onto her. It was difficult; Toby was a big muscular man and outweighed her by almost a hundred pounds. She stumbled as the heat and smoke began to choke her, but someone caught her, steadying her on her feet. At first, she feared it was a Sen, but then she saw the hands that had her were human. Large, long and thin, and lightly freckled along the backs. She squinted up at the familiar face looming over her through the curtain of smoke. She immediately recognized the pale rain blue eyes. "Quinn?" she said, almost afraid to believe that it might be true, that he'd come back for her.

"There's no time to talk," he said matter-of-factly, his voice muffled behind a handkerchief tied cowboy-style around the bottom half of his face. He took her arm. "We need to get out of here *now*." He looped an arm under Toby's armpits and hefted him to his feet.

"Take his other side," he said, and Sasha immediately raced to his other side and took as much of Toby's dead weight as she could.

Together, the two of them started down a long tunnel so smoke-filled it made Sasha gag. "Are we going the right way?" she asked, blinded by smoke. It seemed like they were walking right into the thick of it, and further down the tunnel she could see the glimmer of flames.

"This is how I got back in, so yes." Quinn directed them into a branch tunnel. Suddenly it was easier to breathe. "Keep moving," Quinn advised. "We need to get out of here. It'll only get worse soon."

Sasha kept going, each step a struggle with Toby's mostly unconscious weight pressing on her. The smoke gradually lessened, and then at last she saw daylight further down the tunnel. It galvanized her like nothing else. She could not wait to escape the Sen's caverns and see the open sky and breathe fresh air again!

They charged into the jungle with its myriad of buzzing insects and its fresh damp earth smell, then stopped when Sasha crumbled to her knees, gagging until her throat felt like rough sandstone. Her head swam and she realized she was on the verge of passing out. She was surprised to suddenly find herself in Quinn's arm.

"My darling," she heard him say or thought she did. Then all was darkness and silence.

| 25 |

It was all like a bad dream. Sasha opened her eyes and looked up at a clear, dark tropical sky full of strange birds she had never seen before. A huge orange orchid lazily dripped water onto her cheek. She tasted its unfamiliar nectar and sat up.

They were camped at the foot of the Sen's mountain. For a moment, her heart thudded in her chest in panic. She glanced around, afraid a Sen might swoop down on them at any moment. Instead, she spotted Quinn a few feet away, working on starting a fire for the oncoming night. Toby lay beside her, breathing roughly but alive when she checked him over.

She was too dizzy to climb to her feet so she crawled through the jungle debris to Quinn's side. She watched him spark a small flame in a pile of dry sticks with the flint in his pocket. He worked steadily at kindling the fire, without looking at her. She had judged him harshly, she knew. She'd assumed he would leave her and Toby to die. She'd assumed he was full of hate. She'd been utterly convinced of it. And the realization made her ashamed.

"Quinn," she finally said when the silence became too much.

He ignored her. He was not classically handsome like Toby. He was too tall, too gaunt, middle-aged, freckled, redheaded pale, and perpetually unsmiling. He looked rough, like the lot of them. He smelled of jungle and time and trials. He gave off a faint vibration of rage at all times, like a man who might do anything. And yet...he'd saved her. He'd treated her with enormous tenderness. She'd kissed him and nearly swooned like some silly heroine in the romance novels. He infuriated her, confused her, and the more she learned about him, the more she wanted to know.

"Quinn," she said again. She thought about touching his arm, but she didn't know how he would react. He might brush her away. "Quinn, is it safe here? What if the Sen return?"

"They won't," he answered tersely. "The cavern is all smoked out."

"Will that stop them from returning?"

"The Sen navigate by echolocation, and smoke interferes with their senses. They won't fly anywhere near here until the smoke clears out, and that will likely take all night. By then, we'll be away." He sat back on his heels. "In fact, the smoke will probably keep most of the animals away from us until morning."

She just looked at him. "How did you know that? That the smoke would work?"

He sat with his back to the mountain, hugged his knees, and watched the flames like they were the most interesting things in the world. "I remembered how bushmen flush bats out of caves in Africa. They smoked them." He shrugged his thin but powerful shoulders. "It worked, didn't it?"

She knew she ought to check on Toby, make sure he was doing all right, but she didn't want to leave Quinn just then. Quinn had saved her. Again. She didn't know what to say, how to apologize for what she had said—and thought. But she had to say something. She swallowed and found her courage, courage that Quinn himself had taught her. "You came back for us."

Finally, he looked at her. He looked hurt, as she had expected he would. "Did you think I would *not*?"

She stared down at her hands clenched in her lap. "I don't know what I thought."

The silence pressed in. She could feel him staring at her, his gaze so piercing it hurt.

Finally, he said, "Your young man hates me."

"He's not..." she began. Then she stopped. She didn't know *what* Toby was to her. "He doesn't hate you, Quinn."

"Yes," Quinn said. "He does." He looked back at the fire burning so fiercely before them. "Perhaps it would be best if we parted company here."

Sasha's heart lurched. "What? What do you mean?"

"It would perhaps be more...advantageous if I went one way and you and Toby the other. We could cover more ground that way, and if one of us found your friend Dr. Ulysses, we could devise a signal of some kind. A smoke signal, perhaps, something that could be seen for miles."

"Quinn, I really don't think that's a very good idea." She stood up. It was important they found her friend John—Dr. John Ulysses of Cornell University in the States. He was perhaps the only man who could get them home, and she knew Quinn's logic was flawless, but she also knew he was doing this for reasons other than convenience. "Let's discuss this at a later time. Please. At least until we reach the coast. Right now we need each other." She touched his shoulder, but he was cold, so cold.

| 26 |

By morning, Toby was better. Not perfect, perhaps, but he insisted he was fit enough to travel. Since the Sen could return at any time, they packed their camp and were off.

It was a painfully silent journey out of the jungle and across the open plains. Sasha had everything and nothing to say to Quinn. Toby seemed to sense that something was amiss but chose to say little unless he saw something truly amazing. Sasha and Quinn knew what to expect—they'd been this way before—but for Toby, the incredible variety of dinosaurs perambulating along the plains was something new. He gaped at the ship-sized sauropods in massive, earth-moving herds, the giant armored stegosaurus, the small, quick-witted dinosaurs no larger than cats that darted in and out of their paths. Some of the creatures seemed to follow them for a way before bounding away toward their companions. The only creature to stay with them throughout was Newton, the little orange mammal that had attached itself to Sasha one night while she and Quinn were sleeping in a cave. He stayed on Sasha's shoulder and played the part of the lookout. If any dinosaurs wandered too near, he would chirp excitedly until everyone went on alert, manhandling the new, flint-headed javelins they'd made until whatever curious creature was drawing near changed its mind.

Sasha thought about the night they had found Newton—or, rather, Newton had found them. It had been a good night. A wonderful night. Quinn had kissed her for the first time, and they'd fought, and she'd wanted to kiss him some more. Now it was nearly impossible for her to look at him and not want to kiss him, to touch him, which was patently ridiculous. He was the most infuriating man she had ever met, and it was ridiculous that she should even feel this way. At least in Miss Austen's novel *Pride and Prejudice,* Mr. Darcy had been fantastically beautiful and romantic as well as abrasive and proud. It came as something of a mystery to her as to why she felt any kind of attraction to Quinn at all. Perhaps, she thought (not for the first time) she was fevering from some unknown jungle disease.

They camped in a cavern of the volcanic range they had utilized the first time they'd traveled this way. The remains of their past campfire were still there, and Quinn had only to add to it and spark a flame. As he slipped into the back of the cavern to refill their waterskins from the underground pool they knew was there, Sasha checked on Toby. He was still weak from his days as a prisoner of the Sen, and she couldn't help but feel responsible for him. She brought him a waterskin, made him as comfortable as possible before the fire, and promised him that Quinn would soon return with food.

Toby took her hand and pulled her down so she was facing him. He looked at her with his handsome, sun-bronzed face, his wavy dark hair, and warm buckskin brown eyes. It was the face of the boy she had grown up with, but it was also a man's face. The face of the man she had once wished to marry if only society would let them. She expected to feel a little pulse running in her throat at the warm touch of his hand, but something had changed between them. "Thank you," he said. He still sounded hoarse, exhausted, but he was almost well again.

"You should thank Quinn. He's the one who smoked the Sen out."

"Perhaps I misjudged him."

"We both did," she said, and it sounded more solemn than she'd intended. She was changing, she realized. Becoming harder, more resolute, more pragmatic. And she knew now, more than ever, what she wanted. Home. Safety. And someone to break the chain of long, lonely years. Quinn no longer accused her of acting like a child. She hadn't felt like a child in some time, she realized.

It seemed like years since they'd landed here, in this primordial world.

Toby watched her intently. "Sasha…remember when I told you I had something to say? When you first returned with Quinn?"

She did not want to hear this. "Yes," she answered cautiously.

"All the days you were gone…it left me thinking. I realized how much I'd missed you. And how free this world is."

Sasha swallowed. Her throat was suddenly dry despite the water she had drunk.

"If we stayed here, we could be free. Really free."

"Stayed here?"

"Have you thought about it?"

She didn't know what to say. The only thing that came out was, "But if we stayed, I'd miss Papa."

He thought about that. "You would, wouldn't you?" He smiled, a little.

"Yes, of course." She stood up. He released her hand, inch by inch. "I should see if Quinn needs help with dinner."

After they'd eaten the fish that Quinn had caught, and the berries that Sasha had picked, they turned in early. There would be more walking in their future and Quinn wanted to make an early start of it, when the day was still cool. Sasha had learned to cushion her head on her own hair, and the sandy cavern floor wasn't nearly as uncomfortable as it had been in the beginning, or she was toughening up, which was a distinct possibility.

She had a strange, disorienting dream of trying to find her way through her Papa's gardens, except that they seemed to stretch in every direction, bordered on all sides by thick, impassable hedges. There seemed to be no way out. She ran down one twisty-turny corridor of hedges after another, searching frantically for some escape until she saw him. Her Papa was seated on a gazebo that looked like a painted white island amidst a sea of tall golden grasses. He was watching some enormous African elephants wandering past.

"Papa!" She raced up the steps of the gazebo as she had when she was a little girl and her father would sit out in the garden in the evenings and smoke his pipe. He used to say, "Jump, little Sasha!" And Sasha would jump at him and he would catch her and hold her on his knee.

"Little Sasha," Papa said in welcome and held out his arms to her. It was so good to see him again! She flung herself into his arms and he lifted her with a laugh before bringing her down for a kiss. She looked down into his eyes and realized they were the vast, all-consuming blue of African skies, not brown like her own. It was Quinn who held her, kissed her. She wondered how she could have made such an obvious error, but right at that moment an elephant made a terrifying trumpeting noise.

Sasha sat up in the cavern. She was lying on the floor, blanketed by Quinn's frock coat, and she was awake and feeling vaguely mortified by her dream. It was improper, indecent...and so very real. But underlying her shame was a sense of fright. The trumpeting noise had been real, she realized, long and mournful and threatening, much like a hunting call in the night, only darker, like some vast, angry creature was weeping.

Suddenly her heart was in her throat and her whole body was shuddering with a light, cold sweat. She climbed stiffly to her feet, pulled Quinn's coat close, and moved cautiously to the mouth of the cave. There was only the plains darkness to greet her, the dead blackness of a primitive world with no candles or lanterns or electric lights of any kind, a world full of chittering, crying noises that she was almost used to. Almost. Newton made a *tsk*-ing noise like she ought to go back to the fire and ducked behind her ear.

Someone touched her from behind and she nearly jumped out of her skin. She whirled and almost didn't recognize Quinn beside her. It was more by the scent that she recognized him. Quinn smelled of the jungle and flowering life. It clung to his skin like cologne. She touched her heart. "Oh, dear God," she whispered savagely, "you gave me a fright!"

"Then you should be more observant," he said.

"I know," she answered.

Quinn liked to laugh at her, to challenge her. But not tonight. Some moments passed in awkward silence. Then he took her hand and pulled her aside and said, "You should stay away from the entrance at this time of night. Something might scent you."

"Something already did," she said, her heart fluttering in her chest, but for an entirely different reason. She stepped back so her back was to the wall of the cave and the darkness cloaked her completely. Quinn followed, still watching her with interest...and appetite. He cupped her chin, moved his roughened thumb across her lips, and bent to kiss her. He did not ask her permission, but she found she hardly cared. The familiar, comforting feel of his rough cheek sparked something deep inside of her, and she tugged on him, pulling him flush to her body. He kissed her hungrily like he was starving and she food. He breathed into her.

"I love those little catlike noises you make," he admitted almost shyly.

She made those little catlike noises for him. He kissed her lips and chin and eyes and even her hair, gathering great swaths of it up in his fingers and inhaling her scent as he did so. He said in a breathless little hush, "I'm still very cross with you, Sasha Strange."

"Yes," she answered. "I want you to be cross with me, Quinn. I want you to be *most* cross with me."

He laughed then, a soft rumble she could feel deep in his chest. She wished she could see him laugh. He almost never laughed. Suddenly, she felt tears welling up. She sniffed at them, grateful for the almost absolute darkness. In the dark, he couldn't see her crying like a little girl. "I'm sorry," she told him, clinging to him. "I am so sorry. I should have trusted you wouldn't leave us, Quinn."

He held her close, stroking her hair as he contemplated her apology. "Ah well, trust is earned, is it not, little Sasha?" He cupped her cheek, kissing her with all the hunger and desire he felt. He was *very* cross with her, so cross that his hands wouldn't stop moving over her, touching her delicately through the tattered remnants of her debutante dress, and he kept flicking his tongue over her teeth in a most delightfully wicked way. She held him, sliding her hands down his long slim back. She could feel the ugly scar tissue there, old scars from beatings he'd received from his evil father. She held him, hoping to comfort him. She wasn't afraid. She trusted him, truly. And wanted him fiercely. The realization startled and frightened her.

"Sasha…" he said cautiously as her hands glided over him, enlivening him. He sounded concerned, though his hands and lips never stopped moving.

A faint bellow echoed out over the plains and made them both hesitate. She leaned back against the wall, listening carefully, though her heart was thudding too loudly in her chest for her to hear much of anything. In the dark, the cry had sounded so vast. "Listen."

"It sounds like a hunting call. A large predator."

"She?"

"Or a creature like She."

"What if it is She?"

"It cannot be. It simply cannot."

"Why not? You said the death of her husband would destroy her. I *heard* you."

Quinn swallowed, his throat working. Suddenly he looked uncomfortable. "The loss of her mate could have changed the boundaries of her territory. She could be looking for a new mate."

"Or she could be looking for us."

He fell silent at that.

Sasha fingered the large claw around her neck, a gift to her from Quinn when they had first killed She's mate. "What if she's hunting us, Quinn? What if she hates us for killing her husband? Maybe he was her great love."

He snorted. "She's an animal, Sasha. She has no concept of...what are you proposing, revenge? That's rubbish." He looked at her sternly, the mood broken. "Let's get some sleep. We have a long trek ahead of us."

| 27 |

The following day they reached the coast of the vast inland sea where Quinn and Sasha had killed the Ceratosaurus. The moment Toby saw it, his face alighted with wonder—it was Sasha's understanding that he had never seen such beautiful, sugary white beaches or clear, aquamarine waters before, having spent most of his early life in the filthy heart of London. He immediately threw off his rucksack and rushed down the beach to the water's edge. The morning tide swept in, wetting his boots.

Sasha likewise dropped her provisions and raced after him, but for an entirely different reason. She was terrified he would throw all caution to the wind and dive headlong into the warm, beautiful, *beast*-infested waters. She reached him just as he was pulling off his boots. "Toby, wait!"

"What is it?"

She pointed out to sea where some enormous whale-like beast was breaching a few hundred feet from shore. Toby stared in wonderment and terror, sitting on the sand with one boot on and one off. Were it simply a whale, he might have looked merely amazed, but it sported jaws like a crocodile that the beast snapped reflexively at the open air as it rolled its bulk in the water before diving back into the cool, dark depths of the untamed sea.

"What...is that *thing*?" Toby cried.

Sasha shielded her eyes from the relentless glare of the sun. "*That's* what I was trying to warn you about. I believe it's some form of plesiosaur."

"Another dinosaur? There are dinosaurs in the seas, too?"

"It's not a dinosaur. It's a marine reptile…"

"It looks like a dinosaur."

Quinn had finally joined them. He dropped his pack on the sand but kept his homemade javelin close at hand. "So, boy, can you tell this is no mere swimming hole?" he joked, smiling grimly at Toby.

Toby glared at him but said nothing in return.

| 28 |

That night, they camped in one of the many sea caves that dotted the coastal cliffs. Sasha chose the one where she'd first found Dr. John Ulysses's chalked letter on the wall informing any English-speaking passersby that he was following the coast. Toby read the missive about how he was traveling to the possibly mythical "Valley of Song," thought by some to be a holy place, a deep river valley that experienced unusual weather patterns. It was Sasha's secret hope that John had found it, that perhaps he was even now working on a way to manipulate the winds to produce the proper vibrations needed to open a gateway home.

Toby examined the small, cramped script. "Dr. Ulysses is your friend?"

"Yes," she answered.

"Muk talked about him, but he didn't have much good to say about the bloke."

"He did trick Muk into letting him go." As they stood in the shallows and watched the sea lapping at their feet, she pointed out the place where She's husband had died, torn apart by gigantic sea reptiles. She had filled Toby in on most of the details of their little adventure the day before, as they crossed the plains, though she'd left out a few details, like the things that had gone on between herself and Quinn. Toby wouldn't understand. In fact, she wasn't entirely sure *she* understood. "John is a very smart man," she said.

"Smart enough to get us home?"

"I hope so." She was hoping to catch up to John despite his three-month head start on them. Of course, it was possible she would never find him, especially if he'd run into trouble. She shook her head. She couldn't think that way. John was alive. She had to believe that. She and John were their only hope for finding a way home. The two of them together had built the Tuning Machine, the device that had brought them here in the first place, and she had a feeling that only the two of them working together could get them home.

After they had eaten the fish that Quinn had caught, and refreshed their supply of water, Sasha went down the beach for a walk. Quinn was concerned about hidden dangers, but none of the larger animals could walk on the soft sand without sinking, so she had a certain level of protection, she figured. But to be on the safe side, she took her javelin. After weeks of being chased by giant predators, she had learned that there was no such thing as paranoia, only perfect awareness.

It felt good to be alone, to think. Staying well ahead of the tide, she knelt in the sand and used the point of the javelin to draw some blueprints for her machine. She frowned over the drawings. It had taken her months of hard labor to build the Tuning Machine in her father's conservatory, and she'd had almost everything she needed at her fingertips. In London, anything could be bought or sold. There was no way she could reproduce her Tuning Machine under these primitive conditions!

She angrily struck out her drawing and stood up. She looked toward the evening tide, the sea wind tearing at her long hair and biting through the remnants of her dress with its salty little teeth.

Something was struggling amidst the rocks of the shoreline only a few hundred feet away. Newton began chittering excitedly in her ear. She reached into her pocket and offered him a berry. Setting him down on some rocks, she started toward the shoreline, trying to keep an eye on the vastness of the ocean in case predators were swimming just offshore.

As she drew near the rocks, she thought she recognized the creature as a smaller species of marine reptile. It was seven or eight feet long and had oily grey skin like a seal. It looked like a species of long-necked plesiosaur. In one of the many science periodicals she'd read, paleontologists referred to plesiosaurs as looking like "a snake threaded through a turtle," and that was very much what this creature resembled, though this plesiosaur seemed to be quite young. She watched it flounder amidst the rocks it had become hopelessly moored upon.

She stopped a few feet away from the creature. It looked at her with big, dark winsome eyes. Its flippers beat helplessly against the rocks. She had to remind herself that it was a prehistoric creature, a potentially dangerous animal. But in that moment, she felt a certain kinship with it. She was as trapped here as the plesiosaur. She reached into her pocket, extended her arm, and offered it one of Newton's berries.

The plesiosaur snaked its head out awkwardly, its sleek, cold grey snout brushing her fingers as it inspected the berry. Its jaws yawned open remarkably wide and Sasha saw a lot of small but very sharp glistening teeth. She wondered if this wasn't a very bad idea, then the plesiosaur snatched the berry and swallowed it. It looked at her again and flapped its flippers against the rocks.

She offered it another berry.

"Sasha? *What* are you doing?"

She turned to find Quinn hurrying toward her, his javelin in hand. He tested its weight as he bore down on the plesiosaur, a keen, disgruntled look on his face. Sasha turned to intervene, grabbing his arm before he could plunge the javelin into its throat. "Quinn, stop! It's only a baby!"

"A baby that intends to eat you, my dear."

"Quinn, no!" She gave him a narrow-eyed, surly look, an expression she had borrowed from the man himself. "If you kill this plesiosaur, I shall never speak to you again!"

Quinn offered her a half-smirk. "Now you know that isn't true, Sasha. You've tried in the past and it hasn't worked out at all."

"I shall try harder!" She held his arm to restrain him and create a wall between him and the plesiosaur, which had started making alarming lowing noises. "And you're frightening the baby!"

Quinn, looking angrier than ever, dropped his javelin. Sasha released her hold on his arm and he took that moment to snatch her by the shoulders, lift her off her feet, swing her around, and deposit her a safe distance from the shore.

"What are you doing?" she said, struggling in his embrace. "It isn't going to attack me, Quinn!"

"No, but that is." He pointed a few hundred feet offshore, where a great dorsal fin at least as tall as a man had broken the surface of the choppy dark water. The creature—whatever it was—was zeroing in on the baby's distress.

"Oh, dear God," Sasha said as she struggled to slip past Quinn. "We've got to get the baby out of the water!"

"Out of the water?" he cried, trying to hold her back. "Are you insane, woman?"

But she'd already shoved past him—she was small and quick, and he had trouble holding onto her—and then she was sprinting into the knee-high water where the baby was making pitiful noises and flapping its flippers with wild abandon. She didn't think. She just raced up to the baby, took its slick long neck in an embrace, and tried to drag it over the rocks and onto the safety of the beach.

It was like the baby was made of stone. Slippery stone. She couldn't budge it more than an inch.

"Sasha!" Quinn was furious, not that that was anything unusual. "Sasha, you're mad!"

"Help me get her to shore!" she said, trying to angle herself so she had a better hold on the baby's neck but was still able to keep an eye on the dorsal fin growing larger by the second. Her hands kept sliding off the slick surface of the baby's skin and she felt her frustration mount moment by moment. The baby mewled pitifully. "Quinn!" she cried. "Please! You've got to help me!"

"Mother of Mercy," Quinn said, but he raced dutifully into the foamy grey water to help her rescue a prehistoric reptile from another prehistoric reptile. He grabbed the baby around the bulk of its body and started shifting it along the slick rocks, straining with every inch.

"Quinn, please hurry!" Sasha said as she continued to tug on the baby's neck.

The baby began screaming, its whole body electric with fear.

Quinn huffed and puffed. "Sasha, my dear, I'm rather fond of you, but if you don't be quiet and let me work, I'm going to leave this baby of yours to the shark!"

"Do you think it's a shark?" Every time she glanced out to shore, the dorsal fin seemed to grow bigger, the shark that much closer. The fin alone was as tall as a sailboat's sail. She shuddered to think of the size of the creature it belonged to.

"Sasha, get out of the way!"

"I won't leave you!"

"Sasha, get out of the way *now* or this 'baby' of yours is going to crush you."

Nearly whimpering with fear, she shifted out of the way.

Quinn was much stronger than he looked. With a great cry, he flipped the baby up off the rocks and onto the soft beach with a puff of sand, where it started floundering. "Help me," he said. Together, the two of them started rolling the baby through the sand like a beer barrel while it mewled in alarm. Quinn said, sweating and sand-covered, "How does this thing survive on its own?"

"It's an apex predator."

"Really? It looks rather foolish to me."

"Maybe it gets smarter with age." Panting, she stopped rolling the baby through the piles of sand to check on the shark, which was practically right on their heels. It was as monstrously big as a whale, the shallows barely reaching its gills. The moment Sasha saw it she screamed. She screamed at the size of it. She screamed at the size of its teeth. She couldn't help herself. The only thing keeping the shark from coming right up on the beach were the rocks that had moored the baby plesiosaur. The creature was a nightmare of huge black mechanical eyes and a mouth so large it could have swallowed a man whole.

Quinn snagged her wrist and pulled her to him. They were on an incline now, the baby floundering in the sand at their feet. They tripped, and then all three of them started rolling down the beach Jack and Jill style. The world turned round and round. It was a bumpy, painful ride that didn't end until they were halfway to the sea cave. Quinn did his best to cushion her fall. Unfortunately, the baby rolled right over him, leaving him dazed in the sand with Sasha landing atop him in a very unladylike sort of way. He let out his breath in a grunt and stared up at her.

They were less than an inch apart, her legs straddling his hips, her hands flat to the hard muscles of his chest. He had a small cut at his temple where the baby had cuffed him. She found her handkerchief, soaked from the sea, and used it to wipe away the bit of blood there. Quinn flinched when the salt entered the wound. She expected him to be furious. She expected him to berate her. Instead, the most peculiar expression overcame his face. Instead of angry, he looked positively elated.

"Quinn..." she said, feeling his hands move to clutch her shoulders and draw her closer. She had absolutely no idea how to finish that statement. Luckily, she was saved when the baby started crying and rolling helplessly in the sand next to them. She slid off Quinn, who sighed with regret by the sudden turn of events as she stood up to attend to the baby.

And just in time, as Toby had appeared at the mouth of the cave, looking tousled and confused. "What in hell is going on?" he asked. Then his eyes widened when he spotted the baby plesiosaur floundering in the sand. "And what in hell is *that*?"

| 29 |

First, they got the baby plesiosaur centered on Quinn's frock coat, then he and Toby started pulling her down the beach toward an isolated shallow with Sasha following after. She toted a waterskin and she poured water over the baby's back to keep her skin moist under the scorching sun as they pulled her along.

"Sasha, I really must protest your habit of collecting pets. This environment isn't appropriate for such sport," said Quinn, his teeth clenched as he tugged the enormously heavy creature a few more inches down the beach. The softness of the sand didn't help much. It had been soft and deep enough to trap the Ceratosaurus knee-deep, and it wasn't conducive to pulling a half-ton creature through it. They were leaving quite a rut.

"Dotty isn't a pet. I don't mean to keep her. She's just an animal in trouble," Sasha explained simply.

"You named the damned dinosaur?" Quinn cried in horror.

She frowned at Quinn and offered Dotty another berry. "She's not a dinosaur. She's a marine reptile." Dotty took the berry gracefully, swallowed it down, then flapped her flippers in the hopes that more would follow. More did.

"How do we know this thing isn't going to turn on us, come up the beach one night while we're all asleep, and eat all of us?" Toby asked. He'd stripped off his dirty white work shirt and sweat gleamed against the sun-bronzed muscles of his arms and chest as he yanked Dotty a few more painful inches down the beach.

"Dotty doesn't eat humans. She eats fish and crustaceans," Sasha explained.

"Are you certain of that?"

Sasha hesitated. "I'm fairly certain."

"Fairly?" Quinn said. "You don't know?"

"The periodicals allude to an all-fish diet."

"Well, as long as the periodicals *allude* to the beast not eating human flesh, it must be true!"

"Quinn," she said, getting exasperated now. "Your sarcasm is not welcomed."

Toby elbowed Quinn. "Don't talk to Sasha like that."

Quinn gave the boy his now-familiar disgruntled look. "I should have left *you* to the Sen…"

"Please," said Sasha with a long, weary sigh. "Stop."

Quinn almost started saying something, then thought better of it. Instead, he concentrated on the work at hand, though his eyes periodically shifted to Toby, taking in the boy's physique as he worked as if he were assessing him. When Toby pulled, Quinn pulled harder as if it was a contest between them. Although Quinn wasn't built like Toby, who'd worked his entire life with horses, he was strong and wiry, without even an inch of fat on his body like so many men his age. At times it was difficult to believe that he was twice her age; he strained the seams of his shirt very nicely.

That wasn't a proper Christian thought she realized and dutifully turned her back. Closing her eyes briefly, she said a little prayer that God would lead her out of the path of temptation. She'd already given in too many times where Quinn was concerned.

They were coming upon an incline, which she knew would help some. If they could get Dotty over the ridge, they'd be able to roll her down to the water's edge. "Give her a push, old boy," said Toby, and Quinn pushed, though his expression remained as sour as ever. Between the two of them, they managed to roll Dotty down the incline and into the lagoon. A natural row of rocky outcroppings a few hundred feet offshore made the lagoon impenetrable to large predators—there was no way they could get their enormous bulk around the rocks—but it would allow a small predator like Dotty to maneuver easily. She seemed very keen on getting back into the ocean, and within seconds was slicing through the water.

The two men waded out into the water to stand beside Sasha. "I hope she'll be all right now," Sasha said, watching Dotty dive for fish.

"Bloody hell," said Quinn under his breath. "I can't believe she named the bloody thing." With a huff, he walked away.

| 30 |

After a supper of roasted prehistoric crustacean—she thought it might have been a sea scorpion of some kind—Sasha excused herself and went down to the water's edge to check for signs of Dotty. She wasn't very hopeful. Surely, the plesiosaur would have swum out to the open sea, lured by the prospects of more kinds of fish. But after standing on the shore for a few minutes, she spotted a small head on a long snakelike neck breaking the surface and gliding through the water of the secluded little shallow.

The water was a clear blue-green and glittered in the setting sun like it was full of diamonds.

She turned to glance behind her. Both of the men were still occupied with after-dinner duties. Quinn was gathering and itemizing their supplies for the trek ahead of them tomorrow, and Toby had taken one of their homemade javelins for protection and had gone down the beach to hunt for crustaceans. She was alone.

She glared up at the boiling reddish sun, suddenly realizing how long it had been since she'd felt clean and not covered in sweat and brambles from walks through jungles, or had sand in her shoes. With no one watching, and the secluded little lagoon stretching out in welcome, she stripped off her once-white debutante dress—it wasn't much more than brown rags now—then her chemise, stockings and shoes, and quickly dived into the water before she had any second thoughts. It was much colder than she'd anticipated; she came up gasping and shivering, her skin pebbling all over. But oh, it felt so good to be wet and cool and clean!

She swam a few laps, circling close to shore and keeping an eye out at all times for potential dangers. The larger marine reptiles might not be able to draw inland, but that didn't mean there weren't smaller dangers lurking about. Primitive jellyfish, sea scorpions, even prehistoric eels could present problems if she tangled with them.

Dotty skimmed by her at high speeds, then made an arc around her before swimming further out on her never-ending quest for fish. Sasha wasn't afraid of Dotty. Much. Dotty wasn't much larger than she was. She wouldn't think of making a dinner of Sasha Strange, would she?

Something slippery brushed past her leg and she nearly jumped before noticing that the water teemed with fish. All kinds of fish, of so many varieties and colors that they looked like little living jewels glowing in the water. For all the danger and fear this place generated, it still managed to serve up an amazing variety of beautiful things, like the glittering fish and clear, tropical green water. She could *almost* love this place...

A splash made her jump and swing around, bobbing in the water like a top. At first, she thought it might be Dotty playing with her, but then she spotted a second set of clothes crumpled on the beach beside her own. Like her, someone had decided that an evening swim was in order. The problem was, the clothes were too far away to see whose they belonged to. "Quinn?" she called. And then, "Toby?"

No answer. And no one broke the surface. She was alone.

Sasha felt her heart trip in her chest. Suddenly she was cold, and this little swim didn't seem like such a good idea anymore. She had just started stroking back to shore when someone touched her leg. She jerked away with a cry, splashing water compulsively. If it was Quinn, she was going to kill him for frightening her! But when a head finally broke the surface, she saw it was tanned and smiling and had longish brown hair plastered down over boyish dark eyes.

"Toby!" she said, getting angry now and splashing him. "You frightened me." She kicked at the water, putting space between them, suddenly acutely aware that she was very much naked. Toby smiled cheekily and swam a few paces closer, which only made Sasha splash back a few more paces. "What are you doing?"

Toby treaded water, smiling his charming smile. It occurred to her that he was probably as naked as she was, though the water came up to both their chins. "Swimming."

"I'd prefer to swim alone," she said, "if you don't mind."

"I don't. But don't you think it's a bit dangerous to swim alone? There could be anything in these waters." He offered her his beautiful, lopsided grin. It made her remember him as a little boy, climbing trees with him, catching fireflies. All those nights she'd snuck books out to him in the stables where he'd smiled like this in welcome. He looked like a boy and a man all at once. Her charming Toby. But that didn't mean she wasn't angry with him.

"Dotty's looking out for me," she said, hoping to chase him out of the water. "I'm in no danger."

"I think Dotty's off fishing." He swam that much closer.

Now she had a decision to make. She could swim farther out and take her chances with whatever might be skulking in the deeper parts of the lagoon, or stay where she was. It seemed ridiculous that she was even thinking about running away. Toby couldn't be any more frightening than anything that might be out there.

Toby swam right up to her, which put them in an awkward, intimate space as they both dog-paddled to stay afloat in the water. She couldn't find the sandy bottom of the shallow lagoon at all anymore. They were most certainly in depths that were becoming treacherous. Toby gave her his lopsided smile, leaned in close, and flicked some wet hair off the side of her face.

"Toby…" she began.

"What's wrong?" he asked, sounding concerned suddenly. "We used to swim at your aunt's farm, remember? Remember when you invited me to see her horses?"

They'd climbed the trees, and fallen, and ridden the horses, and fallen off those too. They'd swum in the beautiful lake that bordered her aunt's pastures, and had managed to conquer all of that in just one summer. She gave him a sidelong look. "We were children then."

He splashed closer and Sasha kicked away, turned, and started swimming back toward shore. Toby followed, staying abreast with her. Like her, he was a strong swimmer. He looked amused, playful. As they drew closer to the shore, and the water became shallower, he grabbed her around her wet, bare middle to stop her. She snapped around and he pulled her closer like they were children in her aunt's lake again, though she had a feeling that the games of the past, the dunking and laughter, were not on his agenda today. He smiled cheekily at her as he drew her against his cool wet body and she felt things that made her blush all over. "Did you think about what I said about how different this place is?" Toby asked, sounding almost breathless. "About how there are no rules here?"

She knew what he meant. She was naïve, perhaps, but she wasn't stupid. "I thought about it," she said quietly. "But I haven't made any decisions about it yet."

His face darkened. Over the years, much had changed about Toby. He was a man now, and she'd heard stories that he could drink and fight with the best of them down in the East End pubs. She felt a pulse of anger from him. "Sasha…"

"Toby, please, don't. We have to keep our heads straight at the moment." She didn't want to go on. She didn't want to have to explain Quinn to Toby. But maybe he suspected something, because he gave her a dubious look. "You know how I feel about you, Sasha. Do I have to spell it out?"

"Please, Toby," she said, raising her hands between them to break his hold.

"Why are you pushing me away?" He glanced at the shore, then back at her. His eyes clouded over. "Is there something between you and Quinn?"

"Toby, don't. Please. Not now."

"Is there?" he demanded to know, his voice growing hoarser by the moment.

She didn't know what to say to that. She couldn't sort out her feelings for Quinn at all. She was drawn to him, body and soul, that was all she knew. The Chinese believed that an invisible red string of destiny bound one soul to another. Yet it seemed ridiculous; Quinn was everything in a man she disliked. She had never so hated and wanted a man in her life. She had vowed to keep her distance, yet the more she tried *not* to think of Quinn, the more she did.

Toby's whole face clouded over. "That evil old git? That old drunk? You *like* him?"

His words stung. Her first impulse was to tell him he was wrong, that he didn't know Quinn at all. Quinn had saved both their lives. But then Toby's attention was drawn away from her. The subject of their conversation was heading down the beach toward them, carrying his javelin and unbuttoning his shirt, ready to fish for more traveling food before they moved on. He watched them both, looking churlish.

Sasha started swimming for shore.

Quinn tossed the chemise to her. "I have fish to catch if you two wouldn't mind." He glared at Toby, the hostility in his eyes burning brighter than the sun overhead. "You two would best be getting back to the cave. You'll only disturb my fishing."

Sasha ducked under the water to slip into her chemise and to give Toby the privacy he needed to get to shore and dress. When she finally popped back to the surface, Toby was halfway up the beach, dressed and carrying his boots, and Quinn was watching her reproachfully. She felt like a small child that had been caught doing something wrong as she climbed from the shallows to gather the rest of her clothing up.

Quinn scrutinized her up and down but said nothing. She was happy not to receive another verbal scolding from him—after all, he'd laid no claim upon her and it wasn't fair. She picked up her shoes and hurried back to the cave, and it wasn't until she was halfway up the beach that she realized the water had made her chemise diaphanous.

| 31 |

John had left no more cave notes; Sasha made sure by exploring the inside of every cave they came upon. She did find primitive, worn pictures on the walls in some of them, mostly simplistic men chasing and hunting simplistic animals. That worried her some. She knew from the periodicals she'd read that something with humanlike creativity had painted them. That meant humans might live here—or some form of human, anyway. She thought about Neanderthal men, huge, hulking creatures almost more beast than man. Neanderthal were expert hunters. They wouldn't stand a chance if they encountered one.

Sasha kept her concerns to herself as they migrated down the coast. There was no reason to worry Quinn and Toby, after all. The cave drawings had looked faded. They could have been years or decades old, made by a people who had long since moved on to other territories. Only if she saw additional signs of habitation would she warn them.

She was also afraid to add more fuel to the fire already burning a half-mile high between them all. They had been friends once—or, if not friends, exactly, then at least allies. Now they were all angry with each other. Toby was angry with her since their swim; she knew his pride was hurt, and probably his heart. Quinn was angry with her since seeing the two of them together. And, of course,

Toby and Quinn disliked each other immensely. She'd never realized until now how much. They ambled along with their respective packs carried over their shoulders and javelins in hand, occasionally talking to her, but never to each other, and any task they were forced to do as a team became a competition.

It was sad, a hardship, but Sasha endured it. When the men became overbearing, she spent most of her time talking to Newton on her shoulder or trying to spot Dotty along the coast. Since leaving the secluded little lagoon, Dotty had followed them. Sasha picked the big juicy pro-gooseberries wherever she could, both for Newton and in the hopes of luring Dotty to shore. At least *they* weren't angry with her!

There were fewer dinosaurs along the coast. There was little vegetation for them to eat, and most of the heavier animals were too afraid of the sinking sands to draw near. For that, Sasha was grateful. On the first day of their trek, they saw some Rhamphorhynchus gliding overhead and diving for fish, that was all. On the second day, they encountered a herd of young Iguanodon on the beach, scratching for sea kelp that had washed ashore. Sasha stopped to observe the tall, bipedal herbivores, trying to memorize everything about them.

Some years back, two life-sized reproductions of Iguanodon had been built at the Crystal Palace in London. Sasha had gone to see them twice. But now she saw how inaccurate the statues were. The creatures had been depicted as elephant-like quadrupeds, their thick, horny thumb spikes reassigned as nose horns. She watched them feed, and since she had no notepaper, sadly, she tried to memorize everything about them in the event they ever made it back to London. Eventually Quinn urged her to move on. He didn't touch her, only said, "The tide is moving in. We should be moving along." Which, in Quinn-speak, meant that the larger sea predators would be swimming closer to shore. Already she was able to spot their huge sail-like dorsal fins on the horizons, and a part of her started to worry about Dotty all over again. Immediately after they moved on, the young Iguanodon had the same idea and started moving inland.

As they trekked onward, Sasha no longer described the habits of the dinosaurs they encountered as she had in the past. Since none of them was speaking to each other, it seemed a pointless venture. Each of them had their assigned tasks; each concentrated on that. Quinn was their hunter, fisherman, and tracker. Toby prepared their shelter, tended their fires, scaled or skinned the prey that Quinn caught, or did any manual labor that Quinn wasn't strong enough to do. Sasha's job was to prepare the food, monitor their supplies, refill their waterskins, and play lookout anytime the men were to be exposed to the environment for any length of time. Newton helped her stay alert for danger, chittering excitedly if anything dangerous drew near. Even Dotty did her part. Sasha had learned that when Dotty breached, it meant the waters were clear of predators. If she couldn't find Dotty anywhere on the sea's horizon, it meant she'd dived to avoid a confrontation with something larger or hungrier than herself.

But the silence and tension weighed on them all.

On the third day, Sasha woke from a sound, exhausted sleep and sat up in the early, predawn hours of the morning, looking about the cave they had chosen for their nightly camp. Even though Quinn was still cross with her, he continued to cover her each night with his frock coat, always after she'd fallen asleep—presumably, so she could not protest. It was almost a ritual now. The frock coat was more holes than substance; in no time, there would be no coat left at all. She stood up and restlessly moved to the entrance of the cave. She listened intently for a repeat of the noise that had stirred her, but it didn't come. Was it She's call that she'd heard in her sleep? Sasha couldn't be sure. Maybe Quinn was right; She was just an animal. There was no way her little primordial brain could have developed a vendetta against them.

Taking a deep breath to steel herself, she stepped outside the cave. She was still damp from her swim the evening before, her hair hanging in heavily saturated ropes around her shoulders. Quinn sat on the beach just outside the cave, a small bonfire burning fitfully beside him. Maybe he too had heard something and couldn't sleep. He was designing a primitive bow and several homemade quivers. They weren't perfectly straight quivers, but they *were* functionally close, and each tipped with a diamond-hard piece of flint. She knew he was making them a more effective way to hunt and fish. He was very practical that way.

Sasha knelt beside him and picked up the heavy Bowie knife with the ivory handle that he'd been using to carve the quivers. She fingered her long, wet, cumbersome hair. "I should cut it," she said. It was too long, always windblown, and full of debris from their daylong treks. When she swam, it took forever to dry, and when it finally did, she had no way to untangle it. It was snarling up on her.

"Don't. Let me," said Quinn, setting his half-finished bow aside. He gathered the fullness of her hair up in his hands, and it was almost more than he could handle. Sasha waited patiently while he divided her hair into small sections and finger-combed it, then began braiding each tiny piece. It took a long time, but it felt very good to feel his fingers working through her bothersome locks, to feel his warm touch on her again.

"What are you doing?" she asked after a time.

His voice tickled the back of her neck, raising goosebumps. "All across the African continent, you'll find women who wear their hair in cornrow braids. It keeps the hair neat in otherwise rough and primitive conditions. Often, beads or small cowry shells are woven into the hair, but I'm afraid we don't have those available."

Sasha laughed, couldn't help herself. "How did you learn to style women's hair, Quinn?"

"Gabrielle wore her hair that way during the summer months. She..." he stopped speaking as if he suddenly realized what he'd said.

Gabrielle. His woman back in Africa. The woman he'd planned to return to since breaking off their engagement. Gabrielle was one of the reasons she had refused to take any direct orders from Quinn. If Quinn's heart belonged to the mysterious and probably very beautiful Gabrielle, then he had no claim on her and she had no obligation to obey him. She fell silent and let him work on braiding her hair while trying very hard not to hate Gabrielle completely. She imagined Gabrielle was tall and bold and curvy—everything Sasha was not. Why else would Quinn reject Sasha as a suitable wife? The thought made her angrier than ever.

She glanced down at herself. She was nineteen, almost twenty years old, and yet she still looked like an underdeveloped child. She had never given it much thought until now. But, really, how could Quinn ever love someone like her? The thought was ridiculous. Her eyes were welling up with unwelcomed tears by the time Quinn declared her done, her hair bound up in all these beautiful tiny braids. She was trying to be brave, to be everything Quinn wanted, and here she was, ready to cry and run away. She turned to face him and the braids spilled over her shoulders. "Quinn, am I pretty?" she asked, trying not to let the worry show in her voice.

Quinn's eyes halved as he considered her. "Very." He ran his hands along the sides of her head, smoothing the braiding there. "You look like an African princess, my dear."

She felt her heart lift. She looked directly into Quinn's pale azure eyes. In the near dark, they were full of the flames of the fire. Fire and ice, she thought. She thought about kissing him then, but the trumpeting noise that she both dreaded and yet somehow expected rang out in the feral night like a clarion bell, making them both jump. The sound seemed to vibrate in the air between them and Sasha found herself shuddering in its aftermath. "It's She," she said.

"It can't be She," Quinn answered angrily as he struggled to see past the firelight. "There is no way she can cross this beach. The sand is much too soft."

"She's out there, Quinn, somewhere beyond the beach." In the dark, Sasha's hearing was almost painfully acute, and she *knew* that sound. "She's following us. She's waiting..." She had to struggle to find the words. Her heart was beating so rapidly in her chest that it hurt. "She's waiting for us to go further inland, and..."

She didn't say the rest, that She would hunt them down and consume them all in retribution for what they had done to her mate. She waited for Quinn to protest, to call her a fool, but he stood up instead and grabbed his javelin. "Go back inside. I'll bank the fire." He didn't say what she thought, what they both knew to be true. The creature knew the light of the fire meant they were close at hand. She knew they could hear her. She knew they were afraid.

She was stalking them, haunting them, terrorizing them. Waiting for her chance to strike.

| 32 |

In the morning, Quinn developed the brilliant idea of hunting She.

"But don't you see that's what she wants, what she's counting on?" Sasha gestured wildly and—she feared—Ineffectively at the open plains beyond the beach. She looked to Toby for support, but he was hunched down on the beach, putting his pack together, and he refused to meet her eyes or offer any kind of assistance. "She *wants* us on the plains, Quinn. That way, we're in her territory."

"Precisely," he said.

"You've gone completely mad!"

He gave her a veiled look as he adjusted the pack on his back. "You remember how we trapped the male by luring him onto the beach with carrion. This is the same principle. Except, in this case, I won't be using carrion, since our friend seems to be a bit smarter than her mate."

She just stared at him. "You're going to use yourself to lure She down to the beach and try and trap her?"

"By my estimation, She is nearly twice the weight of her mate. That means she's likely to sink twice as fast."

"She's also likely to run twice as fast."

"There's a risk in anything we do to capture her." Quinn fingered his javelin. "At least our theory about the beach is workable. We've tested it and found it to be true."

He could be so bloody arrogant! "But why do we have to capture her at all?"

Quinn looked surprised like she ought to know the answer to that question. "You said yourself she's hunting us. I say we turn the table." He glanced at the sun, his only timepiece now that his pocket watch was long gone. "It'll likely take me a day to track her, and another to lay some kind of ambush. So I'll be back around this time in approximately two days."

If he came back at all.

He gave her a falsely cheery smile, looked her over in her ragged dress and braids like he'd like to eat her, and stalked off, trekking across the sands of the beach. Sasha waited exactly five minutes before grabbing up her pack. Newton jumped to her shoulder, and together they followed Quinn's footsteps.

Five minutes later, she'd caught up to him.

Quinn looked over and frowned. "What are you doing?"

"Helping you to capture She." She was carrying a new javelin she had made. She showed it off by jabbing at the open air. She was very proud of it.

"I don't need your help, Sasha."

"Yes, you do."

"No. I don't."

"Yes. You do."

They stopped and faced each other in the sand like adversaries. Between them raced a small bipedal dinosaur the size of a dog chasing a giant dragonfly. It disappeared over the next ridge.

Quinn stared at her ferociously. "Sasha, I command you to go back immediately!"

"Quinn," she stated simply, refusing to wither under his look. "Who is Gabrielle?"

He looked taken aback by her change of subject. For some time, she knew not how long, they simply stood there, glaring at each other.

Finally, Quinn frowned. "That is not your concern..." he began, but she immediately cut him off.

"Is she the woman you mean to marry?" She would not be put off. They'd stand here all night if need be until she had the answers she needed.

He looked stunned. It wasn't the expression she had expected to see. She saw a deeply buried hurt leaking into his very blue eyes. "Oh, Sasha," he said at last. "Gabrielle was my first wife. She died in Africa fifteen years ago, during an outbreak of Malaria." He hesitated, and his eyes turned inward. His face twisted for a moment, painfully. "Along with our son Percy." He closed his eyes, seemed to armor himself mentally against the past, then continued. "They both died within days of one another. Gabrielle was only a little older than you. Percy was two years old at the time."

She was dumbfounded. "But you said you were going back to Africa to see Gabrielle."

"Gabrielle and Percy are buried in Africa, Sasha, on my estate. I go back there every few years to see them, to be with them." He hesitated as if he'd said something very foolish. "I enjoy being near them and talking to Gabrielle. They loved Africa almost as much as I did. I suppose you think I'm a fool. An eccentric."

Sasha felt her shoulders slump. All the fight went out of her with Quinn's statement. "My mother is buried on our estate. I visit her mausoleum all the time. I even bring flowers." She hesitated. She had to try very hard to remember her mother after all these years. "My Papa says I remind him of her. She was very willful, he said, always getting in trouble. She died when I was very young so I never had a chance to find out if that was true." She stopped and smiled. She took another deep breath. "Your son was only two years old?"

He looked whimsical for once; it was a very odd expression for Quinn to wear. "When I see Gabrielle's grave, I always talk about Percy, about how he might have lived, the man he might have become. He would be seventeen years old this year, almost a man." He stopped and stared at the sand at his feet and seemed to consider. "He might have been planning for marriage or continuing his studies at university. Perhaps it isn't healthy, but I can't help but wonder." He looked up, his eyes sincere. "I think about Percy all the time."

"I'm sorry, Quinn." It was all she could think to say.

"You are, aren't you?"

"Yes, of course." She jabbed the javelin into the ground between them and boldly took a step toward him until mere inches separated them. She reached out and brushed her fingers against his scratchy cheek. He closed his eyes to her touch. "When my father originally planned for your arrival, he told me you were perfect for me, that I ought to give you a chance. I didn't believe him, of course. I thought you an evil old git."

"I am an evil old git," he admitted. He smiled, then set his warm, heavy hand on the hand that touched him. "And now you should be off. Back to camp, with you."

"Quinn..." she began, but before she could finish her statement, she spotted Toby hiking toward them over the sand dunes, bearing his pack and a javelin of his own.

"Lovely," said Quinn with his customary drollness.

"Quinn, we're all a team, all three of us. And we'll hunt She together as such."

"Sasha, I really must insist..."

She stood on tiptoe and kissed him, briefly. "You are *not* my husband, Quinn. Therefore, you have no say in the matter."

He frowned. "One day I may have to rectify that oversight."

She was about to question his statement when Toby reached them. Together, as the team, they were off.

| 33 |

John had three months head start on them, so spending three days walking the plains on the edge of the beach wasn't likely to have a very big impact on catching him up, Sasha decided. Unfortunately—or maybe fortunately, depending on how one was looking at these things—after three days they saw no signs of She.

Well, that wasn't *exactly* true. Almost from the beginning, they found She's calling cards. Sasha wasn't even sure why she thought it was She killing the beasts, but she was. On the first day of the hunt, they found the half-eaten carcass of one of the Iguanodon youngsters. The following day they stumbled across an adult, as well as a young stegosaur some distance off. In all cases, the carcasses were being systematically picked over by small, opportunistic predators. She had killed for sport rather than food. Or in anger, Sasha thought with a shiver as the horrendous fumes poured off the remains, keeping them at a distance. The stegosaur bore the scars of a horrific battle, bite marks covering most of the body. Some of its tough armor plates had been bitten clear off. Sasha didn't think anyone but the ferocious She could have done that. Muk, the leader of the Sen, had called She a dark goddess. Sasha was finally beginning to understand why.

On the third day, they were heading back to their camp down on the beach, when Quinn suddenly held up his hand, halting both Sasha and Toby in their tracks. They'd been moving unevenly through a plain of tall yellow grasses as big as they were. "What is it?" Sasha asked, suddenly on alert. She swatted at some insects trying to land in her eyes for a drink of the fluids there. Had he spotted She, or some other great predator?

Quinn raised a finger to his mouth for silence, withdrew his hunting knife, and parted the grasses using the blade. Through the almost perfect blinds, they could see the beach ahead, and, a little way down, their camp. A figure moved in their cave, a large, agile figure examining the weapons that Quinn had been working on, the javelins and spears and primitive bows and arrows. Sasha thought automatically of Neanderthal and wondered if they were in any immediate danger.

The figure emerged from their cave, Quinn's bow and a quarrel of arrows carried over one shoulder. It was a tall, sturdy young woman with long hair. She looked human enough. Her skin was bronzed from constant exposure to the sun, her hair a sleek dark auburn that Sasha envied, and her eyes all liquid darkness. She was wearing a short, primitive sari of some roughly woven material. Sasha had expected it to be animal skin, then thought better of that theory. Wearing animal skins would only attract predators. The girl—she was Sasha's age—crouched down to examine the remains of their fire and their footprints leading away from it.

Quinn caught their eyes and made a circular motion with his finger, indicating he meant to circle around the sand dunes out of sight until he was closer to the cave entrance. Sasha nodded and patted the air near her knee to indicate they would stay here. They were working automatically, almost on a psychic level, she realized, just like a tribe of people. Quinn meant to drive the strange girl toward them. She and Toby would capture her. Toby nodded and reassured his hold on his javelin, though Sasha sincerely hoped they would not have to use it. The girl looked fierce and strong, but not dangerous.

Quinn darted soundlessly into the tall grass and Sasha moved closer to Toby. She thought about taking his hand, but he might misconstrue the gesture. "Is Quinn insane?" he breathed in her ear. "What are we going to do with a girl?"

"Talk to her," Sasha whispered. "Maybe she's from our world, another visitor."

"Is that possible?"

"I don't know, Toby."

They waited, hardly breathing. Quinn was fast. Less than five minutes later, the girl jerked upright on full alert and glanced at the sand dunes, though Sasha had no idea if she had heard Quinn or sensed him in some other way. A moment later, she bolted right toward them. "Here she comes," Sasha said, trying to get ready and wondering how she would capture the girl without actually hurting her. Then an idea came to her. She got down on her knees and ducked her head. A few moments later, the girl dived blindly into the tall grass, hit Sasha's side, and blundered over her, falling right into Toby's grip.

It was over in seconds. Toby had her locked in his embrace, his arm under her chin to restrain her. The girl made breathy, panicked noises and bit him like an animal. Toby roared and the girl began to fight, loosening his hold on her.

Sasha immediately stood up and held up her hands to show she was unarmed. "Stop! Please! We won't hurt you."

To her surprise, the wild-eyed girl stopped struggling. She seemed to be of some mixed racial descent, Sasha noted. Her face was wide and exotic, her coloring dark, yet her uptilted, Asian-inspired eyes bright blue. She was unfairly curvy, in Sasha's opinion. "We won't harm you," she stated again in what she hoped was a kind voice. The girl would be listening to her tone of voice, not the words, after all. She had probably never encountered an English-speaker before. "We just want to talk to you."

The girl grew very still. She tilted her head as if she were thinking about what Sasha was saying. She glanced at the bow still slung over one of her shoulders, then said in heavily accented English, "I no stealing, only borrowing!"

| 34 |

The men wanted to drag the English-speaking native girl back to camp by force and interrogate her, but a sharp look from Sasha changed their minds immediately. Instead of forcing her, Sasha invited the girl back with them, promising her that she could keep Quinn's bow if she'd spend a little time talking to them and answering her questions. The native girl, whose name was Naja, agreed to come back to camp with them, but only because Sasha had invited her, and only if she could keep the bow and quivers close at hand.

As Quinn set the loin of an unidentifiable reptile to roasting over the fire, Sasha asked Naja all the pertinent questions. Naja was reluctant to answer at first, but Sasha offered her more weapons, and this Naja accepted, much to Quinn's chagrin, seeing how he'd worked so hard on making them. Naja, it turned out, was on the run from her people, called the Moja, who meant to sacrifice her because, unlike most of her tribe, she had red hair, and the "redhairs" were routinely sacrificed to Bolaja, "the One Below." She said this while watching Quinn tend to the cooking fire, commenting that she could not believe that Quinn had lived to see adulthood—Quinn, whose ginger hair caught and held the flames so well she called him "the man with the fire hair." Sasha thought it was rather appropriate, considering how fiery Quinn's temper could run. She had to suppress a smile at how that annoyed Quinn.

To Sasha's intense surprise, Naja knew Dr. John Ulysses—"the man with sun hair," as she called him. He'd been with Naja's tribe for a short time some months earlier. That was how Naja had come to understand a little English, though she admitted to wanting to improve herself. She called the bow and quarrels a "great gift," as the bow would bring her "much meat." Sasha had to assume that in this world, there was no greater treasure.

She did not learn a great deal about John, much to her disappointment. He had joined the nomadic Moja for a short time because he'd been lonely from his travels. Sasha could understand that. She couldn't imagine being trapped on this alien planet with no one human to communicate with. John had earned his keep by acting as the Moja's witch doctor, treating the injured braves who hunted the big beasts, though his desire to find the Valley of Song had pushed him on after a time. The Moja's bloodthirsty traditions did not sit well with him either. But all this was more than two months ago. He'd stayed with the Moja for a little over a month, so by Sasha's estimation, he was only a month ahead of them, which relieved her greatly. She thought it was possible they might catch up to John in a few weeks if they didn't linger in any one place.

After the four of them had consumed the roasted beast and the course, potato-like roots that Naja had dug from the sand and declared edible, Sasha went down to the shore to toss berries to Dotty, who'd surfaced to offer her greetings. Naja followed her. She was cautious until Sasha explained that Dotty was "pet," not "enemy" or "food." It was an unknown term to Naja. She was fascinated by the concept of keeping animals for companionship only. Sasha suspected that her tribe was so busy keeping themselves alive, they'd never even considered domesticating animals.

"What other animals you keep as 'pet'?" Naja asked with interest.

"At home I have horses."

Naja frowned.

"Large, tame grass-eaters." When she saw that Naja did not understand, she stretched her arms out to indicate the size. "They have long faces and long legs and hair like you and I have."

Naja laughed and Sasha could see her trying to imagine the animal. "You eat this animal too?"

"No! Quinn is so much like you," she said with a reproachful grin. "He wanted to eat both Newton and Dotty!"

"Quinn is your mate?" Naja asked suddenly, observing her.

What an unexpectedly odd thing to say! Sasha turned to look more closely at the young woman standing beside her, a woman no older than she. "No, we're not married."

Naja did not understand the concept of "marriage" any more than "pet." She said only, "He is your man?"

Sasha was at a loss for words.

Afraid that Sasha did not understand, Naja added succinctly, "He is the one you make your young with?"

Sasha flushed and looked out to sea where Dotty was playing amidst the whitecaps. She fed Newton a berry from her pocket. It was silly to be so mortified, she knew. They were just two girls engaged in "women talk," as they called it back home. She had known young women who were just as straightforward as Naja, though she'd never been one of them. She'd never dared to be like that.

"Why are you upset?" Naja asked with genuine concern. "Does Quinn not give you meat? Is he a bad hunter?"

"It's not that," she answered. Naja was just curious, she knew. But until now, Sasha had never really thought of Quinn as "hers." Well, that wasn't *entirely* true. When Quinn had confessed those things about poor Percy to her, there was a brief moment when she wondered what it would be like to hold Quinn's child to her breast, to watch him grow into a man before her eyes. It was a ridiculous fantasy. Sasha said, "It's....I don't know what it is."

"I do," Naja said. She glanced back at their camp, but Sasha noticed that her gaze was wavering from Quinn to Toby, who was busy stringing a new bow for their frequent hunting expeditions. Since watching Quinn do it, Toby had gotten very good. He had stripped off his shirt, and Sasha could tell that Naja was admiring him, calculating his worth as a hunter. "Quinn has chosen you. And you him. That is good. Quinn is a hunter and will give you strong sons and much meat."

Sasha looked at the girl. "Do you think so?"

"Yes," she answered immediately. "He is good and fierce. He will be good to your young. You go to him at night and take him." She made a fierce snatching motion.

Sasha laughed. She had a fantasy of going to Quinn in the night and spiriting him away. The idea made her giggle so loudly that Naja flashed a beautiful and mischievous grin that seemed to light up her whole face. "Is that what women in your tribe do, Naja?" she asked. "Do they take the men they want?"

"Yes. Good hunters with good spears who bring much meat are rare." Suddenly, she lost her fierce grin. "But take care with hunter Quinn."

Sasha stopped giggling. "What do you mean?"

"Your man has fire hair. Your young may have fire hair as well. And then you will all be hunted." She looked sad.

"Hunted?"

"The Moja will take your mate and young and give them to Bolaja." She indicated the sea. "Take hunter Quinn and go to lands where there are no Moja. Eat good meat and make strong sons." She sounded very authoritative as if these were the greatest things in the world, the things to strive for in life, and maybe they were. Sasha was fiercely jealous of the Moja. Their life seemed so simple compared to her own.

Then Naja smiled again and the dark mood was broken. Her blue eyes flashed with a sly predatory light. "And now you will tell me about Toby. Is he a good hunter too?"

| 35 |

The following morning, the four of them started out again, hoping to pick up She's trail. Quinn took the lead as usual, but this time, instead of walking single file with Sasha in the middle, Sasha walked alongside Quinn while Naja fell into step beside Toby and practiced her English on him. For the first time in days, Toby seemed more like himself, less stiff and aloof. To pass the time, he showed Naja how to string her own bow, and Naja asked many questions about this new hunting method. Sasha wondered if it was the beginning of something good for Toby.

"Sasha, stop daydreaming and be careful," said Quinn, taking her arm and steering her away from the edge of a ravine. She turned her attention back on Quinn and blushed. After that, she endeavored to pay better attention, hoping she looked more like a huntress than ever in her braids, toting her javelin—even if she *was* in danger of falling into holes in the ground.

"You seem rather quiet," Quinn stated some time later. He razed down some tall grasses with his knife. "Daydreaming again?"

Ahead of them, in a large clearing, roamed a herd of giant hadrosaur with long, bony crests rising like backward crescents from their foreheads. Although they were strictly herbivorous and weren't especially dangerous (at least, according to the periodicals she'd read), she knew from past observation that they spooked as easily as horses. They would need to be on guard as they passed the giant beasts. It only took one hadrosaur to set off the whole group, and then they'd have a dangerous stampede on their hands. "I was thinking about the hadrosaur," she said, pointing.

She mentioned the danger they presented, hoping to impress Quinn. He agreed they ought to make a wide berth around the creatures. Then she added the potential dangers of the Moja tribe that Naja had warned her about. What if the tribe followed them to take Naja back? Naja had said that her tribe had sacrificed so many red-hairs to their god that there were scarcely any left anymore. "We need to protect Naja, in case they come for her," she told Quinn with absolute authority. "And ourselves. We should have a vigil stationed at night from now on. We need to be aware of our surroundings at all times."

"I think you're right," Quinn said, sounding impressed. "But if the Moja come for Naja, don't you think they would likely take me first?"

"If they took you, it would be terribly inconvenient."

"How so?"

"Because then I would need to rescue you."

"You would rescue me, Sasha?" he said, barely able to conceal a little smirk of amusement.

"Yes, of course," she answered, jabbing at the open sky with her javelin. "I'm not afraid of anything!"

Thankfully, nothing untoward happened to them that day. Neither She nor the Moja put in an appearance. But dark storm clouds began rolling in later that day, darkening the sun and setting the air electric. It was just the beginning of the Storm Season, as Naja called it.

They decided to camp early in one of the caves, only just making it as the first rain began to fall, and the first forks of lighting cracked the slate grey skies. Quinn went seaside fishing along with

Naja, leaving Sasha to tend to the cooking fire and keep it from going out in the rain. She watched the two of them disappear over a sand dune and felt a spark of irrational anger. She ought to be the one going with Quinn to catch fish! But Quinn and Naja were the best fishermen and could bring the most fish in the least amount of time before the storm rolled in. That left her and Toby to tend to the camp. She didn't know why she should be angry about that, but she was.

Toby watched her but said little. She wished she could talk to him as she had in the old days, but something had changed between them. Something had shrunk, or grown, or made them different people. He seemed more at ease with Naja than anyone. She was both happy and sad about that.

After supper, everyone bedded down early as the long trek took its toll. Quinn took the first watch, sitting just outside the cave entrance. Sasha lay in the dark by the fire, waiting, listening, armoring herself in courage.

Take him, Naja had said. *Make him your man.*

She breathed in and out, in and out. She was resolved. She was not afraid. She waited until she was certain that Toby and Naja were asleep. Then she sat up and unbuttoned her dress, pairing herself down to her chemise. It was cool, but not cold, giving her skin a delightful chill. She bound her braids up, gathering them off her neck, hoping it made her seem older, more sophisticated. She had swum earlier with Dotty and smelled like sea and sand and sun. She was still small and underdeveloped, but there was nothing she could do about that. She took a deep breath and stepped outside the cave.

Quinn was resting with his back to the entrance, his eyes steady on the distant seas. His face looked younger and smoother in profile. But the moment he sensed her, he turned and looked, and looked again. The familiar keenness of his lean, wise face made her heart flutter up near the root of her tongue.

"Sasha," he said.

She didn't answer him. She had resolved not to speak. If she started to talk, she would only babble herself into embarrassment. Instead, she dropped to one knee and wreathed her arms about his neck. His scent and warmth filled her senses. She angled her chin and kissed him, a long, slow and—she hoped—sensual kiss, remembering everything he had taught her in past kisses. She kissed him with her lips and tongue and all of her.

At first, she was uncertain, afraid. If he rejected her, she would feel like a fool. But he responded like there was a trigger in his heart. Less than a second after she'd drawn back to gauge his reaction, he took her and pushed her down into the sand so forcefully her breath was gone in a sharp gasp. Then he was atop her, kissing her mouth and chin and the line of her throat while his hands moved over her, touching her intimately through her chemise.

He did not ask if she had thought this through, if she was even a sane woman, and for that, she was grateful. She didn't want to argue tonight. She did not want to mull over every uncertainty, every consequence. She had done that already and had come to this conclusion. She wanted him. She had chosen him. She wanted to feel him close, closer, feel his hands and mouth on her, the delightful scratch of his beard, the sound of his breathing in her ear. She wanted to taste the wild, flowering sweetness of his lips and skin.

He palmed her cheek and kissed her nose. She kissed his face all over and ran her fingers over his wild, mussed ginger hair. She guided him, and he followed, and he gave, and he took, and all of it was soft and warm and sweet and thrilling, and it was nothing at all like the stories she had heard from the married women her age, the terrible tales of the first-times, the men who hurt them. She made the soft kitten noises he delighted in and Quinn laughed. He was gentle and silly, and he pressed his kisses to the side of her throat as they came together. There was no need to communicate; she knew exactly what to do as he brought her the gentlest of pleasures.

He seemed more than a little drunk, more than a little satisfied when they finished and she lay quietly nestled in his arms, her frayed, half-braided hair lying in loops and whorls over them both. She ran her fingers down Quinn's arm. He had the softest hair she had ever felt, and she rubbed her cheek against his arm like a cat. Her heart was thudding in her throat like she had run a mile. She had half expected to feel like an entirely different person as if Sasha Strange the child should cease to exist with the advent of Sasha Strange the woman, but it wasn't like that at all. She felt no different, only complete with him, safe and secure. She was surprised to learn the child and the woman could coexist inside of her skin like this.

Quinn took her hand and kissed the inside of her wrist, then the side of her neck. He liked her neck very much. She closed her eyes and listened to the roar of the sea only a few hundred feet away. Out on the plains, the night creatures lowed, and the darkness was alive with the sounds of a million prehistoric insects in flight. The busy, ceaseless noise had frightened her once; now it was commonplace, a comfort, a sound of things alive and living.

"Look," she said, pointing toward the sea. Farther down the beach, several huge turtle hatchlings were clambering out of a shallow nest and through the thick sand, making their way down to the ocean. "I believe those are Archelons, prehistoric turtles."

"Those are big turtles."

She rolled over onto her belly in the sand and rested her chin on her folded hands to watch them. Quinn moved up beside her, keeping his arm around her protectively. "They're just little ones," she explained. "The adults are huge, as big as elephants. Imagine, one laid its eggs on this very beach and tonight the young are going to fight their way down to the sea."

Quinn stared in wonder as the young hatchlings with their soft shells raced each other toward the water, the night tide lapping at them in welcome. "Will they attack, do you think?"

She glanced at him slyly. "Well, I don't know. They might if they're hungry enough. It's best if we stay very still and very close, just in the event they do. We might have to stay like this all night."

Quinn looked concerned, then saw her teasing smile. He rolled over and drew her up and over him so she was astride his hips, staring down into the dark seawater blue of his eyes, her hair tenting them in together. He cupped her cheek, kissed the bareness of her throat. "My Sasha, my clever little cat," he said, looking up at her so fondly. He took the claw about her neck, using it to guide her mouth down to his for a slow and gentle kiss.

"Will you love me again?" she asked almost shyly when he had broken the kiss.

"I expect all this means the wedding is on again, yes?"

"Yes, Quinn," she said with absolute wisdom. No *little Sasha*. Only *my Sasha*. She smiled to herself in the dark. "It most certainly is."

| 36 |

After a week, they found no more evidence of She. It was almost a relief. It meant they could follow the inland sea once more. It meant that She might have given up and gone her own way.

They resumed their journey, and their lives began developing rhymes and patterns. Sasha was pleased about this. Where once they were strangers traveling across the face of an unknown world, bound together by a need for survival, now they were a community, almost a family. Toby and Naja were her best friends, and Quinn was her lover. A hundred times a day she had to stop and remind herself of that fact, it felt so strange.

Quinn must have spoken to Naja about new arrangements, because the day after Sasha had visited Quinn, Naja became their land hunter, often taking Toby with her to hunt small prey on the plains and leaving Sasha and Quinn to do the fishing amidst the shallow lagoons where they camped. She was not very good at first, but Quinn was a patient teacher, and she was very strong and fast from the work of living off the land. Soon she could spear even the fastest fish.

After all the fish was caught, Sasha would often swim in the shallows if she saw Dotty was on lookout nearby. Quinn would sit on the beach and watch her, always alert for signs of danger. At first, she thought he was being careful, or only self-conscious, until he sheepishly admitted that he couldn't swim. Sasha couldn't imagine it. He seemed good at everything else.

On that occasion, she swam up to him, dressed in only her chemise, and stood up, inviting him to join her. She knew the chemise was diaphanous when wet. On that day, she learned that Quinn's desire for her was stronger than his fear of the water. He paired himself down to his trousers and stepped cautiously into the water until he was waist-deep. Sasha swam up to him. He tried to catch her, but she ducked away as quick as a seal, swam in a circle around him, and embraced him from behind. That seemed to both calm and excite him at once.

She ran her wet arms up and down his bare chest. She loved the warm, slender slickness of him, the heat and strength in his body, the way he yielded to even her smallest touch. "Aren't you going to teach me *anything*?" he finally asked with mock irritation.

"I thought I was," she said, leaning against his back and resting her head on his shoulder.

Dotty streaked by, splashing water at them with her flippers. "Sasha," he stated with sudden alarm. "I really must insist you do something about your pet before it eats me."

"Dotty doesn't eat people, I told you," she laughed, pulling him around so they were face to face. If anything, having Dotty nearby was a comfort, as Dotty became very excitable when danger was near. Sasha gave Quinn her coyest look, the one he couldn't resist. He leaned down to embrace her and she put her arms about his neck and yanked him under the surface with her for a watery kiss.

Several moments later, a very wet, very cross Quinn tromped back to shore, vowing never to go in the water again if she acted in such a despicable manner. Sasha followed, laughing. She pulled herself ashore beside him and lay on the sand, letting the sun dry her hair and chemise before she redressed. Quinn watched her, his anger withering in seconds. She laughed at his expression, the way he ranted at her, the way he tried to stay angry and failed horribly. When she felt he'd suffered enough, she opened her arms to him. He needed very little persuasion. His skin was warm and still wet from the sea as he pressed himself against her. She rubbed her cheek against his chest and held him close. "Sasha, you really are the most extraordinary girl," he said. He held her, running his hands over her wet braids with exquisite care and tenderness.

She tried to kiss his neck—she liked his neck too—but he suddenly held her apart. He cupped her cheek and looked into her eyes. "You know," he said, "I still mean to return to Africa, assuming we ever make it home."

Her heart stuttered and she felt her spirits wither as a thousand miserable things flew through her mind. She thought about him leaving, about being alone again. She wasn't sure she could bear it. Then she saw his secret smirk, the way he was teasing her as she had teased him in the water. Turnabout was fair play, she expected.

"You will come with me?" he asked.

"Am I invited?"

"No, Sasha. I plan to return to the Continent sans my wife." He gave her a droll look. "What do you think?"

She kissed him quickly. "I think I shall like to see Africa with you, Quinn." She kissed him again, deeper, slower. He moved to embrace her, but she broke the kiss and sat up. "Can we have an elephant?"

"An elephant? Yes, of course."

"I shall like to meet bushmen as well."

"Certainly."

"And may I have a laboratory and a library? I should like to continue work on the Tuning Machine...more carefully, of course."

He bit back a smile. "Anything you wish, my dear."

She was in good spirits when they returned to camp. But Toby looked more miserable than ever, and Naja was less talkative than usual. Sasha wondered if they'd had a disagreement of some kind. After the supper cleanup, she followed Toby out onto the beach. He sat on some rocks precariously close to the shoreline, his head cocked skyward where a myriad of unknown constellations glittered overhead. "Toby," she said, coming upon him. "Is everything all right?"

"Yes, of course," he answered too quickly.

Distantly, she could hear something that sounded like a steady, manmade beat, a sound almost like…drums. She listened carefully, but the night fell still. All she could hear were some diplodocus bellowing across the plains. "Toby?" she said again.

He turned and smiled at her, but it was a mere shadow of his former smile, a soulless smirk like the kind Quinn had favored before they had become lovers. It looked…pained. Sad.

"What's wrong?" she asked, suddenly concerned.

"Nothing," he said, shaking his head. "Did you have a pleasant swim this afternoon?"

She didn't know what to say to that. Had Toby seen them together? She was almost prepared to ask when Toby offered her a dark look that made her cold somewhere deep inside. "He is going to get you killed, Sasha," he said. "He is going to hunt the big one until she turns on him, on all of us."

She swallowed against the lump of fear and anger in her throat. "No. He's careful, Toby."

He gave her a doleful look. "How can one be *careful* with something like that?"

"Toby, please…"

"Your handsome, adventurous hero," he said in a mocking tone. "Will he protect you? Will he save the day?"

"Stop it," she told him. Anger had won out over fear. "Leave him alone!" Toby was acting like a child, and she would endure it no longer. She returned to the cave and lay down by the fire. It was not yet her watch, though she wished it were. She would never get to sleep now. Early on, she had insisted, woman or not, that she partake in the watch duties like everyone else. After all, it had been her idea, and it was only right that she contribute. Naja was taking the first watch. She thought about switching with her, but she didn't know if she would be any good right now. She could feel tears burning up her eyes, and her heart was almost leaden with worry. She didn't understand Toby at all anymore, didn't know if she wanted to. In the dark, Quinn moved closer to her, as was his way. She often woke with him pressed against her back, his arm curved around her waist, snoring into her hair. But he must have sensed something was wrong, because his embrace was tighter and more intimate tonight, and his voice whispery soft against the back of her neck. "Sasha?"

"I'm fine." She was proud of the steadiness of her voice. "I'm very tired. Goodnight, Quinn."

The walking and fishing had taken their toll, and she fell quickly asleep despite her concerns. When next she awoke, it was near morning, the early grey ocean light filtering in waves into the cave, and she realized she'd overslept and missed her watch. She sat up, rubbing at her gritty eyes and clutching Quinn's coat close about her shoulders. Toby and Naja lay together near the dwindling fire, still fast asleep, and that was the first indication that something was wrong. It was part of the watcher's duties to make certain the fire didn't go out, even if it was a warm night. The fire kept any lurking animals out of the cave. They seemed to have an instinctual fear of fire.

Sasha climbed stiffly to her feet, took up a javelin, and approached the cave entrance. "Quinn?" she called softly. She received no reply. Now she knew something was wrong. She shrugged out of his coat and stepped outside the cave, but no Quinn was there as he usually was, sitting in the sand, working on some new weapon or tool. "Quinn!" she cried, truly concerned now.

A blast of hot fetid air made her turn.

Standing on the rocks overtop the cave entrance was She, balanced precariously with her enormous, oversized head fully extended. In that moment, Sasha found herself face to face with the open mouth and bloodied teeth and stinking gullet of the beast. The Ceratosaurus roared, the sound ripping through Sasha like knives. Before she could turn or even scream for help, She struck, her teeth clamping over Sasha like a steel trap…

Sasha sat bolt upright, so shivering cold and disoriented that it took her a moment to realize she was still alive, still in the cave, that it was still the dead of night, and the fire was high. Dear God, she felt sick. She climbed unsteadily to her feet, knowing that she'd never get back to sleep without checking on Quinn. She took up a javelin, feeling a queer stab of déjà vu, and approached the cave entrance, being more careful before stepping out onto the sand. She craned her neck to make certain there were no dangers perched atop the cave, but nothing was there but a pair of roosting Rhamphorhynchus. The moment the small flying reptiles spotted her—they were barely larger than blackbirds and no danger at all—they fluttered up and away.

She turned to glance over the moon-silvered beach. "Quinn?" she called, but no one was there. No one answered. Sasha's heart fluttered like the birds far above. "Quinn!" she screamed, sounding hysterical now.

Within seconds, Naja was at her side, her bow and quivers ready, with Toby not far behind, looking bleary with sleep. "What's going on?" he asked.

But Naja was already down in the sand, studying what looked like a scuffle of footprints. Sasha felt her heart speed up, ticking loudly in her throat, and she thought once more of the dream. She shivered violently. Most of the footprints were similar to the primitive boots that Naja wore. There looked to be four or five pairs of them. But one pair was more familiar. Quinn's boots.

Half buried in the sand was Quinn's survival knife. "Dear God," Sasha said, picking it up. He never went anywhere without it, and she didn't need Naja to tell her what she already knew. Sometime in the night, the Moja had taken Quinn.

| 37 |

They followed the footprints for several hundred feet down the beach. They had likely gagged Quinn because no one had heard anything in the night, but it was obvious from the placement of the footprints and drag marks that he had struggled the whole way. Sasha was very proud of Quinn. He had fought them, and fought them hard. Finally, they reached a spot where the sand was splattered with droplets of blood—Quinn's blood. Sasha stopped and looked at it, her spirits sinking.

"The Moja hit him here," Naja confirmed. They had finally given up and struck him, probably in the head, and he had bled quite a lot. Sasha swallowed and reminded herself that head wounds did bleed a lot. He was probably all right. Probably.

"What happened after that?" Sasha asked. There was more scuffling, but she couldn't tell much in the confusion, not the way Naja could. But then, Naja was a tracker.

Naja pointed up a steep ridge. The footprints resumed, this time wending up the beach toward the cliff heads. She pointed out the marks that indicated that Quinn's unconscious body had been dragged. The Moja had taken Quinn over the cliffs, through a line of horsehair conifers, and out onto the plains beyond.

Sasha shielded her eyes and stared out at the plains. It was warming up quickly, which meant the cold-blooded predators were slowing down and seeking shelter from the sun—she knew from experience that they preferred hunting at dawn and dusk—leaving just the big sauropods and smaller armored dinosaurs to wander the plains. The smaller dinosaurs seemed better able to regulate their body temperature, and the huge sauropods, like the pod of Diplodocus in the far distance, were so vast they threw off body heat better than the fast-moving predators. But that didn't make her feel any better about leaving the shelter of the beach and traveling across the plains. Out there, somewhere, was She. And she was waiting for them.

As if sensing her distress, Newton put his nose to her ear. She petted him. If she went out there, Newton would be her only alarm to ambush predators. She didn't know how she felt about putting her life in the hands of a tiny prehistoric mammal.

"Why would they take Quinn out on the plains?" she asked Naja. "Isn't it dangerous out there?"

Naja raised her face and almost seemed to sniff the air. "There is much danger. But also much meat. My people make their stays on the plains."

"You mean camp."

"Yes," Naja answered with a short nod. She still struggled with her English.

"How do they survive? I mean, amongst the big predators?"

"My people move much. Not stay in one camp often. And we have ways." She narrowed her eyes. "There are scents big ones don't like. And we use fire sometimes. The meat is good on the plains."

"Do you know if there's a camp nearby where they might have taken Quinn?"

"There were drums the night last. They are near. Out there." She pointed east, where the sun was almost fully up. "Beyond mountain, maybe."

"You don't know?"

"Moja may have moved on now. They will go to the sea soon. They will go to sacrifice to Bolaja, the One Below."

Again, Sasha shivered. Naja had said they sacrificed their redhairs to Bolaja, their sea god. They would most definitely sacrifice Quinn; he had the reddest hair she'd ever seen.

She swallowed against her sore, tired throat. "How long...how long before they'll take Quinn to the sea?"

Naja shrugged. "I do not know. There will be a ceremony first, the Moja will eat and dance, but it could be very short or very long."

"So there's time," she said. "Maybe there's time." She didn't feel better, only slightly more hopeful.

"We're not going out on the plains," Toby stated, stepping up beside her. He'd been so quiet she had nearly forgotten he was there. He put a hand on Sasha's shoulder as if he would restrain her. "You saw what that...thing did to those animals it killed. You'd be mad to go out there."

Sasha's grip on her javelin increased until her knuckles turned white. "Toby, I can't *not* go out there. They have Quinn."

"He could be dead already. They might have killed him on the beach."

She shuddered, closed her eyes for a second. She couldn't afford to believe that. "He's not dead. They don't want him dead. They need him for a sacrifice." She turned, but Toby's grip on her shoulder increased. She looked at him. Her face felt like stone. "Toby, unhand me."

"You can't go out there!" he shouted. "Either She will kill you, or the Moja will."

"Then come with me." She looked to Naja, then back at Toby. But it was obvious to her that they were far too frightened to go out onto the plains. She felt the first nibbling of despair, then sucked back at the sudden tears in her throat. She would not fall apart. She would not be afraid. Not when Quinn needed her to be strong, a huntress. She shrugged off Toby's touch. She had her answer. But she had no more time to waste.

Turning her back on Toby and Naja, she headed back to camp to collect supplies for the long, lonely trek ahead.

| 38 |

She took two waterskins, a supply of food that would keep her three days, and two javelins. She bundled everything up in her homemade rucksack and shouldered it, testing the weight. She took up her favorite javelin for protection. Before she left, she stripped away the remnants of her dress so she was paired down to just her chemise and the homemade Moja boots that Naja had made for her. She was done with modesty, and the shredded dress was becoming more a hindrance than anything else. For protection against the night's chill, she took Quinn's frock coat, tying it about her waist. She had everything she needed for at least three days of hard travel. Newton leaped up onto her shoulder as if to assert that he was ready. Newton, her only alert to danger on the plains. And now, her only companion.

She emerged from the cave and saw Toby and Naja waiting for her on the beach. They too were ready to move on, though they'd be going in a different direction today.

"I wish you wouldn't do this," said Toby. His face was lined with worry. He kept compulsively clutching his bow. "I told you he'd get you killed."

She stared at him. She refused to be afraid. "I have to find him, Toby." She swallowed, hard. "I love him."

Toby looked infinitely sad. "You do, don't you." He saw how serious she was, how hard her eyes and spirit were. "You won't survive out there, you know."

"Maybe."

"And even if you do, how will you ever rescue him?"

"I'll think of something. I'll negotiate. I'll show the Moja how to construct better weapons in exchange for Quinn's freedom. I'll show them how to get more meat."

Naja looked sad. "They will not listen."

She waited for one or both of them to offer her assistance, to join her in this dangerous task, but they only looked on her with pity and sadness. Naja was afraid; she had escaped her people because she feared for her life. And Toby did not care if Quinn died. She was alone in all this. In fact, she'd never felt so alone in all her life. "I have to go," she said. "Goodbye, then." With a heavy heart, she pushed past them both and hiked out into the plains toward the distant mountains, alone.

39

She'd gone perhaps two miles before she spotted a lumbering pod of Diplodocus, one of the largest groups she had ever seen. She counted at least thirty adults and twelve juveniles. They filled the plains, somehow making it seem less vast as they bullied each other and switched their long tails in communication. The ground trembled with their passing. Quinn would have suggested moving with the herd for protection but keeping a reasonable distance. If she kept walking east without taking many breaks, it was possible she'd make the mountains in a few hours with the Diplodocus acting as a living shield. No predator would dare approach such an imposing herd as this. It was difficult keeping up with such gigantic land-shakers, but, by nightfall, she was within a few miles of the Moja camp, and she could hear the distant thudding of drums.

Newton became more agitated then, and Sasha stopped to let him off in a tall conifer. At first, he was reluctant to leave her, but Sasha shooed him away. If she was taken by the Moja, she wanted Newton, at least, to have a chance at life.

She hiked on alone, taking pains to listen to the drums, which were increasing in volume and steadily picking up rhythm. By the time full dark fell, she was perhaps a quarter of a mile from the looming black mountains and she could see a myriad of small fires lit all across the Moja's camp. Naja said the Moja used fire to stave off the night predators, but some of the bonfires were larger than others. She had a sinking feeling there was some religious significance to them. She moved to the shelter of a stand of conifers and started to climb. At least this way, she was hidden from the Moja and still protected from ground predators.

From the higher bows, she could see the camp more clearly. It covered the whole foot of the mountain and was comprised of perhaps three hundred individuals of various ages, all of the same overly large, sturdy genetic stock as Naja, all dressed in similar crude saris, men and women alike. They were maintaining at least ten large ceremonial bonfires, with a great many people dancing and offering up praise to their gods. The rattling drums and primitive twittering flutes quickly frightened off any animals that drew near the camp—which was likely its original purpose, Sasha thought. The reverie was likely intended to keep predators away from the camp at night, but like people everywhere, the Moja had attached religious significance to the songs and dances of their people until one day they began taking on a life all their own.

The Moja were nomadic, Naja said. As a result, there were no permanent structures, only a handful of crude wigwams—small, dome-shaped structures built of branches or bones and covered in hides or palm fronds, easy enough to deconstruct and carry with the tribe when they chose to move on. In the middle of the camp, surrounded by a circle of wigwams, was a large, painted man bearing an elaborate mantel of bone around his shoulders. He was directing the largest number of dancers, and she thought he might be the tribal leader.

Sasha watched for over an hour as the chief directed his people to add burning branches to the already enormous bonfire. They danced, and sang, and strengthened the fire until it was as high as a pillar. Then he pointed at the largest wigwam and four of the largest men ducked inside. Sasha felt her breath catch when they emerged. They were dragging a much smaller man with them who was fighting fiercely to be free of their hold...a man with hair as bright as the fire they were feeding.

Quinn.

| 40 |

Sasha followed the tribe down to the inland sea, staying as hidden as possible amidst the cycads and conifer pines. She thought many times about rushing into their midst and trying to negotiate for Quinn's freedom as she had told Toby and Naja she would, but it wasn't long before she realized how futile that would be. The ceremony was reaching a fever pitch, the Moja shouting and dancing in ever more ecstatic patterns as they marched Quinn with enormous ceremony down to the sea. Some seemed so possessed by their religious zealotry that they began convulsing with the sheer power of song and dance. She was afraid if she approached them now they would simply kill her, or perhaps add her to the sacrifices to Bolaja.

On the beach, they lit an enormous bonfire, the light so great it filled the sky like noontime and spilled across the sand and turned it golden. No animals were willing to approach now. They tied Quinn to a sturdy saltire cross that looked like it had weathered many ceremonies similar to this, then fed their fire higher and danced about him, brushing fans of brightly colored feathers against his face.

Sasha slipped behind some boulders on the edge of the beach and watched and waited. She knew she was likely running out of time, and she wondered if she'd be able to pass as a Moja in her dark braids and tan just long enough to get close to Quinn and cut his binds with her knife. But each time she thought the Moja were distracted enough to allow her to creep down to the beach, one broke away from the rest and approached him, flicking him with incense or fluttered their ceremonial fans in his face until he grimaced and looked ready to bite the next Moja who approached him.

She waited another twenty minutes, but no opportunity presented itself. She was running out of time. She was going to have to take her chances by directly infiltrating the tribe. She dropped her rucksack on the ground and stabbed her javelin into the sand. She slid Quinn's knife into the obi-style belt holding her slowly disintegrating chemise together and started down the beach.

And that's when the hands fell upon her shoulders.

| 41 |

Gripping the knife in her belt, Sasha turned, ready to strike the person behind her…only to recognize the familiar plains and worry lines in Toby's face. She nearly shrieked in surprise, clapping a hand over her mouth to stop herself. "What are you doing here?" she asked, then spotted Naja a few steps behind him. She looked as worried as Toby.

"We came down to warn you not to approach the Moja now," Toby explained. "Naja said that Quinn is now a 'sacred object' to be sacrificed. Anyone who touches him will make him 'unclean' to be sacrificed to Bolaja."

Sasha let out her breath. "Isn't that a good thing?" She looked at Naja, but Naja shook her head vehemently.

"If Quinn is made unclean by your touch, they will kill him right now," she said.

"They're going to kill him anyway!"

Naja gave her a serious look. "They will not kill your Quinn. They mean to send him to Bolaja."

"What does that mean?"

"You will see."

"I don't need to see!" she hissed. "I need to save him before they do…whatever it is they plan to do to him!"

Naja pointed to the horizon where a craggy collection of rocks projected from the sea. "In the early hours of the morning they will take him there and bind him to the rocks, and then call Bolaja. But they will not remain to see. The Moja fear Bolaja too much to look upon him."

Sasha looked at the other woman. "So I'll have time to rescue him?"

"You may if you can swim very fast. Bolaja is…very fast."

She thought about that. Her head hurt from the continuous rolling thunder of the drums. "I can swim. But Quinn can't." She sat down on the sand and clapped her hands over her face. How would she *ever* tow Quinn to shore in time? She was strong, an excellent swimmer, but Quinn was heavier than he looked, and the swim was at least a thousand feet.

Naja gave Toby a meaningful look. After a moment, he sat down beside her. He took a deep breath that almost seemed to pain him and said, "I'll help you get Quinn to shore."

She looked at him in surprise. "Why?" She knew he hated Quinn. She did not even think he cared enough about him to help her at this point.

Toby looked unsure of himself, but a glance from Naja spurred him on. "Because I owe Quinn."

She shook her head. "I don't understand. Is this because of what he did in the Sen cave?"

He stared at his feet a long moment before glancing up at her. He hunched his shoulders as if he were expecting physical blows to fall upon him. "No," he said. "I asked Naja to cut a piece of Quinn's hair off while he slept and deliver it to a Moja scout."

The words made no sense to her for a moment. She looked at Toby. She looked at Naja. She said, "I don't understand."

Naja averted her eyes.

"When the scout saw his hair," Toby explained, "the Moja decided they wanted him, that they would hunt him."

"I still don't understand." She stared long and hard at Naja, her friend. The woman who had told her she must take Quinn if she wanted him. "Why would you do something like that?" She stood up and took an unsteady step toward her. "Why would you want to hurt Quinn?"

"It wasn't Naja," Toby said, standing up and moving closer to Naja as if he meant to intervene between the two women. "She likes Quinn, Sasha. She only did it because I asked her to."

She looked at Toby. She felt numb all over.

Toby held her steady gaze. "I lied to Naja. I told her Quinn was a very bad man in our world, that she'd made a dreadful mistake in encouraging your relationship with him." He took a deep breath and ran his hands over his face and hair. "But I knew it was all a mistake when I saw you run off like that. I knew it was wrong."

"It was my mistake too," Naja said, turning her careful attention on Sasha but lowering her eyes in deference. "I should have trusted he was a good man. I am sorry, Sasha." She went to one knee and bowed her head in a gesture of contrition.

Sasha stared at them both. She felt a flash of anger so great it made her tremble. "So you made Toby come here," she said to Naja.

"No, I made us come here," Toby said, his eyes burning with an unfamiliar pain. "I want to make it up to you. I want to help Quinn, Sasha."

"I trusted you. Both of you." She shook her head, hateful tears filling up her eyes. "How could you do this? We were all together in this. We were *friends*." She looked directly at Toby.

Toby took a step toward her. "Sasha, please…we want to help you…"

"Leave me alone!" Sasha pushed past them both and walked away.

| 42 |

Near morning, Sasha had turned things over in her mind a million times. Her anger hadn't cooled, but it had gone from a rolling boil to a low simmer. She still felt sick to think of what Toby and Naja had done. She was trying very hard not to think of the world as a bleak, unhappy place full of ugly, untrustworthy people. She knew that wasn't true, but, at the moment, it *felt* true. The ongoing mental tug-of-war had left her frightened and exhausted, and she had never felt so alone in her life, even amidst friends. *Especially* amidst these friends. But at the same time, she had to look at the practical side of things as Quinn himself would. She needed Toby to help her tow Quinn ashore, and she needed Naja to act as lookout in case the Moja returned or Bolaja appeared. She had to bite her pride, swallow it. She had to work with Toby and Naja or Quinn was going to die.

She peered out to sea. In the grey, pre-dawn light, she could just make out a group of Moja canoeing toward the rocks, their place of sacrifice. Wedged between the big, dark, painted braves sat Quinn, looking hunched and tired and small from the long night of relentless ceremony. Wiping the worry and hurt from her heart, Sasha turned to the two people standing at nervous attention behind the boulders. She looked them in the eyes and said, "All right."

They didn't look happy. They did look relieved.

Together, they waited impatiently as the Moja dragged Quinn out of the canoe and marched him up a slippery stair of rock. Quinn was no longer fighting the men. He was probably frightened half to death of slipping and falling into the ocean, and having his hands bound together behind him wasn't helping in the least. He simply let them guide him along until they reached the largest, most jagged outcropping of rock standing at least twenty feet high. There they untied his wrists and slipped them into crude manacles permanently affixed to the rock via long handmade chains.

"I wonder if the Moja even belong in this place," Sasha said, more to herself than to anyone.

Toby, standing beside her, said, "What do you mean?"

"The chain and manacles the Moja use look almost medieval," she said. "And the canoe design is similar to the ones that natives in North America build. Yet the Moja cannot even construct permanent shelters. I wonder if it isn't possible the Moja are descended from displaced people like us."

"You mean they came from our world?"

"Maybe," she said. "A small handful of people may have…slipped sideways into this world long ago. That may be why they know how to construct chains and canoes." She shook off the thought. It was an interesting theory, but she didn't have time for such speculations. The Moja warriors were scurrying like frightened children to get off the rock and back into their canoe. They paddled madly back to shore, practically leaping out of the water.

The tribal leader moved to stand in the shallows and raised a great conch shell to his mouth, releasing one long, low note that sounded too much like an animal in distress for Sasha's liking.

"The chief is calling Bolaja to feed," said Naja. "He sent my brother and mother to Bolaja." Her voice sounded low and pained. "I will not let hunter Quinn be taken as well."

"I'm sorry," Sasha said. She had to force herself to sit still and wait until the Moja began to retreat from the shore, so frightened of their god that they did not even want to witness his arrival. Naja muttered something in her language, bowed her head, and drew some sacred symbols over her heart. It sounded like a prayer of deliverance, and the sound of her words made Sasha's skin prickle as the knife-edge of fear scraped down her back.

As soon as the Moja had vacated the beach, the three of them started down, with Naja on lookout. She'd warned that Bolaja, whatever he was, could swim fast, so the moment Sasha reached the shallows, she kicked off her boots, scouted for immediate dangers, and, finding none, dived straight into the shockingly cold seawater with Toby not far behind her. She surfaced long enough to take a deep breath, then dived back down into the cold silence of the sea. She knew she didn't have much time, and the rock that Quinn was chained to seemed endlessly far away. Swimming under the water was far faster than cutting through it.

"Sasha!" Toby called breathlessly from several yards away, trying desperately to keep up with her. She'd always been the stronger swimmer, and she didn't have time to wait for him. She kicked and clawed at the water, and each time she raised her head, the rocks were a little bit closer. But along the way, something bumped her leg—and it wasn't Toby, who was still lagging far behind. She stopped kicking and simply treaded water, trying to hold very still. Something cold brushed her leg again and she jumped, feeling her heart climb up into her mouth. She wondered if it was Bolaja. She wondered if it was something worse...

Then Dotty broke the surface of the water and swam in a tight circle about her, chattering excitedly like a seal. Sasha was immediately relieved. "Dotty!" she said and grabbed hold of the plesiosaur's neck. "Dotty, Quinn!" She pointed, hoping the creature would understand in some arcane way. "We need to swim to Quinn!"

But Dotty chattered and started swimming in the *opposite* direction, which only made sense, Sasha supposed. Dotty knew to swim away from danger. "Oh, Dotty," Sasha said, letting her go. She dived back under the water and started clawing her way toward the rocks again. The hour was getting late and she had to get to Quinn, with or without Dotty's help.

It seemed forever before she reached the rock and started scrabbling up the rough wet side, desperately seeking purchase anywhere she could. The sea seemed to be getting darker, choppier, and she was deathly cold by the time she reached the top where Quinn was chained. The moment he saw her, he seemed to come alive and started pulling desperately at his chains. "Sasha? *What* are you doing here?"

She raced up to him and flung her arms around his neck, hugging him tightly. "I'm saving you, silly man."

"What took you so long? I waited all bloody night..."

She kissed him. That shut him up. He tasted like salt and sea. She freed his survival knife from her belt with a smile. "Won't be but a moment." She went to work on the manacles, which were made of crude metal that had simply been bent around Quinn's wrists with incredible strength. They were weak from use, but not yet at the breaking point. Sasha hoped to change that.

Quinn watched her. "You know, my dear, this is doing absolutely nothing for my male ego."

"Oh, shut up," she said as she concentrated on bending the steel without accidentally stabbing Quinn with the blade of the knife.

Toby had finally reached them and was pulling himself up the rock. "Sasha!" he cried, pointing frantically off toward the horizon.

Sasha stopped to glance up, her heart back in her throat. Not far off, perhaps a quarter of a mile, an enormous wake was headed their way as a gigantic creature cut through the water, zeroing in on the rock.

Bolaja was here.

| 43 |

"Sasha, I really must insist that you go now," Quinn said. He sounded amazingly composed as he watched the sea creature heading their way. "It really is too late."

She ignored him. She jammed the knife into the little space between the manacle and Quinn's wrist and kept prying at the slowly weakening metal.

"Sasha…"

"I'll go when you're free!" she said sternly, her panic mounting moment by moment. The wake was growing closer by the second. She started smashing the weakened manacle against the rocks, putting everything she had into it. "I wish you'd be less argumentative."

"I am not argumentative."

"Yes, you are."

"No," he argued, "I'm not."

She gave a cry of victory when she felt the metal give and the manacle fall away from Quinn's left wrist. But just when she thought there might be a chance they'd all live through this, an enormous wave came up and slapped them all. Bolaja was close, almost upon them. She started frantically on the second manacle.

"Sasha," Quinn said, his voice unusually calm and demanding.

She turned to look at him.

He was smiling, though his eyes were deadly serious. He put his free arm about her waist and drew her close to him, all the plains of his body familiar as they pressed against her. He slanted his mouth against hers and kissed her deeply, tracing the seam between their lips with his tongue. "I love you, Sasha," he said, moving his hand around until it finally came to rest at her wrist, where he deftly liberated his knife from her. "Remember that, my darling."

"Quinn..." she began, stunned speechless by his words. She clung to him even as they were both sprayed with seafoam from the slowly building wake. She would not let him go. If she had to die here, so be it. She would die with him.

Quinn looked beyond her to Toby. His face was resolved, peaceful. "Take good care of her, boy," he said. "I care very much about this girl." Then, still smiling a little, he pushed her hard, backward, off the rock and into the ocean.

Sasha screamed.

| 44 |

"Toby, let go!" she said, trying to wriggle out of his hold. But Toby, who had dove into the sea seconds after her, had an iron hold on her. He was trying to drag her back to shore on Quinn's orders, but, every time he pulled on her, she twisted in his arms to make him release her. "I'm not leaving Quinn!"

Toby put his mouth very close to her ear. "It's already here, Sasha. There's nothing more we can do."

"No!" she screamed. She kicked at him, almost managing to get free, but it was futile. They were both picked up and flung halfway back to shore by an enormous wall of water as a creature as vast as a whale breached like a mountain before them—a mountain that bellowed with a voice like thunder. Sasha screamed, and then the ocean sucked them under and the world became nothing but light and darkness and silence and terror. Sasha kicked, but she had no idea which way she was swimming; she could only hope for the best. She searched for light and swam in that direction.

She broke the surface seconds later—it felt like years—and gasped for breath. Toby sprang to the surface beside her, and for that, at least, she was grateful. They were both now closer to shore than to Quinn and she could see the creature looming over him clearly. It looked like a giant, primeval crocodile. "What in bloody hell *is* that?" Toby cried in horror.

She shook her head in disbelief. The creature seemed to be some form of pliosaur, a short-necked plesiosaur, and one of Dotty's distant relatives. "Dear God," she gasped, watching the gigantic creature snap at the open air before sinking back into the sea. Quinn was busy working on his second manacle with the knife, trying not to look, trying not to panic, she knew.

Dotty, frantically circling them both, gave her another friendly bump. Sasha grabbed hold of the plesiosaur's slick neck, wrapping her arms tightly about it. "We have to help Quinn, Dotty," she told the creature, whispering close to its ear. "You're the only one who can do it."

"Sasha, what are you *doing*?" Toby demanded to know, trying to snatch at her.

As if spurred by her words, Dotty started sprinting toward the rock, though her whole body shivered with fear, and Sasha could see poor Dotty's big black eyes flickering nervously in her head. Sasha held on, letting Dotty tow her on. They were cutting so quickly through the water that Toby would never be able to catch her now. She prayed Dotty didn't lose her nerve. She could never swim fast enough to get there on her own.

The sea was very still around them, too still. Sasha had a terrible fantasy of Bolaja circling beneath them, then streaking upward to consume them both whole and alive. The thought made her whole body break out in a cold sweat. The journey seemed endless and nightmarish.

Bolaja resurfaced, but it was again near the rock. Possibly the beast was attracted to the color red, and maybe *that* was the reason the Moja sacrificed their red-hairs to the creature. It snapped wildly at the open air around the rock where Quinn was crouching, still working slowly and awkwardly on the manacle. But the creature's neck was too short to give it the angle it needed to bite its intended target. Bolaja's enormous, pointed jaws could only snap at the tip of the rock, chipping off a large chunk that knocked Quinn's chain loose. Still cowering, Quinn slid sideways off the rock and into the sea.

"Quinn!" she shouted and started to kick, hoping to direct Dotty toward the place where Quinn had gone under, but Dotty had other ideas. With a cry, she broke away from Sasha and swam directly toward Bolaja, so fast that Sasha couldn't stop her. With a cry of her own, Sasha dived—there was nothing else she could do. She swam just as fast as she could, trying to keep an eye out for Quinn, but the dark green waters were so stirred with debris it was nearly impossible to see.

She surfaced and glanced around frantically, but there was nothing to see. Gasping, more panicked than ever, Sasha dived again, hoping to spot something...*anything*. Then some huge thing grabbed her around the middle and she screamed and swallowed what felt like a gallon of seawater. She kicked, half expecting to feel prehistoric teeth piercing her flesh, but the pain never came. She kicked and swam and struggle, dragging herself to the surface, and it was only then she realized a choking, half-drowned Quinn was attached to her, his arms wrapped so tightly about her ribs she could scarcely breathe.

The moment they were up, Quinn heaved water all over her—which, by her estimation, was the *second* time he had thrown up on her. "Quinn," she said and turned to face him, trying her best to support his weight above the water. He looked miserably half-drowned and about as terrified as she had ever seen him. "Quinn, are you all right?"

He choked again and clung to her. "Dandy..." he said, not sounding dandy at all.

"I'm going to try and swim us back to shore," she told him, "but you're going to have to let me breathe, please."

"Yes, of course," he managed, slowly releasing his death grip on her.

Before she could orient herself and aim for shore, another wave hit them, almost capsizing them. Twisting around, she was able to confirm what she feared—Bolaja was sinking back under the surface of the water. She had just started to wonder how they would ever out-swim that monster when Dotty surfaced again. She chattered excitedly and surrounded them in a whirlpool of frothy water as if they didn't already know they were in terrible danger! "Dotty!" Sasha shouted. "Dotty, run away!"

This time she obeyed. She whimpered and swam off...right toward Bolaja.

"Oh, Dotty," Sasha said, feeling her heart sink inside of her. She bit back the desire to cry and turned back to the task at hand, the one thing she was capable of doing. Gripping Quinn around the shoulders, she began backstroking them both toward shore as quickly as possible. He was cumbersome, and it was difficult to keep them both afloat, but she was saved Toby joined them and took much of Quinn's weight off her. Together the two of them towed him along until they'd reached the shallows. There Toby took over, pulling Quinn ashore, allowing Sasha to rest in the ankle-deep water and look back.

The only thing that had kept Bolaja from following them was Dotty. She was swimming in beautiful, slick circles around the beast, which kept breaching and clapping its enormous jaws at the tiny plesiosaur. Dotty wheeled in and out of the waves, sometimes leaping ten feet into the air. Finally, she turned back toward the sea and streaked off, as fast as an eel. Bolaja immediately gave chance, his mountainous body cutting deep into the water as he dived after her. He was bigger and much faster than Dotty. Sasha watched with her heart pounding and her mouth as salty and dry as sand as Dotty surfaced for the last time, mewling in fear. Then Bolaja's huge jaws came up beneath her and clamped shut. Sasha waited, eyes burning, breath stuck on a sob.

Bolaja dived, then surfaced a moment later and flung Dotty's bloodied carcass high into the air before catching it between his teeth and disappearing under the waves for good. Seconds passed and the water stilled as if nothing had transpired. As if nothing was there at all. Sasha, sitting in the shallows, bowed her head, put her hands over her face, and wept.

| 45 |

She was tired, worn to the bone, and she wanted to go home. She didn't feel like a huntress. She felt like what she was—a ragged little girl who wanted someone to hold her and make things right. It was such a relief when Quinn lifted her into his arms and carried her ashore. She couldn't have walked if she needed to. She put her arms about his neck and rested her tearstained face on his soaking wet shoulder. As Quinn turned, he came face to face with Toby standing in the shallows, looking on with concern. He immediately stiffened and she could feel him bristling all over. "Don't touch her," he said, his voice a threatening growl. Toby grew absolutely still. Quinn pushed past him and strode with her in his arms toward the beach cooking under the early morning sun.

When they had gotten as far from the shoreline as possible, Quinn set her down in the soft, warm sand. He held her close and let her cry until she was all washed out. "All these tears for a bloody dinosaur." He sounded exhausted, as worn and finished as she felt. And then he reconsidered. "Or is it a marine reptile?"

She sat up then and looked him in the eye. She sniffed back the tears. "I'm being silly, I know."

"You are a bit of a silly thing," he admitted, though something warm and fierce and proud burned in his eyes.

"I'm sorry. I don't mean to be."

He brushed the greatly matted braids off her face. "I should hate it if you weren't." He had turned his body so he shielded her in a very chivalrous manner from the view of the others, she and her tears and her diaphanous chemise, which was torn almost to shreds now. He said low, almost a growl in her ear, "That was a very stupid rescue, you realize. You could have been killed. I shouldn't want to see you do that again." He gave her a stern look.

"I'm sorry," she said, though she was not. She had come so close to losing Quinn forever. The realization made her want to cry all over again. "I was so afraid, but I knew I had to do something."

Quinn brought her hand to his lips. "Funny, the whole time I was with the Moja, I wasn't frightened at all."

Her eyes widened. "You weren't?"

He smirked, a little. "I was too miserable to be afraid. I kept thinking about not seeing you again. That seemed a more terrible fate than dying, somehow." He paused as if the words embarrassed him terribly. He looked away, but not before she recognized the fierceness of love in his eyes.

"Quinn..." she began, but he interrupted.

"I really do mean to make you my wife, and I'm sorry to say you'll have to obey my every word. No derring-do's, no big escapes, no rescues." He smiled then, a teasing, genuine smile, and tapped her nose for emphasis. "I shall have to be very firm with you, I think. It will be a difficult task, but I'm sure I can make a proper wife of you."

She tried to imagine Quinn "taming" her; the thought just made her smile through her tears.

He stared down at her in that all-consuming way that he had like she was the only thing in his world. "My brave Sasha," he said. He leaned down, took her face in his big hands, and kissed her, a kiss that seemed to reach deep inside of her and make her heart flutter and her insides feel honey warm She marveled at the roughness of his hands and voice and the tender carefulness of his kisses. She was still cold and shaking and miserable, but it felt so good to have Quinn near, pressed against her, kissing her, keeping her safe. She would have given almost anything just to go to Africa with Quinn, to see gentle elephants and to talk to bushmen with him at her side.

She had almost lost herself in the fantasy of it all when she saw Naja hurrying toward them through the heavy soft sand, her javelin at her side and her bow jouncing over one shoulder. She looked pale and worried, her dark blue eyes wide in her face. She stopped, breathlessly, and said, "We must leave now. The Moja are returning."

| 46 |

There were only four of them and over three hundred Moja. Somehow, the odds just didn't seem stacked in their favor today.

"Can you run?" Quinn asked her, gently and seriously.

"Yes," she answered, though she wasn't at all sure. She ached everywhere as if someone had dragged her behind a horse. She pushed upward and Quinn helped her to her feet. She weaved dangerously and he kept his arm about her waist.

"Sasha..."

"I'm fine," she told him, trying to convince herself.

Toby had rejoined them by this time. He and Naja gave each other meaningful looks, nodded in unison, and moved to stand as a barrier between the oncoming Moja and Sasha and Quinn. A line of Moja braves crested the beachhead and started down the sandy slope toward them, armed with spears and javelins. Toby took Naja's hand and stood tall as Quinn looked on in confusion at this act of bravery on Toby's part. "This is all my fault," he said by way of an explanation. "Sasha will explain everything." He swallowed hard, armoring himself in courage. "Naja and I will try and negotiate for your release, Quinn."

Quinn climbed shakily to his feet, clutching Sasha close "We'll stand together. I'll just need a weapon."

"No, you'll stay." Toby looked to Sasha for her support.

Sasha nodded and took Quinn's hand. Neither of them was strong enough to fight at the moment. It would be a miracle if they could even run. And she well knew it.

Quinn said, cautiously, "Thank you, Toby."

Toby hefted his bow. "My pleasure." Without waiting for further protests, he turned and started down the beach toward the Moja. Naja followed a few steps behind, sometimes glancing back at them to make certain they weren't following.

Quinn fell back to the sand with Sasha in his lap. It was then that Sasha realized he was bleeding from multiple wounds. His wrists were scraped raw by the manacles, and one even still dangled from his left hand. Bright red wounds were bleeding through the holes in his trousers and scrapes decorated his face and arms. She found her handkerchief and busied herself with attending to the worst of the scrapes while Quinn kept his eyes steady on the horizon. "That boy is going to get himself killed." He looked at her. "What did he mean, this was all his fault?"

She told him. She kept her words clipped, letting no emotion leak into her voice. She was no longer angry with Toby or Naja. She was just tired and finished and afraid. She wanted to be away from this place as soon as possible. She waited for an explosion of anger from Quinn, but he just sat in the sand and watched the negotiations over her shoulder. "You loved Toby, yes?" he said at last. "When you were still children?"

"Yes," she answered. There was no reason to lie about it.

"Do you love him still?"

She wiped dried blood from the corner of Quinn's mouth. She thought about that. "Yes. I expect I'll always love him. In some ways, he was my first. And he's my friend." She saw a shadow creep behind Quinn's eyes and added, "But I chose you as my lover, Quinn. I chose you as my mate."

"'I am my beloved's, and my beloved is mine,'" he quoted.

She stopped and let out her breath. "Yes."

"I chose you too," Quinn said suddenly.

His words were so sincere her throat closed up and new tears blurred her eyes. No one had ever said that to her before, not even Toby.

Quinn looked worried. "What are you thinking?"

Sasha forced a smile. "I was thinking the first time we were alone together, I hit you with a log."

Quinn mirrored her smile, though much more sheepishly. "You didn't care much for me back then."

"I hated you, actually."

Quinn blanched. She could tell he hadn't expected this much honesty from her. "That log hurt. Did you enjoy hitting me with it?"

She smiled. "Very much so."

"You are a very strange girl, Sasha."

"So they tell me."

Toby and Naja had returned from their negotiations. Toby stopped and reassured his hold on his javelin. He looked...not well. Pale beneath his summery tan.

Sasha stood up. "What did the Moja say?"

Toby shook his head. "I talked to Tojo, their chief. They're trying to decide whether to throw us all into the sea." Sasha started to say something but Toby held up a hand for silence. "Naja and I tried to negotiate by showing Tojo the bow and arrows and promising to show his people better ways to hunt."

"And they don't want to hear it," Quinn guessed.

"They said their god hasn't been appeased, and until he is, they won't let us go." He looked to Naja, who nodded him on. "We think that's just a way for Tojo to recover his pride. He's lost face among his people since Quinn escaped Bolaja."

Sasha let out her breath and shuddered. She glanced up at the long line of powerfully built warriors watching them so intently. It was conceivable that they might be able to outrun the Moja, though she didn't know if they would ever truly be free. The Moja might send scouts to retrieve them. The Moja might follow them. Naja had said they were nomadic.

Toby, as if sensing her unease, added, "So I challenged Tojo for his place as tribal leader."

Sasha started. "Are you mad?" The man was a giant.

Toby's face was grim and stony, nothing like the carefree boy she had once known. But then, they'd all changed so much since this little adventure had begun. "Possibly. But if I kill Tojo, all of you will be free to go. Including Naja." He took Naja's hand and squeezed it. He turned to look at them all. "It was the least I could do to make up for my mistake."

"Toby..." She started to reach for him, but Quinn pulled her back, allowing Toby to walk hand-in-hand with Naja back to the waiting Moja tribe.

"Let him have his pride, Sasha," he said.

"And if he doesn't kill Tojo, Quinn?"

Quinn smiled, bitterly. "Well, then, we all die together as one big happy family."

| 47 |

Everyone gathered down on the beach and the Moja set a ring of small bonfires around Tojo and Toby.

Tojo was as tall as Quinn but twice as wide as Toby. He came from the same mixed genetic stock as Naja—dark-skinned, dark hair and dark blue eyes. He was built like an Irish boxer. A hard, nomadic lifestyle had chiseled Tojo into a mountain of hard muscles and harder, unsmiling expressions. His face, and body, crawled with arcane tattoos and body piercings full of jangling bones and fearsome bits of metal. According to Naja, Tojo was not tribal leader because he had been born into it, or because he had been elected, but because he brought the most meat to the tribe. He was the Great Hunter, a title of enormous respect among the Moja, who valued hunting above all other skills. As Great Hunter, Tojo had his pick of meat and woman, and all in the tribe deferred to him. One of his duties was to appease the gods and to ensure they all saw good hunting on the plains in the coming season, hence the reason for all the sacrifices to Bolaja of late. Quinn's timely escape had rattled the people's faith, and Tojo had lost face. Thus, Tojo was a very angry young man.

Sasha sighed at all that wounded male ego eyeing them so savagely.

Tojo wore only a loincloth and had a wicked-looking dagger made of some large carnivore's tooth. Toby was bare-chested and bore Quinn's knife, which Quinn had, by some miracle—or only by pure stubbornness (Sasha was betting on stubbornness)—managed to hang onto, even during their swim. Sasha, Quinn, and Naja stood clustered together at the edge of the circle with powerful Moja tribesmen keeping a close eye on them. If Toby failed, they were all going back into the sea, including Naja, now considered by her people to be Toby's woman.

Toby looked sure of himself, but Tojo struck first, lunging at Toby and bringing his knife around in a whirling arc. Toby caught Tojo's wrist, halting the flashing knife inches before it would have reached his face. The Moja braves screamed jubilantly as the two men scuffled in the sand, egging them on.

Sasha's first instinct was to help Toby. She took a step toward him, but Quinn grabbed her around the middle, holding her firmly in place. *Let the boy have his pride*, he'd said. She tried not to worry. Toby was a scrapper. He'd grown up in the East End. He knew how to fight. And today he surprised her. He slid in under Tojo's arm, grabbed Tojo's wrist, and jerked his arm back, throwing Tojo down in the sand. He tried to stomp Tojo's face, but Tojo grabbed his foot and flung him over onto his back. Then Tojo was on his feet again and bearing down with his knife.

Toby rolled out of the way and sprang to his feet. He'd lost Quinn's knife, but he had other weapons. He clenched his fists and made a shield for his face. Letting out his breath, Toby jabbed at Tojo's jaw, driving the bigger man back down to earth. Sand hissed as it was scattered wide and the Moja, both men and women alike, screamed as one and began to chant, obviously impressed with Toby's bare-knuckled boxing method. Tojo shook his head and bounced nimbly back to his feet. His face was like stone. Stone that bled. He screamed, a primal note of male hostility, and Toby jerked at the sound, caught off balance by it. Tojo's arm came around, and in it was the knife.

Sasha screamed a warning, but too late. Tojo's knife ripped across Toby's exposed chest, drawing a long garnet line across his tanned skin. Toby lurched backward, almost stumbling into one of the bonfires at his back. But Tojo was showing no mercy. He flung himself at Toby, his knife fully extended. Toby moved, but not soon enough. Tojo clipped Toby's shoulder with the blade and there was a spurt of fresh blood. The two men went down hard in a tangle of limbs, bloodying the sand beneath them. Toby reached up and ripped the doorknocker from Tojo's nose. Tojo screamed and lost his knife. At her back, Sasha could hear Quinn quietly and ardently cheering Toby on.

Suddenly there was a scramble for the knife just out of arm's reach of both men. Tojo's arms were longer; he was going to get there sooner, so Toby reached back, took a handful of burning ash from the bonfire, and flung it at Tojo's face. Tojo roared and flung himself away.

Toby, his teeth gritted against the burning pain of his hand and blood running from his multiple wounds, flung himself atop Tojo, but the blinded Tojo reached up and clutched Toby's throat in a hand nearly twice the size of Toby's. Toby choked, his eyes flaring with pain and surprise, and started scrabbling in the sand for the fallen knife, but it had slipped too far away. Sasha felt Quinn shift behind her and subtlety kick the knife so it spun toward Toby's open, grasping hand. His fingers closed over the ivory hilt and he brought it up and down in an arc, embedding it in Tojo's shoulder. Tojo grunted as more of his blood began to flow, and suddenly he let Toby go. Toby rolled away and climbed unsteadily to his feet, staring in horror at what he had done and choking and rubbing at his bruised throat.

"Stupid boy," Quinn whispered behind Sasha as he watched Toby stagger around in a circle as the Moja cheered him on. "You're supposed to *kill* him..."

Sasha was about to protest that when Tojo reached up and pulled Quinn's knife from his own flesh with no trouble at all, despite the copious amount of blood he was losing. Screaming savagely, his teeth full of blood, he threw himself at Toby. Toby turned at the last moment, a look of surprise on his face, and caught Tojo's wrist, holding it apart. It was déjà vu, almost like the beginning of the fight, except that this time, Toby's eyes went wild and unfocused. He screamed and brought his free hand around, ripping a gouge in Tojo's face with his fingernails.

Now Tojo screamed, a wild, ululating sound like one of the animals on the plains being slaughtered. Toby twisted the man's wrist so hard there was a muted snap and Tojo dropped Quinn's knife. He brought his other hand around, and in it was a second knife no one knew he'd had. Toby only saw it out of the corner of his eye as Tojo aimed it toward Toby's midsection, but he had lost his momentum. He was in too much pain and had lost too much blood. Toby caught the man's hand, reversed the knife's trajectory, and drove the blade into Tojo's belly.

There was a terrible moment when everything stopped and Sasha could tell the Moja were holding their collective breaths, waiting to see if they would have a new leader this day. Then Tojo staggered back, looked at all the blood on his hands from the knife wound in his gut, and dropped to the sand.

Toby fell too so he was sitting in the sand, panting and wild-eyed, covered in a combination of his and Tojo's blood. For a moment, he almost didn't seem aware of it. He didn't seem aware of anything. Then he looked at his hands, his voice hitched once, and he started to cry like a child.

| 48 |

Sasha and Quinn stayed with the Moja for three days.
During that time, the Moja declared Toby the new Great Hunter, the leader of their nomadic little tribe. At first, Toby was horribly maudlin about the whole affair, but after spending a few hours talking with Naja, he was resolved. He said this was where he belonged, helping the Moja learn to survive without the sacrifices. One of Toby's first declarations was that the allies of the Great Hunter—to wit, Sasha and Quinn—should be regarded as great hunters themselves. He promised the Moja that he would protect them from their angry gods and that the new season would be the greatest the Moja had ever know, primarily because of the new hunting methods he would teach them. The Moja accepted this with barefaced logic. In the end, they were all about the hunt.

On the third day, Sasha ducked out of the wigwam she shared with Quinn and walked to the top of the cliff heads overlooking the beach to watch the morning tide roll it. The scouring sea wind blew her long braids back and scuffed across her perpetually windburned face, yet she hardly felt it. She pulled the handmade afghan the women had given her close about her shoulders more for comfort than anything else. Beneath it, she wore the tunic of the Moja tribe and durable Moja-made boots that reached to her knees. Quinn said she looked very beautiful in the primitive clothing.

She watched Quinn and the other young braves down on the beach, fishing in the shallows. Some used javelins and others bows and quarrels. Despite the loss of Dotty and the great upheaval of the Moja tribe, it had been a good three days. Peaceful. She was almost sorry to move on, though she knew Quinn was feeling restless, eager to find John and the Valley of Song. The Moja considered him a great hunter like Toby and called him Amo-Bolaja, which meant "god-killer" in the Moja language. They believed that Quinn had not only escaped Bolaja but had somehow scared him off. And though Quinn was very flattered about the whole thing, she could see the homesickness in his eyes when she looked into them at night. Homesickness not for London, but his beloved Africa.

The night before, while they lay abed together, Quinn had held her close and asked her what her immediate plans were. It was her turn to feel flattered; not many men were willing to put their future in the hands of their woman. She enjoyed the familiar comfort of his nearness and told him the truth: to move on, to find John. To get home. Of course, they would need to do so soon, before John got too far ahead of them. They agreed it was best to leave today, as early as possible. The thought excited and saddened Sasha at the same time. She knew in her heart that she would never see Toby again. Her friend. Her Toby.

Quinn was waving to her as he made his way up the beach. Between him and the young hunters-in-training, they had managed to catch almost a dozen fat fish on a long string. Some of the tribe's children raced down the sandy incline, chattering excitedly about meeting Amo-Bolaja, the great "god-killer," and Quinn, laughing, caught one of the boys around the middle and lifted him onto his shoulders, giving him a piggyback ride up the steep incline.

He looked so happy with the children, so at peace. So why were her eyes wet?

"Is everything all right?" Quinn asked, coming upon her. He looked concerned.

"Yes, of course," she answered, offering him her windburned smile.

He set the boy down and put his arm around her waist, guiding her back inside their wigwam. The space held good memories that made her smile. Last night, Quinn had made love to her here, quietly and ardently, as was his way, while the Moja sang and danced down on the beach and lit their bonfires to the sky. She touched their pallet as she returned to the task of packing. The Moja had offered them a tremendous amount of traveling supplies, homemade weapons and tools for Quinn, and tunics and afghans for Sasha. They would need for nothing in the coming weeks.

"You're concerned about Toby," Quinn said, drawing her close against him.

Sasha stopped packing. "Yes."

"Will you see him one last time?"

She thought about that. Last night the Moja had celebrated, and there had been meat and dancing and festivities in abundance. For a while, the tremendous burden of what he had done had seemed to lift and Toby, resplendent in the robes and mantle of the Great Hunter, looked almost happy, almost young again. She wanted that to be her lasting memory of him, not some sad-faced boy sitting grim and lonely on a seat of power, his face drawn with lines she had never noticed before. She didn't want to say goodbye. She didn't want there to be a last time.

Quinn looked uncomfortable in that way he had like he had unanswered questions.

"What is it?" she asked, looking up at him.

Quinn looked aside, then said it. "Do you regret not being with him?"

She smiled then, truly. "No, Quinn. I have everything I want right here."

By mid-morning, they were packed and ready to move on. The Moja said John was last seen crossing the plains on his way to the valley region, but since the Moja did not go to the Valley of Song where the "sky demons" lived, they did not know how far away it was. Sasha was almost too afraid to ask about that.

As they said their final goodbyes to the tribe and started ascending the beach, Moja supplies in rucksacks over their shoulders and brand-new Moja-made javelins in their hands, Naja joined them. She was resplendent in her sari and robes, an intricate necklace of small bones and talons about her neck to indicate she was a woman of great influence. Naja was the "First Woman" of the tribe, the woman all the other women would look to for advice. Her hair was braided and beaded, and she had dabbed some crude cosmetics around her eyes, making them look smoky and wise. She smiled. "I will miss you, sister," she told Sasha. "And you too, hunter Quinn."

Sasha stopped at the edge of the beach and turned to embrace the woman. "You will care for Toby?"

"I will guard Toby with my life. And I will guide him with it too. This I vow." She drew back and gave Sasha a long, sad look. "I have wronged you and your man. I will forever be in your debt. I will carry this burden forever."

"I don't want you to carry any such burden, Naja. I want only for you and Toby to be happy together."

Naja smiled. "We will be happy. Toby is a great hunter. We will have great hunters for sons."

Sasha smiled back. She couldn't help herself. "Have you *taken him* yet?"

Naja's smile grew, beautifully impish. "Not yet. But tonight, yes!" She swiped at the air with her javelin.

After they had parted company, Quinn drew close to Sasha and said, "What in bloody hell was all *that* about? That *taking* business? It sounds downright sinister."

She smiled secretly and reached up to kiss Quinn's cheek. "Just womens' talk," she said.

| 49 |

Sasha and Quinn moved steadily across the plains on the tail of a huge pod of hadrosaur. Newton, who had rejoined them the moment they had stepped out onto the plains, chattered excitedly on Sasha's shoulder as she fed him berries from her pocket. Hadrosaur weren't the choicest animals to use as shields, as they seemed to be food for just about every predator around, but they hadn't encountered any other animal herds in days.

The fifth day out, they camped at the foot of a butte and lit a tall bonfire to keep the predators away. The butte made for a good camp. A number of shallow crevices in the foot of the mountain made for good rain shelters. Wet weather had been rolling in for days, it seemed, almost like it was following them. That night, as Sasha and Quinn were dragging a young, freshly shot Camptosaurus back to camp, they both stopped dead in their tracks. While they'd been busy hunting, someone had been at their camp. Sasha kept their supplies rigorously organized, but it looked like someone had been rifling through their packs, and some of their travel food looked eaten. In addition, someone had written a message across the foot of the butte in fresh chalk letters five feet tall.

The message read in English:
RUN AWAY!

Together they dropped their kill and turned.

She was nearly on their heels, silently legging it over the plains, over thirty feet of primordial teeth, hunger, and rage. Within seconds the Ceratosaurus that hunted them, that hated them, was upon them. She screamed as she lunged at them, her jaws snapping wildly.

Sasha screamed too.

III

VALLEY OF DRAGONS

In which our heroes must return home.

| 50 |

She screamed in rage, a hackle-raising sound as cutting as a blade being scraped across a bone. The Ceratosaurus was over thirty feet long, ten feet longer than her dead mate, and covered in sharp, armor-like grey scales, her massive, oversized head sprouting bony ridges over both eyes and a long nasal bone at the end of her snout. That spike, Sasha knew, was not a weapon. It was to amplify sound to scare her prey into bolting witlessly at the sight of her. Her mouth was massive, as wide around as a grown man, and her teeth easily six-inches long each. When creatures heard her, they did indeed bolt witlessly. Her head was covered in old scar tissue and parasites. Her yellowish eyes were bloodshot and enraged.

Sasha Strange reflected on the amazing detail she was able to see, then on the utter horror of being able to see it so clearly as She bore done on herself and Quinn. They dropped the young Camptosaurus that Quinn had shot and stood there rooted to the spot for a moment. She hated them, of course; it was Sasha and Quinn who had made her a widow.

Quinn reacted first, pushing her out of the way. Sasha went down hard, a sharp pain in her side that cut off her breath. She had no breath to scream again as She swiveled her head to take him in and lunge.

Quinn cringed. There was no time to run, to even cry out. She opened her massive maw and was almost upon him when the beast shuddered and suddenly stopped dead in her tracks. It took Sasha a moment to realize why.

A quiver protruded from one of She's eyes. It had happened so quickly that Sasha had missed it. A freshet of stinking liquid burst from her eye, and She screamed. She screamed loud and long, her voice ripping the evening in half and making both Sasha and Quinn scramble away. Quinn grabbed her hand, tight. "Come on!" he said, and together they raced for the butte and one of the many small apertures in the rock wall. The first one they stumbled upon was almost too small and Quinn wound up pushing Sasha inside and pressing his body over her like a shield.

She's jaws clacked shut seconds after they'd made it. She pressed her snout to the opening and snorted, instantly coating them in a fine layer of dinosaur mucus. Sasha whimpered and Quinn folded himself down tighter upon her. She nosed into the crevice but fell short by a foot or two. She screamed so loudly that it made the tight little cavern shake and stone and debris fell all about them. She jerked back, a second quiver sticking from the side of her neck. She shook her head, screaming, and trying to claw at the quivers in her flesh.

The unholy sound that She made ripped up and down Sasha's spine. She shuddered and pressed herself against Quinn. Quinn kept his arms firmly about her and rested his chin on the top of her head. "Please, God," she whispered, "please, please let it go away."

And God must have been listening to them that day, because after staggering around a bit more, the Ceratosaurus did indeed wander away, scraping at the bolts protruding from her face.

They waited a full ten minutes before emerging from the crevice. By then, it was full dark, with only the pillar of their campfire to throw any light across the plains of the desert. Insects buzzed in and out of the light, and farther out in the desert, a behemoth bellowed lonesomely.

The Camptosaurus was gone. In some final act of frustration and retribution, She had taken it. But Sasha didn't mind. She and Quinn were alive. That was all that mattered.

"Those quivers," said Quinn, turning in a circle and glancing around the desert. Though it was difficult to see beyond the firelight, she knew what he was looking for. She was thinking they had company. The quivers had looked distinctively Moja-made, the tribe of people they had only just managed to escape from with their lives—and only because her childhood friend Toby had killed their leader.

Perhaps the Moja had followed them, or Toby. She was about to say as much when a tall, slender figure stepped in front of the fire—a man she was unfamiliar with. He was in his twenties and tawny like a man at home in the desert, his skin burnt to the shade of a sunset, though his hair and the fringe of the beard on his chin was like daybreak and dusty sunshine. He was dressed in the remnants of a suit of pale khaki, the type that the lords she knew back home preferred during the summer months, though he wore the homemade boots of a man who had spent time among the Moja tribe. The Planet of Dinosaurs wore your shoes out very quickly. On his head of blonde unruly curls, he wore what seemed to be a homemade safari hat comprised of stiff reeds.

The man smiled wisely at them both, the firelight catching the silvery string of the bow he carried slung over one shoulder, the bow he had shot She with. "That dinosaur doesn't like you two very much, does he?" he said. He spoke with a dry American accent.

"It's a she, actually," said Sasha, taking a step toward the man as instinct brought them all together. One did not run into many humans here.

Quinn kept his hand on her arm. "Sasha, be careful."

"You just faced a Ceratosaurus and you think *I'm* dangerous?" The man laughed. He had a deep, faintly mocking voice that ended on a high note. That was another thing that the Planet of Dinosaurs did to you: It made you slightly mad.

"Sir, in this place, *everything* is dangerous," Quinn stated, insinuating himself between the stranger and Sasha. He sounded like his usual self—imperious, cynical. Suspicious. Quinn was practically at home on the African plains, and pragmatic to a fault. This place had been a challenge for him that he had tackled with great relish.

The man smiled. "I suppose you're right. But I promise I'm not so dangerous, at least to other humans." He indicated the bow he had shot the dinosaur with. He stepped forward and extended his hand. "Dr. John Ulysses at your service, sir."

| 51 |

While Quinn fed the fire to make it higher and more fearsome to any night predators passing by, John moved to sit beside Sasha on a fallen log they had moved closer to its warmth. He had a small medical pack with him. With it, he doctored the various scratches on her face and arms. They didn't hurt very much, but she knew how easily a small cut could become infected in this environment. She let John work.

"So who's the crabby Englishman?" he asked.

Sasha held very still while John dabbed antiseptic onto a somewhat deeper cut on her forearm. "That's Quinn," she answered. "His name is Sirius Quinn." She didn't bother to add the "Lord" bit even though Quinn was technically gentry. Titles meant nothing here.

John smiled, his sunburned face well lined but not nearly as old as she had expected. Then again, they had never met until today, though they knew each other very well. She and John had been penpals for just over two years. Together, they had created twin Tuning Machines, one in England, one in the Americas. Both had managed to transport them to this primeval world. John studied Quinn carefully. "Is he your beau?"

"Why do you say that?" she asked.

"Because you're blushing furiously."

That only made her blush some more. One did not discuss some things, even with friends. So much had changed since she, Toby, and Quinn had arrived here several months ago. Toby had become the leader of the Moja tribe and had married his First Woman, Naja. Sasha and Quinn had become lovers, though she could scarcely believe that at times. She knew her father would be mad with pleasure to learn she and Quinn were betrothed, and that they actually *wanted* to wed. She looked at John, carefully. "He's the man my father picked out for marriage." There, that sounded reasonable.

John looked surprised. "Do people still do that in merry old England?"

"Do the Americans *not* do that?" Sasha asked, fascinated.

John shrugged. "Rarely. Only in the Confederate states." He smiled. "We back east like to think of ourselves as progressive on that front." He finished doctoring her wounds and started putting his medic bag back together. "I only ask because he took a great risk in saving you from the Ceratosaurus. He must care a great deal about you."

Sasha watched Quinn pick up his bow and javelin and start walking the perimeter of their camp, searching for potential dangers. It was true that Quinn never stopped thinking, planning, looking out for her. She would probably have been dead ten times over were it not for him. She turned and looked at John. John was from her world. They had never met before today, but he gave off a feeling of their world, a sense of home and familiarity, books, and academia. She almost felt she might cry. "It is good to meet you finally, John."

John took her hand. He did not kiss it, but he did hold it tight and nod his head over it. "Sasha Strange. It is very good to finally meet *you*. Though I have to admit you were about the last person I expected to see here."

She smiled a little at that. She proceeded to tell John her story, how the Tuning Machine had transported her, Toby and Quinn here, about the Sen who had captured Toby and forced her and Quinn to hunt the Ceratosaurus, and how she and Quinn had managed to kill the smaller male and send She, his mate, on a rampage. John examined the small, orangey mammal sitting on her shoulder with great interest, which spurred Sasha to explain how she had befriended Newton. That led her to talk about Dotty, the baby plesiosaur that they had rescued, a creature that had given up her own life to lead a much larger pliosaur away from Quinn while Sasha rescued him from the Moja tribe. Sasha had to stop for a moment to keep herself from breaking down in tears at the memory. She told herself it was silly and ridiculous. She offered Newton a berry from her pocket and told him the rest, how Toby had won a place as head of the tribe, and she and Quinn had moved on, following the notes that John had left chalked in the sea caves.

"You've had quite an adventure. I'm certainly glad I took the time to leave those missives, then," he said. He stood up and un-slung his bow. Sasha instantly went on alert. She turned her head and saw a small, upright dinosaur sniffing around one of their rucksacks not a dozen paces away. It was long and sinewy. It would have come up to her waist, had she been standing next to it, which she had no intention of doing. The second claw on its foot was a massive talon that clicked as it moved, and its beak-like snout was filled with small but very sharp teeth.

"Deinonychus, a species of raptor, and very common around these parts. Its name means "Terrible Claw." They like the desert, but unlike the really dangerous raptors that live deeper in the valley region, Deenies hunt alone so you don't have to worry about one sneaking up on you." Going smoothly down on one knee, John withdrew his bow and eyed the creature carefully. He let a quiver fly.

It struck the Deinonychus right in the chest cavity, and the creature made a terrible, birdlike noise before dropping to the desert floor. It kicked for some time before falling silent, all bled out through its wound.

Quinn arrived moments later to see what the fuss was all about.

John smiled grandly at Sasha. "Deenies are fascinating, but also very delicious."

| 52 |

While they dressed the Deenie for roasting, Quinn and John engaged in a lively debate on which dinosaur was best for hunting. John liked the Deenies, but Quinn exonerated the merits of hunting Hypsilophodonts, a small, birdlike dinosaur that, though bipedal, were herbivorous and, therefore, much less dangerous to hunt.

"Very true," John said, rubbing his blond beard ruefully as he watched the broad strips of Deenie cooking over the open fire, their drippings making the fire hiss. "But you have to admit the Deenies are bigger. Thus, they provide more meat."

"You sound like the Moja and their obsession with hunting and meat," Sasha joked, trying for levity.

John gestured toward the spit. "Doesn't it make more sense to hunt a larger animal that will produce larger amounts of meat?"

"Not if the animal is very dangerous," Quinn stated. In the firelight his face looked carven and somehow older. "A hungry tribesman in Africa hunts a gazelle rather than a bull elephant for a very good reason. The elephant will provide more meat, of course, but if he wounds it and does not kill it, it might follow him in an attempt to exact revenge."

John lifted his blond eyebrows at that. "You're joking?"

"Quinn has lived in Africa," Sasha said. "He knows."

"Is there any scientific basis for these theories?" John asked.

Quinn smiled humorlessly. "Sir, one does not need science to know when one is being hunted."

Sasha felt they were descending into dangerous territory. Somehow, she had not expected such hostility from Quinn, especially this soon after encountering another human being. She looked at him, trying to give him a signal to back off, but Quinn's predatory eyes were set fast on John. Quinn was a hunter; he did not easily give up his quarry. To change the subject she said, "John, how did you find us? I thought you must be weeks ahead of us."

"I was," John admitted, gracing her with his smile which was just dazzling in its sincerely and intensity. "But about two weeks ago I heard the Moja drums. They have a very complex system, you see, and can send messages for miles. I knew there were newcomers, though I had no idea who they might be." He leaned forward and poked the Deenie meat with his survival knife. It was almost done, almost ready to fall off the bone. "I couldn't resist finding out, so I left my camp at the Valley and traveled back here to see what all the fuss was about."

"The Valley?" Sasha said, getting excited now. "The Valley of Song?" she asked hopefully.

John smiled devilishly.

"You found it!"

"I've been there over a month so far."

Sasha felt a great wave of relief. She looked briefly at Quinn. "We were afraid that Muk had lied about the Valley."

"I think he was unsure, to be honest. The Sen territory is relatively small compared to most other creatures like the Moja. I doubt his people have been very far outside of their own boundaries." He cut off a chunk of the meat and tested it, jerking at how hot it was in his mouth, but Sasha couldn't blame him. This world made you as ravenous as the animals who stalked it. He started cutting off slices and laying them on flat rocks to be dished around. "And I have a theory about that. Muk's people are seldom seen during the day, according to the Moja, so I believe they might be oversensitive to light. Thus, they only travel at night or in the early evenings. They're probably much too afraid of being caught out in the daylight, so they limit their territory to just the land surrounding their mountain. It makes them susceptible to rumors."

He offered her a plate. Sasha took it and thanked him. She was so very hungry. John smiled. He reached out to her and Sasha saw Quinn stiffen. But John was only interested in the dark, heavy talon she wore around her neck. "Large predator," he said, fingering it. "Is it the one you killed?"

"Yes," she answered. "She's mate. The Ceratosaurus."

"I recall Muk calling her that." He looked at her curiously. "Her territory seems awful large."

"We don't think she has a definite territory anymore," Sasha confessed. She glanced aside at Quinn, whose attention was focused on the claw that John was fingering. "We think she's following us. That she means to kill us."

"Kill you?" John said. He sounded incredulous. "For killing her mate?"

"That's correct."

"She's just an animal. A large one, but an animal nonetheless." He let the claw go. "Animals have no sense of vengeance, Sasha."

"This one does."

Quinn interrupted them, and just as well, as the conversation was becoming uncomfortable. "You are a medical doctor?" he asked.

John smiled at him, but it was less enthusiastic than it had been for Sasha. "No, I'm a mechanical engineer at the University at Cornell, in New York. I specialized in electricity. But I've learned quite a bit from the Moja."

"You have a medical pack."

John's smile was more guarded now as if he sensed a challenge. "Well, I came here"—he indicated the desert—"much more prepared than you folks, it seems. After the Tuning Machine opened the gate, I worked at stabilizing it. I practiced by tossing some office items through it first. Then I decided I needed to explore this amazing world myself. But first, I took some camping supplies with me, which was a wise move on my part, it seems. I didn't expect to *not* be able to return to New York."

"I see," said Quinn.

"Tell us about the Valley," Sasha insisted. "Is it very far?"

John looked away from Quinn and centered his attention on her once more. His smile seemed to grow back. "Not very. About fifteen miles as the crow flies. We should be able to reach it in two days if we don't dawdle. Although I must warn you, it's isn't quite as promising as Muk made it out to be."

Sasha felt her heart sink back down inside of her. "You haven't been able to make anything of it?"

"The valley is a natural amplifier, and prone to windstorms, but no rock formation I've found or have been able to construct vibrates the same way the Tuning Machine can. I'm still working on that little detail."

"I should be able to help," she said.

John nodded. "I'm sure you'll be of great assistance to me, Sasha. It won't be an easy task, though. There are...challenges."

"Such as?"

John looked recalcitrant. "Birds."

She raised her eyebrows at that. "Birds?"

"Very bothersome birds. You'll see when we arrive."

They did an excellent job on the Deenie. Afterward, they retreated to one of the caverns that dotted the rock wall of the butte. Even though it was much cooler inside the caverns, it was also much safer, especially with She on the prowl.

Sasha went about the ritual of preparing for the night, rolling out their bedroll and unfastening the extra blankets in their packs. John watched for several moments before unrolling his own spare blanket. She and Quinn had only one bedroll between them, and the implications made her blush so furiously that she made a point to keep her back to John as she prepared their bed. To spare her honor, Quinn announced he would take the first watch and that John could relieve him in a couple of hours, although that was usually Sasha's task. That sounded reasonable, she thought. Of course, they would be taking turns on the watch and would only need to carry one bedroll with them.

Sasha fell dead asleep, as she often did after a long walk, but a few hours later, she was aware of the changing of the guard and Quinn's familiar presence as he knelt to extract a blanket for himself. Sasha sat up and held her warm blanket open to him. It had become a kind of ritual between them. The one coming off guard duty would often crawl under the blankets and snuggle against the other until the night chill was gone. After that, whoever was on relief duty would take up the post. It was the absolute worst part of the whole ritual, and Sasha often wondered what it would feel like to hold Quinn all through the night, to lie pressed against him till morning, and if they would ever find a place where they would be safe together, where she would know such a luxury.

"Quinn," she said softly when John had taken up his post outside the cave and was beyond earshot.

He leaned over her and kissed her forehead, pushing aside her long braided hair to do so. His hands, roughened by the labor of pure survival, brushed her cheeks, then moved to pull her blanket more securely about her shoulders. He was good with the javelin, good at killing dinosaurs. Yet he always managed to amaze her with his tenderness.

"Quinn," she said and tried to hold him, but he pulled back.

"We should not act inappropriately," he whispered in her ear. "We have company." His voice was sad, and she had a moment to wonder if he'd have preferred not meeting John at all. He clambered over her and sank down in a far corner.

Sasha lay awake under the blankets of the bedroll for some time, wondering about the Valley, wondering how Toby was getting along, if he was happy. She closed her eyes but couldn't sleep; she missed Quinn's touch too much.

| 53 |

"Sasha, come see this."

She immediately sat up and grabbed at her javelin, lying beside her bedroll. Even though her body was still sluggish from sleep, her mind was whirling and she was already thinking in terms of fight or flight. Then she heard John's voice again, calling her softly at the mouth of the cave, where nearly colorless morning light was filtering in and making shadows of the rocks all about her.

She climbed to her feet and moved silently to his side.

"Look," he said.

In the wash of new light, she could see the desert floor was pocked with small holes, and that creatures the size of rats were darting in and out of them. There was something very familiar about them. On her shoulder, Newton chirped with interest. Then she realized why the little beasts looked so familiar to her.

They were mammals. Not mammals she recognized, but Mammalian all the same. They looked rather like desert rats with elongated snouts and bushy tails. She had seen very few mammals in this strange new world, and she said as much to John now.

"I know exactly what you mean. Would you please bring me my rucksack?"

Sasha did so, and John reached in, his eye set unwaveringly on the mammals playing in and out of their holes, and withdrew a sketchpad.

"You have paper!" she said in wonder. She flipped through the pad, finding all manner of prehistoric beasts sketched in various poses. John was not without talent.

"Yes, I took one with me, but, sadly, just the one. I've been trying to keep a record of the most interesting creatures I've encountered."

"This is amazing, John."

John finally looked away from the mammals to glance at her. She thought he might be blushing under his sunburn. He took the pad from her and a rough piece of kohl from his pocket and began work on a new sketch. While he worked, Sasha glanced behind her and saw Quinn joining them.

"Well, that lot looks like dinner," Quinn said in appreciation. "And we might get some nice catgut from them as well."

John frowned. "We can't eat the mammals here."

"Why not?" Quinn sounded annoyed.

He indicated the creatures with his piece of kohl. "These small creatures might just represent the future dominant species on this planet. We could be altering the history of this world by killing them."

"The Moja kill them," Quinn pointed out. "I know because they gave us catgut, and it bloody well didn't come from one of the big reptiles."

Sasha mused that over. "Quinn's right about that. Any altering has already been done by the Moja tribe."

"Well, let's try not to alter it any *further*. The Moja likely don't belong on this planet any more than we do."

"You've noticed that, have you?" she said, getting excited now.

"That the Moja likely come from our world? Yes. They have a kind of Asian look about them, don't they? Maybe Polynesian. Yet some have red hair and blue eyes, suggesting European ancestry. I'm willing to bet their ancestors stumbled into this world not unlike how we did, through some aperture or gate. The rest is, as they say, history."

Sasha thought about that and nodded. "I thought the same thing when I saw that the Moja had managed to forge primitive chains to keep their sacrifices fixed to the rocks. There is simply no way a people who cannot even construct a permanent shelter would be able to do that."

John smiled and sketched. "You are observant, Sasha. I'll give you that. Come make some notes about the mammals. I think they may be Eomaia of some sort."

Quinn drifted away. Sasha turned to find him putting together his rucksack for the trek ahead. He did not grace them with a single look the rest of the morning. And even after they set off toward the west, toward the Valley of Song, he stayed to himself, ambling along in his lank, graceful height, carrying his sack over one shoulder, his javelin in the other. John talked incessantly and excitedly, pointing out the creatures he'd been observing, challenging her to name them (she knew most but not all of them) and asking her to take notes.

The sun beat down on them relentlessly. They saw more parrot-faced Hypsies flitting about the desert, scratching for food or water, but nothing larger than that. The Deenies who fed on the Hypsies had vanished from this part of the desert. Even the small mammals were gone. The sand became deeper in places, the scrub scarcer, and the land treacherous. Quinn asked about watering holes. John knew a few, but not enough to satisfy Quinn, who wanted specific coordinates. He insisted they not travel more than three or four miles a day and conserve their strength and their water supplies.

The farther they traveled, the more dehydrated they would become. And if they didn't find good water soon, they were going to find themselves in trouble.

"There is a watering hole another four miles due west," John said, pointing off toward the endless horizon. "I passed it on my way here. I know what I saw."

"I'd rather not travel another four miles. Our supply is low enough. And Sasha looks tired," he argued.

"I'm all right," she told them, even though she'd found herself becoming progressively dizzier as they went along. The dizziness was most likely due to the altitude of the land, or a slight drop in blood pressure. The bad signs of dehydration were nausea and muscle cramps. That was something Quinn had taught her. Right now, she knew she was all right, though she envied John his hat and promised herself she would construct something for herself and Quinn the moment they found some reeds or long grasses.

They camped at the foot of some hilly mesas. They were much too tired to hunt and decided to rely on their store of dried and salted meat instead. Quinn worked on building the fire while John sat at the base of the mountain and sketched some scrubby little desert conifers. Sasha helped Quinn gather the wood for the fire while keeping an eye out for predators. She'd expected some acknowledgment from Quinn, a smile at least, but Quinn remained aloof even when they were alone. His silence wore her down worst than the desert. "Are you angry with me?" she asked as she followed Quinn, picking up the smaller kindling he missed as he gathered wood.

"No, of course not," he said neutrally. He had quite a stack of wood, more than they needed, really, but he seemed reluctant to return to camp. He glanced at her. "Shouldn't you be taking notes for John or some such?"

She stopped and stared at him. "This is much more important."

"Is it?"

"You know it is."

Quinn stopped, held the bundle of wood in his arms, and looked very lost. The expression on his face, so very young, broke her heart.

"What is wrong, Quinn?" she asked at last.

He shook his head. "I don't understand *any* of the things you and John discuss," he complained bitterly. "Do you know how bloody infuriating that is?"

"I'm sorry."

He looked away. "Don't be. It's not your fault."

"I'm still sorry."

"Sasha…"

"What do you want me to say? John is my friend. He likes the same things I do. And right now, we need him. I may not be able to get us home without him."

A terrible thought occurred to her then. She and Quinn had been together. They were lovers. What if they got home and he didn't want her anymore? She'd been compromised. She was ruined. Unmarriable. It did not even seem such a terrible fate, really—there was a rumor that her Aunt Margaret was a spinster for exactly this same reason, some summer romance that had ruined her—except that she wasn't like her Aunt Margaret, able to lock herself away with her books and pets and forget all this. Now that she had been with Quinn, loved him, she couldn't imagine her life without him. She tried to. She tried to imagine going back to Strange Manor, taking up her old life, her books, and experiments, and living alone.

The idea was too terrible to contemplate.

"Sasha," Quinn said with sudden concern as he read her face. "What is it?"

She blanked her expression. She would not act all weepy in front of Quinn. "I thought I heard something. We should get back to camp."

She slept soundly that night despite the fears gnawing at the back of her mind. In the morning, she spotted a lone, scrawny Hypsie rooting around their campfire, looking for scraps of food. Quinn and John went off after it, hoping to catch some fresh meat, leaving her alone to reassemble their camp. By midmorning, they returned. They had lost the Hypsie, but John had climbed a butte and spotted a watering hole two miles off, and soon they were on their way.

They refilled their waterskins at the watering hole but did not linger. Quinn had warned her that in Africa, watering holes attracted all kinds of prey animals, which, in turn, attracted their predators. They hadn't heard any evidence of She roaming in the night, but they were reluctant to take chances. They took their water and moved on, while a small collection of Hypsies and a distant Deenie looked on with vapid, sun-shriveled interest.

"But it's simply extraordinary," John commented a few miles on. "How could an animal develop such a strong dislike for two people? It's staggering in its implications."

John never stopped postulating. Sasha had found it engaging once. Now she was tired, worn out, and her mind wouldn't stop proposing some tragic end to her summer romance with Quinn.

"How is it extraordinary?" Quinn asked. He used his javelin to move along like a walking stick, squinting up at the hellish sun beating down like a hot lead weight upon them all. "In Africa, bull elephants walk their victims into the ground. If you harm one, or its mate, it may follow you for years before attacking you."

"You keep saying things like that, Mr. Quinn, but this is not Africa."

"My name isn't *Mr.* Quinn," Quinn said coolly. "It's *Lord* Quinn."

John looked surprised, but not especially impressed. "You Englishmen," he said only.

"What's that supposed to mean?"

"You really do need to get over your self-importance, your imperial *lordship*." John, who invariably walked ahead of their little group, turned and offered Quinn an insouciant smile. "Is Sasha impressed with your title? Is that how you've managed to compromise her?"

Sasha gasped and stopped dead in her tracks. Yet again, she felt like crying.

"How dare you," Quinn answered. He stopped too and even dropped his sack to the hardpacked desert floor. His eyes burned in that way he had, and Sasha just knew he was spoiling for a fight. She knew things would eventually come to a head, she just didn't know how quickly.

Before she could utter a warning, Quinn was upon John. He was a dirty fighter, and he'd had some training in fisticuffs, that much was obvious. In less than two seconds, he had dealt John a powerful right hook across the jaw and dropped him. Sasha surged forward, hoping that that was all that would come of the fight. But Quinn wasn't done. He kicked John in the ribs, not a vicious blow, a killing blow, but more of a punctuation to what had come before. John grunted and grabbed Quinn's ankle and upended him so Quinn wound up on his back on the desert floor beside him. He let out his breath in a whoosh.

John sprang up, looking extremely satisfied despite the raw red mark across his jaw. "I learned that at West Point, New York, *your lordship*."

Quinn kicked out from his position in the ground, clipping John in the breadbasket. John went sprawling in the dust, coughing.

Quinn sat up and spat. "I learned that at the Lamb and Flag, in the alley off Covent Garden. The East End."

Sasha moved between the two men. "Stop it! What's the matter with you two? What are you doing?"

"We're about to have one hell of a fight, it seems," Quinn answered, climbing to his feet and spitting into his hand.

She saw the looming danger of the two sweating, narrowed-eyed men and moved out of the way just in time as they clenched. For the next three minutes, they ducked and hooked and threw punches, and speckles of blood fell to the thirsty desert floor as they rolled about and kept jabbing at each other's faces and bodies like madmen. It was a very long, tiresome three minutes. Sasha screamed at them and demanded that they stop immediately, that they were acting like children, that this was ridiculous. But the two men were oblivious.

Two Hypsies flitted by, squawking excitedly.

Finally overwhelmed, she picked up her rucksack and javelin and stalked off toward the east, trying not to bawl like an adolescent child. She wondered briefly how her life had come down to this. She was walking through a brutal, alien desert full of dinosaurs and danger with two men she cared about on the ground a dozen steps behind her, beating the tar out of each other.

She wiped at her tear-streaked cheek and kept walking. Somehow, she felt so much of this was her fault.

Five minutes later, both men rejoined her. They walked in silence, blood and bruises decorating their faces, their clothes dirty and disheveled. Quinn had a broken lip and a blackened eye, and John's hat was missing so the bruises that crawled up his chin and jaw were horribly visible. They trudged on, staying a few feet behind her, neither of them saying anything until they reached the Valley of Song at nightfall, some three hours later.

| 54 |

Quinn sat on a rock overlooking the vast canyon below and let Sasha apply astringent to his cuts and bruises, his stony face carved in deep relief by the firelight. The Valley of Song was enormous, chiseled from two tremendously tall, rambling mesas that must have been several miles long. From their vantage point, they could see the gleam of a stream running between the rock walls. The river seemed to go for miles. It reminded her of some of the amazing pictures she'd seen in books of the Grand Canyon in America.

Sasha worked slowly, trying to clean every wound with John's medical pack. "You act like a child," she said, surprising herself with her own honesty and the choked emotion in her throat.

"I'm a child for trying to recover your honor?" he said, sounding hurt.

She dabbed more astringent onto a cloth and applied it to his left cheek where a long, shallow scratch creased it—too roughly, she supposed, considering how he flinched. "I don't have any honor left, so you needn't bother."

He narrowed his eyes. "What's that supposed to mean?"

"Oh, please, Quinn," she said. Her voice sounded old to her, much older than it ought.

She saw his eyes move as he made the connection. "You believe you're a dishonorable woman for having given yourself to me?"

She bit her lip. She would not cry.

"You're ashamed to be my lover?" He sounded surprised and hurt. Hurt, more than anything. He stood up so fast she took a stumbling step back. "Is that true? Is that truly what you feel, Sasha?"

She didn't know how to respond. She didn't know how to voice her fears. These past few days Quinn had been ridiculously aloof. And now the backbiting, and the infighting…how else was she supposed to feel, except rejected? It was like Quinn wanted nothing to do with her, or with anyone. She was almost certain he was having second thoughts about the marriage. He was probably missing Africa terribly, and his dead wife Gabrielle, and his dead son Percy. He had fought for her honor because that was what a gentleman did, especially when it was *he* who had stolen it away.

No, she reminded herself, that wasn't right. He had not stolen her honor. She had given herself willingly to him. And she knew in her heart that she would give herself to him again if she only thought he wanted her. She cast around, searching for something to say, staring at the ground as if it might hold the answer.

Finally, she looked up at him. "Why did you accept my father's invitation to court me?" It was the only thing that came to mind, the one unanswered question.

Quinn looked uncertain, taken aback. "Your father invited me. And we had always been good friends, Albertus and I. You know that."

"But you had plans to return to Africa before he invited you. Why did you come to the house that night? Why didn't you simply turn his proposal down?"

"Sasha…this is useless and inappropriate at the moment."

"I don't think so. I want to know." She watched him. She thought about all she knew about him, his past, the drinking, the brawls and bad gambling habits he'd acquired whilst in London. His terrible debts. And then she knew. She was a smart girl, everyone said so. The fact that she hadn't figured it out until now perhaps proved otherwise.

"My father paid you, didn't he? Or he promised to pay off some of your debts." She bit back a sob. "But either way, it was all about money, wasn't it?"

Quinn shook his head, but his eyes were uncertain.

Sasha knew it was the truth. No one back home wanted her. She was truly and completely unmarriable—and long before she had ever given her innocence to Quinn. No man wanted Sasha Strange as a wife, Sasha the impetuous inventor who frightened all the good unmarried men of London society away. And that would have included Lord Sirius Quinn as well, except that Lord Quinn was deeply in debt and in need of relief. And her father was in a position to offer that relief.

She lifted her chin and pinned him with a look. She would not cry, not over *him*, of all people. "Tell me the truth. I want to know the truth."

"No," he said finally, sadly. "You don't."

"Tell me."

"What? That your father paid me to visit you, to court you?" He raised his eyebrows and stared her down. "Is that what you want to hear, Sasha?"

"I want to hear the truth."

He let out his breath in exasperation. "Your father paid me to spend an evening with you. He paid me two hundred quid."

She stood very still and absorbed that. She had gotten very strong in the ensuing weeks on the Planet of Dinosaurs. She did not crumble. She sucked up the tears in her nose and throat and straightened her shoulders. "And how much did he agree to pay you to marry me?"

"We did not discuss such matters."

"A small matter between gentlemen, then."

"I told him it was highly unlikely we would be compatible and he should not hold out hope for much."

"I see."

Suddenly, Quinn looked sad. "Albertus and I are very old friends, Sasha. We were at university together. If it makes you feel any better, I did it more to placate him than for the money."

"But you needed the money."

"Needed the money. Need the money." He looked about the desert and threw up his hands in fury. "What difference does it make now?"

"It means nothing now," she agreed, glancing at the looming shadows of the desert, the cool wind rustling her braids. "But at least I know my worth. How many people can say the same? Two hundred quid for an unmarriable bride."

She started to walk away, tears welling up in a freshet in her eyes, but Quinn grabbed her arm, halting her in mid-step.

"Do not walk away from me, Sasha Strange."

"Let me go."

"No."

"Let me go, Quinn, or I shall make an even bigger fool of myself!" She was going to cry. There was no stopping that. But she would not do it in front of him. She would not do it *for* him.

He looked at her carefully. "Do you love me?" he asked suddenly.

She breathed in and out, in and out. "I thought I did." She held his eyes but steeled herself. "But I won't be some bargaining chip.

I won't be sold like a draft horse at market. I'm worth more than that, Quinn."

"I have no intention of buying you," he told her. He sounded angry, hurt, as if his pride was being tested. "When we return to London—assuming we do—I have every intention of returning to Africa and reopening the tobacco fields to pay back my debts. I shan't need your father's money. I told Albertus as much that night, but he refused to believe I could do it. Once a drunk, always a drunk, he said."

Sasha stared at him in horror. "But you have no slaves or servants," she pointed out. He was ruined, penniless; he probably couldn't even afford a valet. And he'd told her long ago that Gabrielle had insisted on him letting their slaves go, which Quinn had done for her sake. Gabrielle had believed in the value of human life, something that made Sasha admire her even if they would never meet in this world.

Quinn shrugged. "I'll work the fields myself if need be."

"Alone?"

He smiled grimly. "I've gotten rather strong since this little adventure began. I don't see the trouble. At least I won't be chased by dinosaurs anymore."

She almost laughed then, despite the tears.

He held her eyes, but grew very still, very serious. "I deeply regret that our first meeting was so unfortunate, Sasha Strange. And I'm sorry that I've taken your honor and complicated your situation. I realize the price you will be forced to pay for it."

He closed his eyes and thought for a moment. "I am prepared to make it up to you as a gentleman. Assuming we're able to get home, I'll be happy to render to you whatever profits from my plantation you feel are appropriate for your recompense." He released her arm and took her hand instead, holding it gallantly between his own. "It's true that I'm destitute at present, and deeply in debt—and, frankly, my house is a terrible ruin—but it should not take me very long to turn profits, and then you will have a tidy sum to build your life upon alone or with John. That, of course, will be your decision."

She thought about that. She was very confused by his words, and why he would bring John into the equation. But his offer intrigued her. She shook her head. "I don't want your money, Quinn. But I am interested in a partnership."

He raised his eyebrows at that. "If that's what it takes to settle my debt of honor with you, then yes, of course."

The tears had stopped. She watched him carefully, his desperate, breathing silence, the way he seemed to wait for her response. Her father was a good businessman. And she was his daughter. "Fifty percent of your plantation."

He looked surprised but not exceptionally appalled. "If you wish. If that's what it takes."

"And fifty percent of your house in Africa, even if it is in ruins."

Now he looked confused. "What shall you do with fifty percent of my house? I dare say, it's a pile."

She smiled through her tears. "I thought I should enjoy living in it. Perhaps repairing it and then filling it up." She watched his startled expression. "I mean, with my books at first. But perhaps later with some children. Not many, mind you, as I have no idea what breed of a mother I'll make. I thought perhaps a boy and a girl to start." She waited, her heart clocking so rapidly she thought it must burst from her chest. Surely, Quinn could hear it. "You do want children someday again?"

It was almost impossible to gauge his expression. She knew his history, how he had lost his son and wife to malaria. He knew how much this subject pained him. It took him two tries to answer her. "You...want to proceed with the marriage?"

"Do you?"

He brightened and his face looked younger. "Yes, of course. But...I thought you were cross with me."

"I am cross with you, *Lord* Sirius Quinn," she told him, wagging her finger in his face. "You were fighting with John like a couple of toerags just two hours ago. John is my friend. I shouldn't want you fighting with him over some silly male ego thing."

"I wasn't fighting him over some silly male ego thing, Sasha. I was fighting him for you."

She started then. She looked at him more closely. Was he mad?

Quinn moved his hand from her wrist up her arm to her shoulder, then to her face. He cupped her cheek familiarly and drew her nearer him so all the sun-baked warmth in his clothes engulfed her. His hand splayed over that side of her face and his thumb played briefly across her lower lip. He looked at her in that way he had, like he'd like to eat her like...well, like some ravenous dinosaur.

"You did not notice?" he asked her.

"Notice what?"

"John wants you, Sasha."

"John's my friend, Quinn. My penpal."

Quinn smirked and nearly rolled his eyes. "I keep forgetting how innocent you are."

"I'm not innocent."

"Pure, then."

"I'm not..."

He kissed her, pulling her into his embrace and cupping the back of her head to keep her in place, to keep her silent. He kissed her mouth. He kissed inside her mouth. He licked her and bit her and tried to consume her. And when she clutched him and began making those little kitten-like cries he enjoyed so much, he lifted her up in his arms and settled her down on a shelf of stone outside the cavern and kissed her hair and ear and neck and slid his hands beneath the hem of her Moja-made tunic. He pulled her tight against him so she could feel just how much he wanted her.

"Quinn," she said.

"Yes, my dear," he said, finding her neck very tasty.

"John might see."

"John's hunting a Deenie, Sasha."

"He still might see."

He lifted her and carried her inside the cavern, which was just as well. Suddenly she felt so weak she wasn't sure her legs could hold her own weight. Inside the cave, the light was dim and flecked with spirals of light from some prehistoric version of fireflies. It was cool and Sasha shivered in the subterranean dark.

"Shall I warm you?" Quinn asked in a soft voice.

She loved his pillow talk, how sweet and intimate he could be. She wrapped her arms about his neck and nestled her head under his chin. Quinn carried her to the back of the cavern and pressed her against the stone wall amidst some stalactites and kissed her again, cupping the back of her neck and pushing his tongue deep inside her mouth. When he drew back, he looked as flustered as she felt.

"John could be back anytime, so we'll need to be quick about this," he said, moving his hands under her tunic to cup her backside and lift her weight so it rested partly against the wall and partly against him. "Please don't assume my haste is in any way a reflection of how I feel about you, my dear."

"Yes, Quinn," she answered, kissing his neck and breathing in the warm, damp, male scent of him. He smelled of desert and pine needles and hunting and a unique scent that was just him.

"Move just a little...yes, like that."

"Yes, Quinn."

He kissed her forehead tenderly and ran one hand over her braids while the other stroked her beneath the short skirt of the tunic. "A complacent Sasha. I never thought I'd see the day."

"Spider," she said breathlessly against his neck.

"Spider?"

"There's a spider on your back. A big one."

Quinn's eyes went wide and he nearly dropped her in his haste to brush himself down. He made frightened noises as he did so, and stomped and gasped until Sasha was laughing at his antics. Finally, he'd stomped the spider into bits under his boots. "Why are bugs always so bloody attracted to me?" he cried, running his hands over his hair to check for more.

"Spiders aren't bugs. They're arachnids."

He gave her a surly look.

She covered her mouth with her hands to control her giggles. "They like you because they know you're afraid of them, Quinn."

"I'm not afraid of them," he insisted.

"I'm sure that's why you became so unglued in the beginning with that beetle."

"I did not become unglued," he said with supreme insult. "And that was *not* a beetle. It was a giant scarab...or something." He stomped on the spider a bit more. Then he looked at her again, perhaps a bit sheepishly. "Are you going to challenge every single thing I say after we're married?"

She leaned against the wall and gazed shyly up at him. "Yes." She reached for him, working the tails of his shirt out of his trousers and sliding her hands over his bare skin until he shivered at her touch and his eyes seemed to glaze over. He was a tough, dangerous, cynical man until she touched him. Then he became all soft and tame and sweet. She tugged him close, close enough to breathe his breath and draw her tongue across his bottom lip.

He smiled against her mouth. He had so little in common with the heroes she'd read about in the popular novels of romance. He wasn't young, dashingly handsome, or even very witty. He didn't read books, knew almost nothing about science or poetry, and she wasn't entirely certain he was even very bright. But he *was* funny and irreverent, and he made her laugh when there was very little to laugh about. She loved him. She loved him better, she decided, than any perfect prince or valiant knight or gallant suitor.

"Will you let me win arguments?" he pleaded at a whisper as they came together, his breath tickling the side of her neck as it came in ever-shorter bursts. "At least sometimes?"

"Quinn."

"Yes, my dear."

"Will you please be quiet and just love me?"

He did.

| 55 |

The next morning, she felt Quinn lean over her and shake her gently awake. "You might want to take a look at this," he said in her ear.

She blinked the sleep out of her eyes and was on instant alert. She had gotten very good at transitioning from sleep to full wakefulness in a second or two. In a world like this, it often meant the difference between life and death. Throwing off her blanket, she followed him out of the cavern and up a steep incline. Together they stood on a high cliff overlooking the valley. It was breathtaking when expressed in full lighting—like something out of a science romance, green and verdant. "Where's John?" she asked, squinting out over the valley to see what Quinn was pointing out.

"He went down a ways to look for prey." Last night's hunt had been unsuccessful. When John had returned, he's even commented on the curious lack of animals to hunt in this area.

"Alone? He shouldn't go alone."

"He's been here alone a lot longer than us. I don't think he feels the same way we do."

That was true enough.

She could finally see what Quinn was pointing out.

The Valley of Song stretched perhaps ten miles down the ravine between the two great plateaus surrounding it, following the twisty, snakelike bends of the riverbed. Between the two plateaus were a great number of natural stone bridges that formed loops and eroding curlicues, some small and linked to others, some huge and extending the full distance of the valley. They were obviously natural formations, the results of millions of years of erosion in a huge, natural rock bed, but Sasha had never seen anything quite like it, and there was nothing on Earth that could compare to it. True to its name, the valley caught the wind and channeled it through the hundreds of small arches like a massive flute, creating a dull symphony of noises when the wind picked up. That was the beautiful and amazing thing about it.

The less beautiful and amazing thing about it were the birds.

At least, Sasha *thought* they were birds. They were the size of grown men, had bat-like shapes and sported some kind of rudimentary feather-like coat and enormous crests. Their wingspans must have stretched twenty feet in length. They wheeled almost lazily in the warm updrafts from the valley below, cawing not unlike blackbirds back home and periodically diving down toward the river to scoop up prey in their long, pouchy beaks. She thought there must be two or three hundred of them, at a glance. Both sides of the valley were lined with big, heavy, basket-like hanging nests.

"Dragons," said Quinn observing the birds as if mesmerized by them.

She looked, and her mind instantly jumped to everything she had read about prehistoric birds. "Those aren't dragons, Quinn; they're pterosaurs."

"They look like dragons," Quinn said all big-eyed as if these were the greatest creatures he had ever seen. "I used to dream about dragons when I was a lad. I wanted to be a knight and slay them." He smiled a little as if he felt foolish. But Sasha had learned to treasure those small smiles. Quinn almost never smiled.

One of the birds turned on an updraft and grew larger as it zeroed in on them.

Quinn stiffened beside her. "Are they aggressive?"

"I don't know. There's very little literature about them, and few fossil finds. I did not even know they looked like this. In 1800, a German-French scientist postulated a pterosaur with big round wings—"

The creature took that moment to descend upon them, screaming.

Quinn gripped Sasha around the waist and yanked her down so they both wound up face-first on the hard-packed ground with the beast screeching overhead, the wind from its wings so powerful it tore at their clothes and hair like claws. Sasha screamed. Quinn rolled over onto his back while simultaneously pulling his survival knife from his boot.

The creature jabbed at them, trying to maintain its lift with its stiff, unmovable wings but still angle its enormously long beak toward them. The angle wasn't right for its attack—it was built to catch fish, not humans—so it hung over them like a malevolent kite, rising and falling, screaming in frustration. Quinn muttered a savage curse and sat up, driving the knife at it. The first time, he hit the bird's bony beak and the knife bounced off, doing almost no damage. The creature turned its head, its eyes rolling wildly in its head, and tried to hit Quinn with the side of its beak. Quinn jerked away, then scooted lower in the dust, aiming for its vulnerable breast.

The knife went solidly in and the bird screamed all the louder, so loud that Sasha screamed in response and tried to roll away, but a wing caught her upside the head and she saw literal stars for a moment. Then blood gushed down.

Quinn, still cursing, gripped the handle of the knife in both hands and yanked it upward, unzipping more of the bird's flesh and delicate bones so the beast gave one last yelp and fell solidly upon them, heavier than it looked and bleeding all over the two of them.

Sasha stopped screaming and stared heavenward, the stunned bird lying like a stone upon her chest. Quinn shoved it over so it landed in the dirt, its body shuddering in its death throes, wings curling, crumpling, his knife sticking out of its heart. Then it fell still, just like that.

Sasha let out her breath and looked over at Quinn, who lay exhausted in all the blood and dust. His eyes seemed to swim in his head. Then he refocused and said in a constricted little voice, "Sasha, I don't think I like dragons anymore."

| 56 |

The pterosaur turned out to be rather stringy and tough, and though a large animal, most of its body mass was made of bones and skin. It did not make for a pleasant meal, though Quinn, Sasha, and John did their best. In the wilds of a prehistoric planet, one could not afford to be picky about where one found a meal.

The three of them sat around a fire inside one of the caverns at the foot of the butte and picked the bones of the big bird clean.

"Deenie," said Sasha, licking at the grease on her fingers.

"Much better," John said.

"Hypsies," Quinn said. "Much sweeter." He broke off the last of the meat and offered it to Sasha.

"Thank you, Quinn," she said.

"Camptosaurus," said John.

"Tough," said Quinn. "Fatty."

"Too big," Sasha said. "Hard to hunt."

John was watching her again. He seemed to follow her every move and concentrate on every lick of every bone. She turned to look at him and John smiled. Quinn bristled beside her. He showed no outward indication, but she could feel the fission in the air. Quinn, though, had promised her he would be a gentleman, and if it was one thing about Quinn, it was that he always followed through on his promises.

"So you see what I mean about the birds being dangerous," John said to break the sudden, uncomfortable silence.

John had explained about the pterosaurs. But she never would have believed it had she not seen it with her own eyes. She said, "Yes, were it not for Quinn, I would have been its dinner instead of the other way around."

John's smile slipped. He turned to Quinn. "How did you know to strike at the breastbone?"

Quinn sat up and gave the young, blond American a courtly smile, showing no antagonism at all. "I didn't. It just seemed like a likely place."

"Do you stab a lot of animals in the heart, Lord Quinn?" John asked with mock severity.

Quinn offered him a little smile in return, not vicious but sarcastic. "Only when they threaten my woman."

"John," she said to interrupt, "you said the birds are strictly diurnal, correct?"

John nodded and bit off the last bit of stringy flesh on his bone.

Sasha turned to include Quinn. "That means the birds only come out during the day."

Quinn nodded in appreciation. "That must make working on whatever you're building fairly difficult," he said to John.

John nodded in return. For once, he seemed willing to set aside his differences. "It does. I've only been able to work on the new Tuning Machine at night, and even then I have to be careful not to make any sudden noises and wake them."

"So you *do* have a machine you're building."

John shrugged. "It's little better than a composition of natural elements, but I'm very excited to show it to you, Sasha. Perhaps you can make some sense of it." He turned to glance at Quinn. "It was

Sasha who developed the mechanics of the Tuning Machine in the first place. I only postulated it."

"Sasha is a very smart girl," Quinn said.

Sasha blushed at that.

Normally, after supper, Quinn took the first watch of the night while everyone else bedded down. But Sasha was too excited to sleep and asked John to show her the Machine. The sooner she saw it, the sooner she could begin any needed alterations. And the sooner they might get home.

They had to wait until full dark before they could pull up stakes and begin the journey down into the valley. The idea didn't sit well with Quinn. There were simply too many predators stalking the night, he said. Plus, there was the possibility of encountering She again. He armed himself with two bows, in the event one malfunctioned, and three javelins. He slid his survival knife as well as two backup hunting knives the Moja had given them as gifts into sheaths that hung low on his hips. Sasha armed herself with a javelin and one knife. If it turned out she was unable to use one of the weapons in a fight, then it was probably already too late for her, she reasoned. She didn't have the fighting skills or reflexes that Quinn had. John, laden with notebooks and tools, a great deal of homemade hemp rope and crudely fashioned metal hooks, carried only one small survival knife. Quinn wondered aloud how he'd managed to stay alive these past three months without a sheer artillery of weapons.

"My defense is knowing how the animals of this world behave," he explained, setting his rucksack more comfortably on his back. "For instance, the pterosaurs won't attack until early morning, when they're most active, and the predators down in the valley won't attack anything they don't recognize as easy prey. As long as you don't have any open wounds, for instance, you won't attract them."

"What predators?" asked Quinn, suddenly standing at full attention and clutching the straps of his pack in one hand and one of his javelins in the other.

John lifted his brows with interest. "Velociraptors. Birdlike dinosaurs that hunt in packs, not very large. Smaller than Deenies but more vicious. Once they smell blood, they'll attack a creature and pick at it until it dies of its injuries. I saw a pack of twelve take down a full-grown Camptosaurus just last week. They started eating it before it was even dead." He smiled, grimly. "So I suggest nobody bleeds."

Sasha swallowed hard against the lump in her throat and said nothing.

"More bloody dragons," sighed Quinn, sounding unhappy.

Together, they started down the mountain and into the valley of dragons.

| 57 |

The hike down the mountain took longer than she expected and was more treacherous than it looked, especially in the dark. John had discovered a narrow, eroded path cut into the mesa that zigzagged down to the valley below, but it was little better than a goat path full of loose rocks and sand. In the dark, with only some weak moonlight filtering down, it just looked like a path of darkness carved into more darkness. At one point, the path ran out, and John had to pound his homemade hooks into the rock and secure ropes so they could rappel themselves down one slow inch at a time.

Sasha did not consider herself a cowardly person—at least, not anymore—but the idea of dangling off a cliff face a few hundred feet in the air in the dead darkness with only a rope between herself and certain death was enough to erode anyone's courage. Halfway down, she froze up and could only cling to the knots in the rope, weave lazily, and whimper while Quinn climbed up her rope and eased her down.

She felt like a fool when they finally reached the bottom of the ravine and she could hear the river roaring less than twenty feet away. She sat down on the rocky, sandy ground amidst the scrub and tried to catch her breath and stop her heart from banging almost painfully against her ribcage.

"Sasha, are you all right?" Quinn asked with concern, refusing to let her hand go.

"Yes," she answered after a few moments. She climbed slowly to her feet and weaved against the rock wall. "I'll be fine now."

"It's not very far," John assured her. He led them on, and they walked single file through the canyon, not because it wasn't wide enough—the canyon itself, including the river, must have been a mile wide—but because the whole valley was honeycombed with eroded stone stalagmites that resembled giant broken teeth and the loops and arches of stone they had observed from the plateau. It made travel difficult and gave the valley a cave-like feel, even though there was no ceiling. The river washed down in a white froth to the right of them. Unlike the plateau above, the river fed the valley. As a result, it was as verdant as an oasis, full of tall marsh grasses, rambling, thorny bushes, and the occasional stunted conifer abuzz with insects and small, busy animals clinging to its upper bows. The valley was too rocky for tall trees, so there was no real protection from the birds, no trees to climb or hide beneath. A series of caves pocked the wall of the canyon to their left, each sinking away into utter blackness. John warned them to watch their step and to be sure not to get snagged on anything. "All you have to do is bleed a few drops and you'll draw a whole host of animals to you."

"I have no intention of bleeding if I can help it," Sasha stated, checking herself all over for scratches. Her palms were rubbed raw by the rope, but otherwise, she was fine.

"And try to avoid making any unnecessary noises. The birds up there"—he pointed in the direction of the cliff wall where the giant hanging nests resided—"have incredibly acute hearing. If they think an animal down here is in distress, they'll pounce on it, day *or* night."

Twenty minutes later, John led them up a short series of levels to his cave, his "home away from home," as he called it. Having spent over a month here, he'd furnished the spacious cavern with rudimentary furnishings he'd been able to construct from logs, stones, and other debris he'd found in the valley. He'd constructed a crude writing easel for himself and a hammock to sleep in and had developed a fairly complex pulley system of weights and balances to move a giant boulder up and down to act as a "door" for his cave, a way of deterring the larger animals from getting in at night. By filling a basket with stones, he was able to tense the rope attached to an overhead pullet and then to a homemade metal hook affixed to the boulder, thus raising it. When he removed the stones, he was able to lower the boulder into place. Sasha admired the ingenuity that had gone into the system. She could also appreciate the idea of all of them getting a full night's rest for a change.

John showed her his notes, diary, and blueprints for the Machine, spread throughout the cave, and even stuck in clefts in the walls. After that, he showed them the underground pool at the back of the cave, which delighted Quinn. Because the comfort and security of a cave, and the ingenuity of its owner, meant very little if there was no source of water. It was a small pool, no larger than the duck pond behind her father's house, but John said a series of underground tunnels fed into the pool, producing a continuous supply of fresh water. The water tasted good after their long hike.

"And now, the Machine...such as it is," he announced, leading her out of the cave, down the crude "steps" to the floor of the valley and through some dense vegetation. Sasha followed, with Quinn close behind. Quinn had said very little since their hike had begun, but Sasha knew he was on full alert, looking for signs of danger.

John's choice in camp had not come about by whim or accident. Just past the weeds was a large circle of complex rock formations pushing up out of the ground like a series of giant teeth. At the center was a stone dais. On the altar-like dais was a very complicated-looking tuning fork consisting of fourteen metal spires of varying height set on a homemade wheel-like device. The wheel spun lazily in the soft wind, the whole thing looking rough but effective.

Quinn took in the sight of the stone formations surrounding them, then the tuning fork. "It's very pretty, but what is it?"

Sasha came forward then. "It's a Tuning Machine."

"It doesn't look like one. At least, not like the one you created at home."

"It's the same principle, though." She walked in a circle around the dais, marveling at it. "How long did it take you to make this?" she asked John.

"A month," he said almost sheepishly. "The Moja traded me much of the crude metals for it after I showed them better ways of hunting and did other tasks for them. I refined the metals, which was the hardest part. It was difficult and time-consuming."

"I'm sure."

He moved closer to the tuning fork and spun it on its wheel. When he turned it quickly enough, it produced a high, clear vibration that Sasha felt somewhere deep in her bones.

"And you use the wind to drive it."

"Correct. Though tonight there's no wind." John looked skyward. "However, the Moja shaman has said that the Great Wind is on its way and will appear in about a week. I'm hoping that means the rainy season—which is, apparently, a yearly occurrence. It'll storm and rain for seven days straight, then there won't be any more rain—or wind—for another year." He turned to look at her. "Unfortunately, I'm having a devil of a time harnessing enough wind to maintain the fork's vibration, even though this rock formation"—he indicated the stand of stones—"catches more wind than any other in the valley. I know because I've tested all of them."

Sasha's mind had already leaped forward, trying to devise a way to catch enough wind to keep the fork singing. If she could do that, she might be able to open the gate. Of course, assuming she was able to do any of *that*, she was still faced with the dubious and almost overwhelming task of tuning the fork's vibration so she had the right gate, not just *any* gate. After all, they could find themselves on a dead volcanic world, or a planet without oxygen. The possibilities were grim and frightening.

"So, Sasha," John said with a game smile, "what do you think?"

Sasha spun the tuning fork on its wheel, listening to its tinny song. "I have no idea."

| 58 |

Well, that wasn't *exactly* true, but close.

She had ideas, but nothing practical, nothing she could apply to John's natural Tuning Machine. Sasha spent the next four days in John's cave, sitting at his writing easel, looking over his blueprints and becoming increasingly frustrated. She needed to construct something that would not only maintain wind but also fine-tune it. It didn't seem possible. Every idea she came up with was based on the design of the original Tuning Machine, and that was based on a complex system of electricity. She had nowhere near the resources she'd had when she first created the device, and certainly no way to harness electricity. She didn't even have any metal scraps to work with—John had used them all just to create a functioning tuning fork. She had wood and cloth to work with, stones and bones, weapons and survival odds and ends, nothing useful.

She worked from sunup to sundown, with only two hours of troubled sleep every twelve hours. On the fifth day, she rose from her fitful rest, uncertain if it was day or night, washed the sleep from her eyes with a bucket of water, and crawled to John's writing easel to look over her notes from the day before. She picked up the crude kohl pencil and started to make notations when the tip cracked. She stood up, exited the cave, and walked down to the Tuning Machine. There she collapsed at the foot of the dais and started to cry helplessly, uncaring if anything heard her, despite it being daylight hours.

Five minutes later, Quinn appeared at her side and went to one knee beside her. He carried his javelin in one hand and an old, half-broken umbrella of John's in the other. The open umbrella, they'd discovered, confused the birds if one had to be out and about during the day. He said, his voice soft and measured in her ear, "Try not to make too much noise. The birds are circling."

She put her hands over her mouth to stifle her cries. The pterosaurs wouldn't attack unless they thought something on the ground was wounded. She didn't want to make any more wounded noises. Quinn pulled her against him and she buried her face in his shirt and cried for a while, muffling the noises against him. He set the javelin down, held the umbrella up as a shield, and cupped the back of her head and held her, saying nothing.

That was something else she loved about Quinn. He never offered false comfort. He didn't do stupid things like tell her it was going to be all right when she knew it wasn't. He let her cry and sob and anything else she needed to do. And then, when she was done, *then* he reasoned with her.

When her sobs had subsided into hiccups he said, "Sasha, is it really that bad?"

"I don't know what to do, Quinn. I really don't."

"You'll think of something."

"I have nine days at most." The days were becoming increasingly darker and the heavy scent of electricity was on the air. She knew the Moja shaman was correct. "Nine days until the storm season is over. Then we're trapped here at least another year."

He petted her braids and seemed to consider that. "Then we're here another year. And during that time, you work on different ideas. Next year, you try again."

"If we live long enough."

"We'll make it," he assured her, and she knew he was making no empty promise. "I'll see to it personally that we make it until next year."

"I just don't have the skills or resources to do this, Quinn. I'm only an amateur inventor."

"You're a very smart girl," he said, resting his chin on the top of her head and embracing her protectively in his arms. It was so odd that she felt safer in Quinn's arms on a planet full of prehistoric predators than she ever felt on her own world, alone.

"I don't feel smart."

He was silent for a long moment. "May I suggest something?"

"Please. By all means."

"I believe you may be overcomplicating your designs. You are thinking like a girl from our world. You need to think like a girl from *this* world."

She eased back in his arms and looked up at him. For a moment, all the tension went out of her shoulders and she smiled. "Lord Sirius Quinn, do you know you're a very beautiful man?"

Quinn laughed then, a real laugh. She had never seen him laugh like that before; it was as rare as his smiles. "No one has ever said that about me before. I usually get the opposite end of that."

"All right, then. You're an evil, ugly old git."

"There you go."

Over his shoulder, she could see the birds circling like a collection of kites, riding the updrafts off the valley. They flapped their stiff wings and cawed to each other, their voices bouncing off the stone of the valley and reverberating on the still air.

"Kites," she said. And then: "Sails. They don't fly like modern birds, Quinn."

Quinn nodded, then frowned and shook his head in confusion.

"They use sails."

"Yes?"

She looked at him, intently. "Did you have a candle windmill when you were a boy?"

"A candle windmill?"

"It's a toy, like a little house. You light the candles and the smoke blows the paddles round and round..." She stopped as a rush of adrenaline gripped her, making her entire body hum. She sprang up, breaking Quinn's hold. How could she have forgotten about the candle windmill? It was one of her first toys, and she'd spent days playing with it, figuring out how it worked. "I need to get back to the cave," she said, perhaps too loudly because one of the birds circled closer, eyeing the two of them. "It's very, very important!"

She started running for the cave with Quinn attached to one arm, toting an umbrella turned very much inside out in their haste.

| 59 |

It took them five days to build the windmill. Sasha worked the calculations while Quinn and John did most of the manual labor. The storm season was well on its way by then, and all three of them were getting very used to being wet and wind-buffeted on a daily basis. The rain was cold and drenching, at times discouraging, but the upside of the situation was that the pterosaurs disliked the rain even more than they did, choosing to roost in their nests or cower in crevices and caves further up the plateau, so the three of them had less to worry about.

The rains fell and the winds blew. That, too, may have been a factor in the birds' withdrawal. Powerful, almost continuous wind, ripped through the valley, generating odd, melodious songs from the weird rock formations and sending anything not nailed down skittering into oblivion.

On the fifth day, Quinn and John finished installing the last of the sails in the gigantic carousel that Sasha had designed. The sales were homemade, yet functional, composed primarily of branches fastened together with catgut and pieces of fabric stretched overtop the skeletons. Each of the six sails was over five feet tall and designed to run on a circular rail that Sasha had constructed of young green saplings. She had made everything using the natural resources at hand, as Quinn had suggested. Almost from the moment they fastened the last sail and let the whole device go, the wind began driving the sails in a steady circular pattern about the dais. Immediately, the tuning forks changed their song, depending on how the wind was being interrupted by the sales. Sasha had also designed a stopper, a stick she used to slow the carousel in certain places by grinding it against the rails, thus adjusting the tune to exactly the speed and velocity she wanted. After the sails started picking up speed, she experimented by racing around the carousel and slowing the sails in certain places. She only needed one vibration to open a gate, a perfectly pitched vibration.

Nothing happened the first day, but the second day she was experimenting with it she hit the right vibration and an explosion of light poured out over the top of the tuning forks like some Martial death ray in Mr. Wells's new book. The light caught a passing pterosaur unawares and it vanished in speckles of light, sent to some far-off mystery world, never to be seen again—at least by eyes in this world.

Her two boys whooped in victory and danced in the rain, momentarily forgetting their ongoing feud, stomping their boots in the mud.

Sasha ran over and hugged them both tight.

"Where do you think it went?" John asked.

"I've no idea," Sasha answered, breathlessly excited and dancing with them like they were all mad together. They were going home. They were really going home!

It seemed too much to ask for. And in a way, she feared it was.

| 60 |

On the sixth day of the storm season, they packed their meager belongings and tried to prepare themselves. John was unhappy about leaving so many of his homemade devices behind, but carrying everything with them into the gate would have proved impractical. It was bad enough he was taking his huge satchel of notes along with him, something Quinn was worried would slow him down, should they find themselves in a precarious position.

Sasha let Quinn pack their things while she worked on fine-tuning the Tuning Machine. Her boys were so eager to return home, they seemed obvious to the one remaining issue: she had to find the *right* gate to take them to London. Otherwise, they might wind up in whatever unfriendly place that pterosaur had gone. And there were other considerations. After she opened a gate, she found that it would stay open so long as the sails were not interrupted. During that time, she needed to sit crouched on the dais and play her fingers over the tuning forks while the images above her changed rapidly from primeval forests to advanced civilizations, from creatures to men to things she had no name for. It took many hours before she hit what she felt was the jackpot: an image of a busy London street, probably somewhere in Whitechapel. She watched with rapt attention as coaches raced through the wet streets and newspaper boys and vendors stood on the street corners, hawking their wares.

She promised herself that the moment she was home she was going to ride up and down the cobblestoned streets and greet everyone she met.

She wondered how her father was fairing. He must be sick to death with worry for her, she thought. She had been gone for almost three months. Then she thought of Toby, who had chosen to remain among the Moja and learn their ways, lead them. Inspired, she dug out the one remaining piece of chalk that John had managed to save and jumped to the ground. She crouched low to write instructions for using the Tuning Machine in English on the stone. The Tuning Machine looked very unusual, so chances were good the native people would leave it untouched, thinking it was some holy shrine. And should Toby's wandering tribe ever come by this way, he'd see the instructions and find he had an opportunity to return home, if he chose to.

She was just finishing up when Quinn popped out of the bushes, holding his broken umbrella high overhead. His face was strained and very pale, rain running down in rivulets over it and into his collar. "You'd better come immediately, Sasha," he called over the wind. "We've got a great deal of bother!"

| 61 |

By the time she made it back to John's cave, most of the damage had already been done. It had been raining for five days straight, the ground a muddy bog, and the few trees bending almost all the way over with the assault of the ongoing windstorm that made walking into it feel like a barrier. The river, though it moved fast, had stolen more than twenty feet on both sides of the valley. It carried with it all manner of debris now, including several floundering birds that were being steadily swept downstream.

Some hanging nests had been washed down while she was busy tuning the machine. They must have been old nests, dry, not fixed well to the walls of the canyon. They were just muddy patches of brambles now strewn across the area before the cave, some of the flightless hatchlings creeping through the mud like giant, naked slugs.

None of it was their fault; the three of them hadn't disturbed the nests. But the birds didn't see it that way. Four or five of them were dive-bombing the area where their nests had fallen and their young were struggling. They rose in the air, then tumbled expertly toward the target area before swooping upward once again to repeat the attack. They were screaming hysterically, clacking their enormous beaks at anything that moved.

John, standing at the mouth of the cave, was stabbing at a young pterosaur that had crashed and was clawing its way toward him, snapping at his feet like a rabid dog. Sasha cursed the sight of the chaos all about them, cursed as hard and as badly as she had ever heard Quinn, or her father, curse, and started racing toward the cave.

Quinn caught her arm. "You can't go charging in without a weapon," he shouted through the drenching rain. "Be reasonable!"

"Do you have your bow?"

"No," he said with regret. "I left it in the cave."

All they had between them were two javelins and a broken umbrella.

Sasha glanced back at the dive-bombing birds, each as large as a man. Quinn had been right to stop her, of course. If any of them stepped into that chaotic arena, the irate birds were going to pull them apart. She glanced at the young ones clawing their way across the ground. Inside the cave, John struck the pterosaur on the head, but his javelin just bounced off its bony crest. "The little ones," she said. "We're going to have to kill them, Quinn."

"What will that accomplish?"

"Maybe nothing. But if the chicks are dead, the nesting adults might give up and fly away."

"We'll be fully exposed."

"You'll need to cover me with the umbrella..." She glanced at the flapping mass of holes. "What's left of it."

He looked at her keenly. "Go."

She went, racing as fast as she could toward the nearest youngster, with Quinn at her back, acting as a defensive shield. One of the birds targeted them immediately, but Quinn turned and thrust the broken umbrella at it. The flapping, broken material started the bird and it withdrew for a moment, giving Sasha a chance to level her javelin up and aim it at the chick lying in the mud, crying piteously.

She experienced a moment of regret—she loved animals, and the idea of killing a baby, even if it *was* a dangerous predator, didn't sit well with her. But this was about their survival, and Quinn and John were depending on her. She couldn't afford to falter. She took the javelin in both hands and, gritting her teeth, drove it through the chick's back. It screamed and fell still. She let out her breath, happy it had died so quickly.

Together they raced toward the next chick, which left them even more exposed in the middle space between the weedy jungle and the cave entrance. John gave a cry of triumph, and Sasha knew he had finally killed the young adult. She raised her javelin and slew the next chick, which, regrettably, took two stabs this time.

One of the dive-bombing adults ripped at Quinn's umbrella, sending him reeling into her. She tumbled down in the mud, only barely recovering before Quinn pulled her up. "Hurry, Sasha, please," he said, sounding far more levelheaded than she felt in that moment. "I don't think this silly umbrella is going to stop them anymore. They're no longer afraid."

She raced to the nearest chick, her javelin already raised for the killing blow. There were ten or twelve chicks by her estimation, and she had to get every last one, she knew, even those that had crawled under debris for shelter. The adult birds continued to attack Quinn's umbrella, the cries of their fallen chicks driving them into such a bloodthirsty frenzy that some of the adults began attacking each other in midair. She knew John was eager to help, but the adults had trapped him in the cave. Every time he tried to rush toward them, another adult appeared, snapping at the cave entrance before flapping away in disappointment.

She'd slain half the chicks when the unthinkable happened. One of the adults had gotten tangled in Quinn's umbrella. He was holding it in both hands, so couldn't reach the javelin he'd strapped to his back. The pterosaur, a huge, crested adult, pulled, and Quinn was pulled with it, his boot heels leaving furrows in the mud as it yanked him closer to the marsh weeds that grew in wild tangles alongside the overflowing river.

Sasha, now fully exposed, stopped killing chicks and started trying to kill adults as they swooped down upon her. She screamed, raising the javelin as a particularly aggressive adult descended on her, bawling in anger. Her braids flew, covering her face. She jabbed at the bird, but the bird only screamed and clamped its jaws over the end of the javelin. The wood simply burst apart in her hands. She dropped the ragged stick that remained and started racing toward the cave as John urged her to run, run, *run!*

She was running full tilt by the time she reached him and threw herself into his arms. He pulled her into the cave, and a moment later, she felt a cold wind at her back as the bird on her heels swooped away. But she didn't stay in John's arms, cowering, as she might have some weeks earlier. Instead, she jumped free and turned, calling for Quinn. Surely if he was out there in the rain and wind and flocking, angry birds he would answer her pleas.

But she heard nothing in response.

| 62 |

After a few hours, most of the birds gave up on their chicks. A few continued to wheel over the ground where the young called in hoarse, tired voices, but even animals are capable of seeing the futility of their mission after a while. With no way of rescuing their fallen chicks, and buffeted by wind and the rain they so hated, the adult pterosaurs slowly began drifting back up the walls of the plateau.

The rain continued to fall non-stop and the wind blew even harder than before, making the storm a steady wet sheet of debris. The whole land was in disarray as if a natural disaster had blown through it. She couldn't see Quinn anywhere. She'd been calling to him all through the wait, but she'd received no response. When the last of the birds finally disappeared, she picked up a javelin and ventured out of the cave.

"Sasha, be careful!" John said before his voice was lost in the hiss of the rain.

She stumbled through it and over the boggy land, stomping through the vegetation at the edge of the river. She screamed over the roaring white water of the river, screamed Quinn's name over and over, but there was no sign of him, no blood, not even a scrap of clothing to indicate that he'd been there. She didn't know if that was a good sign or a bad one. A big part of her had feared finding his bloodied body on the ground near the river, and she'd felt a tremendous wash of relief at finding nothing at all. But the more she looked, the more she realized the possibility that he'd been dragged into the river by the pterosaur.

The problem was, Quinn couldn't swim. She'd been helping him with that, but she hadn't been overly successful. Quinn could have drowned. His body could have washed downstream. Or he may have been carried downstream whilst still alive. It was a possibility. Not a big one, but still...she returned to the cave, sat down on a large rock, and just thought.

"Do you know where the river lets out?" she asked John as soon as he'd returned from killing the last of the chicks.

"Raptor Canyon," he said, looking at her with concern.

She stared back in question.

"That's what I call it, anyway. It's a small, secluded canyon about seven miles from here, with plateaus on three sides. The Velociraptors nest there in clans. I went down there one day, turned around, and came right back."

She stood up.

"You're going, aren't you?" he said warily, leaning on his blood-slicked javelin.

"What else can I do, John?" she asked, presenting her hands to him. "I can't leave Quinn here. He might be alive."

"Or he might not. He could have drowned in the river, Sasha. You said he can't swim."

"I know." She got busy putting a rucksack of supplies together, trying to calm her panicked heart. She had to think straight. It was imperative to both her safety as well as Quinn's. The last thing she needed was to go running off willy-nilly and unprepared.

"Let me go with you."

"No, John, stay here. There's less than two days before the storm season is over." She sat back on her heels and looked up at him. "At least that way, if something happens, and we're delayed, you can get back home. There are instructions on how to use the Tuning Machine chalked on the side of the dais. Besides, Quinn might be alive. He might make it back ahead of me."

He nodded his head reluctantly.

"Maybe, if you make it home, at least you can use your machine, or mine, to return for us."

John looked worried. "I'm not certain I'll be able to find this place again."

"John," she said, standing up and adjusting the pack on her back. She looked at him seriously. She felt old and tired and weary beyond measure. "Just do your best. Just do what you can. I'll be back as soon as I'm able."

"And if it's hopeless? If he is dead?"

She took a deep breath and commanded her heart to slow down from its frantic gallop in her chest. "I'll still be back."

John handed her his javelin, the longest, strongest one they had. She took it, then asked for his survival knife as well.

"You love him, don't you?" he said with regret as he handed it to her.

She secured it to the belt of her tunic. "Yes. I really do."

John shook his head. "I can't figure it. He's not young or handsome. He's nothing like you, so far as I can tell. I fear he's not even very bright."

She smiled, grimly. Newton jumped to her shoulder and twittered in her ear. She touched him. "He's my mate, John. He's the man I intend to marry when I get back to London. He belongs to me. I intend to find him."

He nodded. "Good luck, then, Sasha Strange."

She took a deep breath. Then she and Newton stepped out into the wind and the rain.

| 63 |

She had never been so frightened in all her life.

Wind and rain slashed at her, making her progress slow and deadening all her senses. Newton had taken to hiding in her rucksack, so the journey was lonelier still. She could barely see more than a few feet ahead of her, and that distressed her even more. If ambush predators were lying in wait, she'd never see them until it was too late. The best she could hope for was the rain was keeping most of the animals in their hidey-holes. The wind howled constantly through the rock formations with a voice almost human. She couldn't cry out for Quinn; the uncaring wind simply took her voice and threw it away.

A part of her wanted to cry. The part that was the old Sasha Strange, the child. But the woman she was now wouldn't allow for it. She had to conserve her strength, she knew.

She pushed on, sheltered by a homemade umbrella that John had made for her from bamboo and reeds, shivering and watching the frothing river for some sign of Quinn. It was the longest seven miles of her life.

By nightfall she was exhausted and on the verge of giving up, crying, or just pitching herself into the river. She thought she might get where she was going faster that way, and she'd be no wetter than she was now. But common sense reared its head. Instead, she took shelter in a cave, peeled off her soaked-through clothes, and tried warming herself around a fire while the storm raged on. She shivered and pulled a blanket closer about her shoulders and tried not to think of all the bad things that could have happened to Quinn, and how all this might be in vain. And, maybe worse of all, how she would likely miss crossing over with John and be stuck here at least another year. A year she probably would not survive alone.

Sleeping was a very bad thing, she knew, what with no one to guard the cave entrance, but after an hour of worrying, Sasha nodded off, then jerked away when she thought she'd heard something. She waited, her heart flitting in her chest, but nothing slunk into the cave, thankfully. She hoped it was only debris blown into the cave by the storm. She kindled the fire and made it higher just to be on the safe side. And so her night went, sleeping in spurts before jerking violently awake. By morning, she felt even more exhausted and achy than when she'd first arrived. She changed clothes, approached the entrance to the cave, and looked out at the unceasingly stormy weather and just felt miserable.

The pterosaur appeared like something out of a nightmare. It shrieked, so close to her that it made her ears ring. Sasha instinctively flung herself backward and landed hard on her backside while the bird slammed into the cave entrance. It was big and bulky; the cave entrance was small, only a little larger than Sasha herself. She had chosen it for that reason.

The bird, grounded, started wriggling into the cave, clawing at the rocky floor to reach her. Its eyes were black and bright and wild.

Sasha didn't scream this time. She was too tired. She reached back for her pack lying on the floor and dragged it close, unhooking the bow and quivers from it. Quinn had shown her how to shoot. She wasn't good, but at close range, that didn't matter. She took the bow in hand and aimed, letting a quiver fly straight at the bird less than twenty feet away. The quiver bounced off its bony crest as it floundered, thrashing its head from side to side as it tried to crawl awkwardly on its wings and weak little talons. Heart thudding so hard she could barely breathe, Sasha chose another quiver and carefully aimed this time for its breast, puncturing its heart dead center.

The bird went into a frenzy, snapping wildly at the air before falling dead and bleeding out of the wound in its chest and out of its mouth.

Sasha sat stunned for some moments, her body humming with fear and adrenaline. She was either going to fall apart or she was going to get to work getting the bleeding bird out of the cave before it attracted predators. She opted to get the bird out of the cave, pushing at it with her javelin until its heavy wet body had cleared the entrance.

She scarcely reacted when the second pterosaur attacked. It came out of nowhere, swooping down on her as she was jabbing at the dead bird. She instinctively raised the javelin and found it jammed in the second's bird's enormous beak. The creature screamed. Sasha screamed in response but did not loosen her hold on the javelin. If anything, the bird helped her jam it harder into its mouth, forcing it to break off its attack.

The third bird caught Sasha on her blind side. Only its dark, swooping reflection in a puddle of water at her feet made her swing around and jab at the creature with all her might. The javelin stuck into the creature's throat, just under its beak. Sasha yanked the javelin out, its blood spattering her up and down. Her feet slipped on the wet, muddy ground and she went down hard, scooting backward into the cave on her backside. The wounded bird twisted in agony in midair and snapped at her. She grabbed up her fallen javelin. This time she aimed for its breast, jabbing at her target even as the huge beak came down and struck her a glancing blow across the forehead. She saw stars and blackness but kept screaming and pushing the javelin until fresh blood poured over her.

The bird fell dead in the rain.

This time, Sasha retreated to the back of the cave. She was panting, her throat hoarse, her body thrumming with terror. Her mind kept jumping, seeing dark shapes in the peripheral of her vision, seeing shadows that simply weren't there. Newton stayed out of her way, keeping to the rocks higher up in the cavern, and chirped with concern.

Sasha waited, watching the cave entrance.

More birds came, swooping low and snapping at their fallen comrade, ripping off bloody chunks of meat. There was no honor amount pterosaurs, apparently. After an hour, the bird had been picked clean and the carcass was blown over by the wind and ripped away. Sasha's mind worked automatically, numbly, like a lifeless doll programmed for just one task. She picked up the bow and moved stealthily to the entrance. She breathed slowly, steadily, her voice rasping in her throat. Through the sheets of rain, she could see the dark-winged creatures circling. They'd smelled blood. They didn't care about the rain anymore.

The first spiraled lower and she took aim. She hit it somewhere under the wing, and the creature faltered, then righted itself before it could crash. It zigzagged off, too wounded to continue its assault. The next came, a huge aggressive animal that tried to crash right into her, flying so fast she didn't have a chance to restring a new quarrel. So she dropped the bow and took the quarrel in both hands and rammed it into its breast. The beast screamed and its head collided with her and drove her to the floor of the cave. Sasha skittered backward, away from it. It floundered on the muddy ground and the others descended.

While the birds fed, Sasha picked up her bow and quiver and prepared a new quarrel. One of the birds landed atop the dead pterosaur and she shot that one in the throat. The impact knocked the second bird back into the mud. Now the pterosaurs had two birds to feed on.

Unfortunately, she was quickly running out of quarrels.

The birds were back two hours later. She missed two, shot the third one. The third one lumbered off across the ground in defeat, a quarrel sticking out of its side, probably to be picked to death by its comrades. Or so she hoped.

She was out of quarrels. She scratched around by the fire for some kindling she could use as a quarrel, but there was nothing straight enough to be made into an arrow. She tossed the bow aside. It was now useless to her. She picked up her javelin, and not a moment too soon. A small pterosaur had made it through the opening and slithered wetly across the floor, its jaws gaping wide open.

Blanked, erased of all emotion, Sasha roared and jammed the javelin right into its maw. The bird snapped down on the javelin, breaking it at the midpoint, half of it still stuck halfway down its gullet. It began to gag, to die. Sasha helped it along by beating it to death with the broken javelin. She screamed and cursed it out the whole while. She was probably mad; thankfully, she felt absolutely nothing, like a spectator forced to watch some ancient, bloody sport. When the bird was sufficiently dead, she kicked it over and over until it was crammed into a dark corner of the cave. The smell would probably bring others, but she dared not try to drag it out of the cave.

She knew the others would be waiting.

Panting and wheezing, she retreated to the fire that was slowly guttering out and grabbed up a thick dry branch, the fire spurting at the end in flecks of yellow and crimson, sparks flying. In her other hand, she gripped her survival knife, the only weapon she had left. Resolved, trapped, and thus armed, she stepped outside the cave and let fate take its course.

| 64 |

She had seconds, if that, before the rain put out her fire. But it only took seconds for the birds to spot her and react.

She gasped. More nests and wounded young were strewn along the ground. It was no surprise the birds were in such a state. And though she pitied them their plight, she found she could hate them too. None of this was her fault.

As the first one descended, she lifted her torch high and felt a profound sense of satisfaction when it screamed and darted away. More came at her. She swished the burning, guttering torch at them too, making a half-circle about her. The torch was almost out, hissing in the rain, so when something fluttered at her back, she dropped it and turned, her knife at the ready.

All she saw was screaming blackness and the beat of wind and rain. She had a distinct advantage, she realized, a saving grace, if you will. The bird was confused by its target. It wanted to attack her, *someone*, and though aggressive, it was not designed to do more than scoop up fish in its enormous beak. At this close a range, such a long beak was inconvenient, at best. Sasha stabbed at the bird, aiming her knife low as Quinn had aimed low when he stabbed the first bird. The blade of the Moja hunting knife was long, almost a short sword. It went in smoothly at the juncture of the neck and breast. The bird fell back into the mud, its enormous wings beating rain and mud at her compulsively as it floundered.

The others screamed and wheeled in confusion. She had an opening. Biting down on the edge of the blade covered in pterosaur blood, Sasha ran as fast as she could, tearing through the wet sheets of river grasses, dodging trees, and vaulting rocks as the birds squabbled behind her. She reached the river in seconds. She did not think. She leaped into the air and sliced deep into the numbingly cold waters. And for once, all was still and quiet.

| 65 |

Swimming against the storm current was fruitless, she quickly learned. Sasha tried and failed miserably. She then diverted all her energy into keeping afloat as the freezing cold water ripped her downstream at a tremendous pace. Up ahead was a fall-off. She curled herself into a ball as it pushed her right over the edge. Then she was in free-fall, screaming as she was carried in a shining arc over fifty feet down into the frothing pool far, far below.

It was water, but the impact felt like she was hitting packed earth. She instantly hurt all over. She went all the way to the bottom and twisted at the last moment to keep from conking her head on the bottom of the riverbed, then shot straight to the top, so dizzy that for a moment she wasn't sure which way was up. The only thing she was aware of was light. Then her head broke the surface, and she found the rain was less a slashing curtain and more a gentle trickle.

She could see the sun beating down, something she hadn't experienced in close to a week.

She drifted, the knife still clenched in her aching jaw. She was sore and tired, and so weak she felt like she could sink. But sinking wouldn't help Quinn, assuming he was still alive. So instead of giving up, she breaststroked to the nearest short, dug her fingers into the muddy bank, and hauled herself onto the long, wet tangles of marsh grasses. She spat out the knife and collapsed, so exhausted she didn't have the strength to seek shelter and couldn't have cared less if some large predator came along and found her.

| 66 |

Something did find her in the end.

She jerked awake as something closed firmly about her upper body, instantly regretting her short nap. She just knew it was something that had come up from the river or the birds that had followed her. She started to scream and to fight. Her knife, still clutched in one hand, sliced upward in a shining arc.

A human hand caught it. A human voice said, "Sasha...Sasha, stop. Stop! You're safe!"

She knew what the words meant, she knew she could probably trust the speaker, but when her vision began to clear and she saw who held her, she couldn't believe it. She couldn't seem to convince herself of the fact. It all seemed too good to be true. She writhed, clawing at Quinn—or the vision of Quinn—trying to hold her down. She screamed and sobbed and choked, her whole body electric with fear, so that he was forced to hug her entire body against his, to hold her so tightly she could barely breathe. "Sasha," he kept saying. "Sasha, Sasha, Sasha..." He clutched the back of her head, stroked her braids, which were mostly undone.

Finally, the familiar timbre of his voice began to penetrate her. She started to think that maybe he was real. Maybe she was safe. Maybe they both were. She dropped the knife and brought her hand up, clutching him across the back. She sobbed helplessly into his shirt.

They stayed that way for some time.

| 67 |

Quinn carried her back to the cave where he'd made camp. He carried her easily—he'd gotten quite strong in their last month here, and Sasha quite thin. It was just as well, as she was quite incapable of walking at the moment. He set her down beside the beautiful warmth of the fire and started to undress her, peeling the freezing-cold wet clothes off her one piece at a time.

She didn't mind in the least. It wasn't the first time he had disrobed her. He did not have extra clothes, and everything in the pack she'd been carrying on her back had been soaked in the river, so he stripped off his shirt and pulled her arms gently into the sleeves, pulling it around and buttoning it up tight. It was as big as a chemise on her and tattered and full of holes, but it was warm, and it smelled like Quinn. She was shaking with cold, trembling with fear and spent adrenaline. She was sore and hungry and tired, and she knew she was going to cry again.

Quinn forced her head down between her knees. "Breathe," he told her. "Breathe, Sasha, breathe."

She breathed. Slowly the tension in her shoulders eased, and she felt her body go limp the longer he held her. She was still shaking, but not so badly.

"I'm sorry," she said, her voice coming out in little hiccups. "I'm sorry, Quinn."

"Why are you sorry?"

She choked up some more river water. An hour later, and she was still vomiting up water. "You must think I'm very weak."

"A seven-mile journey, a swim in the river, and a battle with...something, based on the blood all over you...yes, Sasha, I think you're incredibly weak," he said with a wry smile.

She looked him over, barely able to believe he was alive, that they were both alive. "Oh, Quinn," she said, grabbing him around the neck and pulling him close. He felt so good pressed against her, warm and safe and familiar and dear and everything she wanted in the world.

"How did you...?" She didn't even know how to say it. She swallowed. "How are you alive?"

"Same as you. I wound up in the river, nearly drowned. But I'd remembered some of what you'd taught me. I was able to stay afloat until I got here." He slowly pried her off him so he could hold her at arm's length and look at her. She wondered if she looked as surprised and desperate as he did. "Do you come all this way to look for me?"

"Yes, of course." She frowned. "Did you think I would not?"

"But what about the gate?" Suddenly he looked angry. "Sasha, that was a very foolish thing to do. There's barely a day left to use it before the storm season is over."

She felt like she might cry again. "I wasn't about to leave you here!"

"Oh Sasha. Don't you realize how easily I could have been dead, drowned? You'll probably be stuck here another whole year with me now."

"I don't care." She sniffed, then told him about her progress on the gate, how she had left John in charge of it. "We have a little time left, ten or twelve hours. We should be able to get back."

He shook his head, slowly. "If I could have gotten back, don't you think I would have tried?"

"I don't understand."

"Can you walk?"

"I think so."

She let him pull her to her feet and lead her out of the cave. She clung tightly to his arm, partly out of weariness. Mostly, because she was still scared.

The rain was nothing but a drizzle now. She didn't feel it at all after her swim in the river. The river itself fed into an enormous lake, and they stood on its banks. It must have been a half-mile across and at least three times that wide. On the far side, she could see canyon walls at least four hundred feet tall. They ran the full circumference of the lake, enclosing it completely. Quinn pointed. "I haven't gone very far yet, but I don't see any breaks in the canyon walls. For all intents and purposes, this canyon is entirely isolated." He pointed down the river, feeding furiously into the lake. With the storm season flooding it, there was no landmass leading into the canyon, only a few lone trees sticking up out of the river where a narrow strip of dry land used to be.

She looked down at the squishy ground they stood upon. A small ring of solid land led down toward the river. There had probably been a ring of land all about the lake at one point, and leading up to the foothills of the canyon, but now it was mostly underwater except for the higher ground they stood on. "We're losing ground," she said.

"Yes, I think we are."

"Another day and the whole canyon will be underwater." She looked up the sheer rock walls. Caves pocked the canyon walls farther up. It wasn't a solution, but it might be a temporary fix. She could foresee them moving upward as the caves closer to the lake flooded, maybe surviving on fish for a few weeks until the water table dropped and they were able to escape the canyon. That's if they could find enough dry kindle to burn to keep a fire going. It would be cold and claustrophobic, but she knew they'd get by, if they had to.

But Quinn saw her looking and said, "Don't bother with that. *They're* up there."

"They?"

"John's Velociraptors. They nest up there, but they only come out at night. There are thirty or forty of them, about the size of geese. They went into a frenzy yesterday when I shot down a pterosaur. In fact…" He turned and returned to the cave, Sasha still clinging to his arm. He bunched up her wet tunic and tossed it onto the fire, which was practically a sin when they had so little clothes between them. "Even dry blood draws them on, so we mustn't hurt ourselves at all." He took her arms and looked her over very carefully. She was covered in bruises and scrapes, she knew, but the river had washed her clean of blood, thankfully.

"I'm afraid to say we're very trapped here."

She thought about that, then spotted her pack on the floor. She finally released Quinn and knelt to rummage through it. Everything was soaked through, but the handmade rope the Moja had given them, all three hundred feet of it, was there, and it was intact. If anything, the river water would only have made the homemade hemp rope stronger.

Quinn knelt, looking hopeful, and took the rope from her. "Good girl!" he said.

| 68 |

"We're climbing up the canyon?" she said dubiously, watching Quinn uncoil the rope and secure it to a homemade quarrel. Quinn had known bushmen in Africa who used similar methods to scale difficult grades upwards and down, he said. He'd also made a homemade bow with some of the catgut in her pack and a quarrel out of a thick, mostly straight branch.

Quinn checked the sun, which had only just crested the canyon wall. It was edging toward midday. "Yes," he answered, shielding his eyes. "I'd have preferred starting out earlier, but I don't think the water table will wait another day." He looked at her. "Still afraid of climbing, my dear?"

She blanked her face. "No," she said. She was frightened to death, but the alternative—drowning in the flooded canyon or eaten by raptors—didn't appeal much to her either. At least climbing she had a chance. She sat down on a rock and watched Quinn secure the quarrel. When he was satisfied the rope was as secure as he could get it, he aimed for a line of scraggly horsehair conifers at the top of the canyon. He had a good eye, but the first ten or twelve times, he tried to land an anchor, he either snagged some branches that were far too fragile to hold any weight or missed the trees completely. Each time, he reeled in the rope and tried again.

After an hour, he was sweating and cursing. The canyon was too far up, and gravity was working against them. He checked the sun, which had just moved past the midpoint of the day, sweat trickling down his forehead and into his eyes. Sasha could see the strain in every line of his face. "I am never going to get this bloody thing right," he insisted.

"Yes, you will. You can," she said. She stood up and came up behind him, close, and put her arms about his waist. His entire body thrummed like a bow strung too tightly. "Slow," she told him, speaking low and intimately in his ear. "Take your time."

His body relaxed inch by inch in her arms. Finally, he let the quarrel fly.

The quarrel hit dead center, embedded in a tree protruding at an odd angle over the canyon, its roots securely gripping the rocks.

"I told you," she said.

Quinn pulled on the knotted rope with all his might, but it held firm. He turned to Sasha. "Yes," he said. "You did." Then he took her in his arms and kissed her.

| 69 |

The climb up the canyon wall was an agonizing experience. Sasha had to use muscles she did not even know she had. Had she been a little fatter, a little weaker, she never would have been able to do it. As it was, she had scarcely gone half the way up before she felt like giving up.

She secured her grip around the next knot in the rope and pulled down while pushing at the knot beneath her booted feet. It inched her up a painfully tiny distance before she was forced to rest again. Meanwhile, the rope she clung to swayed sickeningly like a pendulum against the almost perfectly flat canyon wall as the wind buffeted her. She had to force herself to keep from looking down. If she looked down, she would be sick, freeze, fall, or all of them at once. The one saving grace was the extra weight that Quinn put on the rope. As he climbed after her, his weight pulled the swaying rope taut. His voice encouraged her to climb another inch up.

The sun was sinking low, the light beginning to mellow and fade. They had maybe six hours before the gate closed, six hours to get back to camp. Sasha pulled down and squirmed her way up the rope another few inches, putting everything she had into it. Above her head lurked a narrow shelf of rock, not quite a ledge. Sasha aimed for it, pulling herself up and over it.

The raptor was waiting for her.

It was barely the size of a goose, as Quinn had said, and covered in colorful, peacock blue plumage. It would have been a beautiful bird, had it not been so aggressive. It leaped at her so quickly she never had a chance to scream, much less react. It made a hoarse croaking noise. Then it was stuck in her braids, its weight dragging her over the edge of the ledge. Sasha clung to the rope, wrapping her arms and legs about it and making it sway dangerously. The raptor's talons came swiftly down, ripping gouges in her exposed cheeks and tender scalp. Sasha screamed but forced herself to stay clinging to the rope. She instinctively swung back at the rock wall, smashing herself and the bird against it. The bird, momentarily stunned, fell further still, its weight pulling at her braids in pure, unrelenting agony.

She began to slide down the rope, the raptor's weight pulling her down and down. Quinn was calling up to her, but she barely heard. She slammed into his shoulders and he grunted as he took the combination of her weight and the raptor. "Get it off!" she screamed, the weight of the bird yanking her head to one side so she felt her neck must surely break at any moment.

"Hang on," he said, sounding much calmer than she felt.

She did not care if he had to rip the bird and her braids out at the bloody root, just so long as he got rid of the excess weight. He didn't, though. He drew his survival knife from his boot and slashed the blade upward, perilously close to her face. She felt her hair give, then the weight of the beast as it ripped her remaining braids loose. It fell, fluttering and screaming to the canyon far below.

"Sasha, look out!"

She'd barely had time to recover when the second raptor—a duller-plumed female—launched itself from the shelf above and aimed for her face. Quinn slashed upward, catching the female with the tip of his knife. It knocked the bird's trajectory off and it fluttered over their heads and began to fall like its mate, its claws raking over their backs.

Sasha barely felt the pain. She clung to the rope and prayed there were no more raptors. She was whimpering. Whimpering and hurting.

Quinn gasped, wheezing with the exertion of clinging to the rope with one hand and supporting her weight on his shoulders. "Sasha, we have to get going. You're bleeding."

She gripped the next knot in the rope and eased her weight off Quinn's shoulders. "I don't know if I can go on, Quinn," she sobbed, feeling foolish. "I just don't know."

"You can. You will," he said, echoing her own words back to her. "Go slow. Take your time. Climb, Sasha. Please."

She climbed. She was more cautious when she reached the ledge this time.

Fortunately, nothing popped out at her, though she did spot a small aperture in the canyon wall just large enough for a large bird to pass. From within, she could hear squabbling, not unlike the sound the pterosaurs had made as they ripped one of their own apart. They had very little time, she realized. The moment the colony of raptors smelled their blood, they were doomed.

"There's a whole next of them up here, Quinn," she said, sounding just as panicked as she felt.

"Climb, then, Sasha. Just climb."

She hauled herself up, scrambling up the rope with renewed vigor. Suddenly her wounds did not hurt so much, though she was still bleeding. Above her, perhaps twenty feet up, she saw the dark outline of the tree branches. The sight of it made her cry out in pure ecstasy, kicking rocks and breaking the skin of her knuckles as she scrabbled ever faster toward it like some fabled nirvana. "We're almost there, Quinn!" she called down, but she received no response.

Her heart, hurting with its frenetic beating, seemed to skip a beat and go still in her chest. She glanced down and saw Quinn swaying and twisting on the rope as he used his knife to slash at the birds casually climbing up their rope. Their dexterity was amazing, the way they clawed their way upward utilizing both their giant taloned feet as well as their dwarfed little clawed wings, their tiny reptilian eyes set fast on their prey.

Dear God, Quinn had been staying silent in the hopes that she'd make it to the top. Sasha lunged up the rope, pulling herself over the edge and turning sharply to grip the rope in both hands.

She tried to haul Quinn up but he was too heavy. "Quinn! I'm up. I'm up!"

"Not a moment too soon, my dear," he said, sounding strained as he jabbed at the head of the raptor closest to him.

Sasha climbed awkwardly to her feet, still gripping the rope. "Climb, Quinn, climb!" she cried as she reached around with one hand for their last remaining weapon strapped to her back, the broken umbrella that Quinn had carried downstream with him. She swung it around and tried to jab at the colorful male that was slowly climbing up the sheer face of the canyon wall but only managed to hit Quinn instead.

"Sasha!" he barked, grabbing the rope with both hands and pushing himself upward a few more inches.

"I'm sorry!" she cried. Then screamed when the raptor leaped to Quinn's back, its great claws ripping through his tattered frock coat and flesh. Quinn grunted in agony but dared not let go of the rope. Sasha aimed more carefully and jabbed at the bird just as it snarled at her. It got a mouthful of broken umbrella spokes before the impact knocked it off Quinn's back. Quinn grunted, the back of his frock torn wide open and flecked with his blood.

She extended the umbrella as the other raptors moved nimbly up the rope. "Grab the umbrella, Quinn!"

"I'll pull you down," he said through gritted teeth. He lost his grip on the knife and the weapon went sailing past the raptors and down into oblivion. His eyes swam in his head and she was suddenly terrified he might pass out from the pain of his wounds.

"Quinn, grab the bloody umbrella!" she screamed.

He reached up and pawed at it in a sort of delirium.

"Oh, Quinn, *please!*" she said, leaning down as far as she dared.

He finally got his hand about the end and she pulled, then pulled some more. The raptors were squabbling. She could hear them fighting amongst themselves. She pulled, praying to God He'd grant her just a little mercy, a few more seconds to pull Quinn up. Her feet gave out and she fell flat on her belly, still pulling, but Quinn was also pulling *her* to the edge of the cliff. She gritted her teeth and reached back, wrapping her hand around a rangy branch of the tree. She pulled with all her might. She was strong; she could hold him if she tried, if she didn't give up.

With one final, mighty burst of effort, she pulled and he came, clinging helplessly to the umbrella. He was bloodied and panting like a wild, wounded animal when she got him over the edge of the cliff. The raptors had torn strips of flesh from his already scarred back, leaving deep furrows of glittering merlot wounds seeping horribly. She bent down and pulled him into her arms. He grimaced and trembled with the pain and effort of it all.

"Oh, bloody hell, that hurts," he said.

"You scared me to death."

"I scared me to death too." He sat up gingerly, looking like he might vomit all over the ground. She wouldn't have blamed him if he did. "How bad is it?"

"Bad, but I think you'll live." She glanced over the edge and saw the raptors still coming, snarling and biting at each other with bloodied beaks, fighting over the bits of Quinn they had ripped loose. It was enough to make her want to vomit herself. "We need to get out of here. Can you run?"

"I think so."

"Do."

Several of the raptors had made it to the top of the rope. They eyed her, screaming hungrily, snapping birdlike jaws full of razor-sharp teeth. She scooted back, then turned and scrambled to her feet, grabbing Quinn's arm.

Together, she and Quinn ran for their lives.

| 70 |

The desert was black and vacant and lonely-looking, like the landscape of the moon or some dead world. Rock formations threw long weird shadows across the dark and almost formless deadpan. Sprays of thin grasses and some scraggly weeds clung to the desert floor, but otherwise the abundant greenery of the Valley of Song was missing, along with the constant rains.

Sasha and Quinn fled across the desert, pursued by a half dozen raptors. Under normal circumstances, she would have had no trouble fending them off. But they'd smelled blood—Quinn's blood—and now they were relentless. They screamed and raced with predatory grace after them. Had they been larger, their strides longer, they would have been upon them in minutes. But they were just small enough that a human could stay ahead of them with a bit of a handicap, which Sasha and Quinn had. They were a few minutes ahead of the raptors, but the raptors were determined to close the distance.

Sasha raced across the deadpan as quickly as she could, Quinn in tow. She could hear them squabbling back there in the dark, each fighting to be the first to reach them.

Quinn stumbled over a rock and fell.

Sasha stopped suddenly, stumbling to her already bruised knees, then rolled to her feet and raced to Quinn's side. He was bleeding much worse than before, his frock coat soaked through with his blood. The run must have aggravated his already impressive wounds. He pushed himself up onto his knees and gasped for breath, sweat and blood pouring off his body even as the remnants of his frock coat slid down his arms. "I...can't," he said. "I...just...can't."

"You can. You will." She grabbed his arm. "Get up, Quinn!"

"I can't, Sasha. I just cannot. Please don't make me."

"If you don't get up, I'll stay here. I'll let them get me too, Quinn."

That got him motivated. Letting out a hoarse breath, he climbed shakily to his feet and swayed for one dangerous moment, his blue eyes completely unfocused.

"Quinn!" she shouted, grabbing him to steady him on his feet.

The raptors screamed.

Sasha turned, still clinging to Quinn, and prepared to face them.

That's when She stepped out of the dark.

| 71 |

The night was silent and almost airless. Empty.

And then, like a ghost, suddenly She was standing there, staring at them.

She was bigger than Sasha remembered, or it was only the emptiness of the desert making her seem that way. She was also gaunt as if she'd been eating little, her bones sharp, her skin covered in sores and parasites. Flies swarmed her and crawled across her eyes. She'd been traveling hard, Sasha realized. Following them relentlessly for hundreds of miles. There were battle scars, both old and new, covering her head and neck, and the eye that John had shot out was egg white and running with a black tarry substance. The other was yellow and hate-filled, seeing them and rolling, appreciating well what it was she was seeing.

Opportunity.

Revenge.

Sasha feared her. Sasha pitied her. She wanted She healed, and at the same time, she wanted She *dead*. She would never feel safe again until She was destroyed.

Sasha moved to block Quinn and the gigantic Ceratosaurus closed in on them. "I'm sorry! We had no choice!" she screamed in a hoarse voice, brandishing the useless, broken umbrella, her last and only weapon.

The Ceratosaurus stopped, swaying on her feet. She breathed in and out, in and out, slowly, steadily, hoarsely. She looked weak, on the knife-edge of collapse. And so evil and motivated that Sasha knew she could do it. She could run them down and consume them, despite the masses of flies and parasites eating her alive. And she would. She would follow them the length of this desert, to the ends of this earth, if need be. The great beast lowered its head and bellowed, its sickeningly rotten breath loosening the spare contents in Sasha's stomach. She took a lumbering step toward Sasha, her lips trembling upward in a grimace of broken, rotten black teeth. There was no pity in her eyes, and no escape.

Ironically enough, the raptors saved them. They burst from the dark, swarming foolishly over She's feet and leaping at her pebbled grey hide, biting at her like excited fleas. The birds, oblivious to her size, immediately began ripping small strips of flesh away and consuming them. She reared back and screamed, shattering the night with her agony, her cry amplified to nightmarish intensity by her nasal horn.

Sasha cowered, grabbed Quinn's arm and tugged. "We have to go, Quinn. Now!"

Quinn staggered a moment at the sight of the great creature writhing and biting at the little birds ripping at her, then turned to look at Sasha. His pale eyes seemed to clear and he nodded.

He let her lead him on.

| 72 |

She was following them.

They had only managed to jog a couple of miles when it became obvious they were being followed.

She had thrown away all stealth, Sasha realized. She wanted them to know they were being hunted.

Sasha urged Quinn on. He was being an incredible trooper, her Quinn. Despite his injuries, he had done a marvelous job of keeping up with her. But even Quinn had his limits, and from the look of him, he had finally reached them. She knew she was going to have to decide for both of them soon, either stand and fight She or find shelter.

The earth trembled slightly as She shortened the distance between them.

Sasha thought again of that face, that mask of mindless fury on a creature that no longer lived for its own welfare but only for revenge. The face masked in blood from the raptors she had so savagely disposed of. She decided on shelter.

Ahead loomed the outline of a butte. She thought—*hoped*—that perhaps they'd find some caves there and started steering Quinn in that direction. Most of the buttes in this area were home to hundreds of small apertures. She only wondered if they'd be able to find one before She found them.

"Sasha, my dear," said Quinn, limping along at barely more than a trot beside her. "You look lovely in the moonlight. So fae." He shook his head like he was casting off buzzing flies. "I don't think I can manage anymore."

"Stay with me, Quinn. We're almost safe."

Ahead loomed the rock wall of the butte. She pushed Quinn on, searching frantically for an opening. Behind her, she could practically feel the hot wind steaming from She's bloody mouth, carrying with it carrion and death. She dragged him along the wall until she found a serviceable entrance. Unfortunately, something hissed and spat at them from within, gazing out at the world with vapid yellow eyes. She moved on, tugging Quinn along.

Behind them, She breathed hoarsely, snorting into the cold of the desert night.

The next cave she came upon looked almost too large, large enough for a small elephant to crawl into, but they were officially out of options. She dragged Quinn inside, and mere seconds later a much larger shadow filled the cave entrance, snorting and growling as it tried to wedge itself inside. Sasha held her breath, but She was simply too large.

She and Quinn scrambled to the back of the cave and collapse in the dust and rocks. Quinn fell against her like a dead thing and she held him and prayed they'd figure some way out of this predicament.

| 73 |

Sasha dampened a swath of Quinn's shirt in a small pool at the back of the cave and applied the cold, wet material to his back, wiping away some of the blood. He grunted but hardly reacted at all. The water was icy; it would help staunch the bleeding. Or so she hoped.

"Does it hurt very much?" she asked. It was a stupid thing to say. Of course it hurt. But she needed to keep Quinn with her. Otherwise, his sense wandered.

"Not so bad I cannot handle it," Quinn answered. He lay on his stomach on the floor of the cave while she applied the improvised cold compresses. He must have sensed her unease because he added, "It's nothing I haven't experienced in the past. My father...he liked the martinet. Did you know you can entirely flay a horse alive with a martinet if you try?"

Sasha grimaced. His father beat him. The old Lord Quinn had beat his son with what was probably the most painful flogger ever evilly devised by a human mind. Years of abuse had left scars on his son's body as well as his soul.

"Do you know I'm actually rather numb there?" Quinn rested his cheek against the stony floor, closed his eyes, and shook with a number of tearless sobs. "Oh, Father..."

Sasha knelt beside him and stroked his hair until the moment of weakness passed and sense returned and Quinn's powerful sense of will began filtering back into his eyes again. His body grew still and he looked utterly sick and exhausted.

With the wet strips of cloth she worked on binding his wounds as best she could and trying to prevent, or at least stave off, infection, though she knew her work was inadequate. Quinn needed medical attention and she had nothing to help him. Then there was nothing more she could do except help to ease him up. He flinched when his back encountered the wall of the cave. She listened to the despondent drip of water from somewhere inside the cave and just looked at him. He looked pale and gaunt and there were feverish dark circles under his eyes. She didn't say as much, but she had a terrible feeling that if they didn't get back to London soon, Quinn would likely die of his wounds.

They had maybe four hours left before the gate closed. And She was out there in the desert, waiting for them both to venture outside. Sasha could feel her in her bones, at the back of her mind, an insistent shadow as somber as the Grim Reaper himself.

"So here we are," Quinn said, trying for levity.

Sasha smiled. There was nothing else left to do. It was either smile or cry, and she was tired of crying. She moved to sit across Quinn's lap and rest her head on his shoulder, carefully trying not to apply pressure to him or aggravate his wounds.

"Do you regret not staying with Toby?" Quinn asked very seriously. He reached up and pulled her tight against him, probably tighter than he was comfortable with. But if his wounds pained him, he didn't show it. He buried his face in the side of her neck.

"No, of course not."

"Really."

"I chose you, and you chose me, Quinn. That's what Naja said. And Naja was right."

"The great huntress."

"That's right."

"But I'm a bit of a disappointment, yes? Not such a great hunter…"

"Quinn, you're perfect. You're beautiful and funny and sincere. I love you."

For once, he had nothing sarcastic or self-effacing to say. She glanced up and saw his head was bowed as if he were trying very hard to control his emotions.

"Quinn…"

He raised his head and pushed himself back against the wall as if the friction and pain were tools to clear his head. He looked at her with steady, dark eyes. "Do you mean that?"

"Yes, of course."

His hands tightened almost painfully around her. "I would do more than die for you, Sasha. I'd kill for you."

"I know that," she said, blinking away the tears that threatened to erupt in her eyes.

"I love you, my darling." He cupped the back of her head and kissed her, a slow and very sweet kiss that left them both breathless. He said, his voice a hoarse whisper near her ear, "I want to live in my old decaying house in Africa with you and raise children and live and die there with you by my side."

"Yes," she answered simply. "We'll do that, Quinn. We'll do everything."

He sagged and she felt her heart flutter. "Quinn…"

"I'm all right. Only not feeling so well."

"You've already started to fever."

"I'm fine. Not fevering. Not yet. I would know it if I was. I did the first time I saw you."

"Oh, Quinn." She leaned up and placed a soft kiss on his cheek.

"We need to get home, Sasha," he said, sagging back against the cave as if there was no strength left in his body. "It's terribly important. We can't die here."

"We'll never get past She."

"We should try. She could stay here for days or weeks until we die." He thought a long moment, seeming to struggle with it. "How far are we from camp, do you think?"

"Maybe five miles. Maybe more. I don't know!"

"If I distracted She, could you run that far without stopping?"

A sudden terror seized Sasha. She leaned back and looked up at him carefully. "I won't leave you."

"Sasha, She cannot follow us both if we go in separate directions."

"Then I should lead her away! I'm stronger than you right now. I'm not as injured."

He looked at her with enormous feeling, his hand moving to brush her tangled, half-undone hair out of her eyes. "It has to be me, Sasha. There's no question of that."

Now she was angry. She wanted to strike him, to scream at him. "No, it does not! I can do it. I can outrun her. I'm not afraid!"

"Sasha..."

"Please, Quinn!" she sobbed. She rested her head on his shoulder and cried. She did not care if that made her seem weak.

He held her, comforted her, and finally he spoke. And she hated him all the more because his words made perfect sense. "You must have considered the consequences of what we have done. You must have entertained, even for only a moment, the idea that we might have a child between us."

She sniffed as his words seeped into her. It had crossed her mind many times, actually, and, she was ashamed to admit, she was most hopeful, despite their precarious living conditions and the almost constant danger of this world. She would be proud to carry Quinn's child, to nurture him, to see him grow. And if—*when*—she returned home, she would happily face London society a pariah, she and her illegitimate child. She'd go to live in a nunnery, if necessary. It would be preferable to living alone.

But she was honest with Quinn. He deserved that, at least. "I don't know if I'm strong enough to let you go."

"But are you strong enough to reach the gate, Sasha? Are you strong enough to raise our child back home, if there is one?"

She nodded. "Yes."

"It will be very difficult. More difficult than surviving on this world, likely."

"I know."

"Well, then." He gently eased her out of his lap and climbed shakily to his feet. For one bad moment, Sasha was certain he would topple over, but he recovered quickly. He looked down on her, his eyes dire and loving all at once. "Would you like that, to raise our child, my darling Sasha?"

She could barely see through the veil of her tears. "Yes. I would. I'd call him Isaac after Sir Isaac Newton, and he'd likely be very stubborn like me, and probably very ginger like you. My Papa was ginger when he was younger, did you know that? I'm a ginger in disguise."

Quinn laughed, a nice sound, and drew her up and into the circle of his arms. "Yes, actually, I knew that about Albertus." And then he grew serious. "I love him like my brother, Sasha. He is and will always be my best friend." He swallowed hard and continued. "He is the executor of my estate, so when you get home, you convince old Albertus that all I have should be yours, the estate in Africa, my flat in London. Everything. Will you do that for me?"

Sasha shuddered. He was telling her goodbye. But she would be strong because that was what Quinn wanted. "I'll tell him."

"Will you go to Africa? Will you claim the estate, you and our child?"

She nodded once, dourly. "Yes."

Quinn smiled then. "It will be good to know that my house will see some happiness, finally."

"I won't be happy without you."

"Try, Sasha." He drew her close, sank his hand in all her tangled cornrow braids, and kissed her, gently, thoroughly. She put her arms about him for a moment and held him close, kissing him, trying to memorize everything about the moment, everything about him. The time was both long and much too brief. Finally, she let him go and he moved stiffly toward the entrance of the cave. He shrugged his whole body and she could see him loosening up, preparing to run. He took a deep breath. He wasn't well, but he could do it, she knew. He was going to run, he was going to save her from the dragon, the way he'd always wanted to. She...and the child they might have between them.

"Quinn."

He turned to look at her. "Yes, Sasha?"

"I'm sorry I hit you with that log. In the beginning. I should never have done that."

"I love you too, my dear." He touched her cheek in farewell. Then, straightening his shoulders, Quinn stepped outside the cave.

| 74 |

She came barreling out of the dark, bearing down on them like a locomotive, just as she had expected. For a moment Sasha froze. She found herself unable to react as she watched the enormous creature charge them like some nightmare shade, kicking up dust and rocks, her gigantic head lowered and swaying back and forth like a pendulum, her greasy black jaws agape.

Then Quinn, clutching John's broken umbrella, ran straight at her.

She hesitated a moment, no doubt confounded by the small creature with the gall to run at her instead of away from her. But Quinn was resolute. He did not flinch. He reached her in seconds, ducked under her head, took the broken umbrella in both hands, and plunged the ragged tip deep into her belly. She bellowed, twisted her head to follow him, and snapped. Quinn rolled out of the way of her giant slavering jaws. Sasha flinched when she saw his back take yet more punishment as he rolled across the rocky ground. Then he was on his feet again and ducking behind her, making She lumber around to follow him.

Now was her chance, her only chance.

Ripping her attention away from Quinn, Sasha ran. She ran crying and sobbing, but even still, she ran. She ran for herself.

But mostly, she ran for Quinn and the child they both might have conceived in this hostile world.

Ahead loomed the open, unchanging desert, the buzzing insect life, and the long, formless shadows that could be anything. She ducked and zigzagged, trying to imitate the behavior of the smaller nocturnal dinosaurs, hoping to go unnoticed by most of the desert creatures. It was the longest five miles of her life, and she recalled almost nothing about it afterward. She knew she ran into through night, through webs of buzzing insects, over rocks and small, dry ravines. She knew she ran and stumbled and fell and clambered to her feet and ran some more. But she had few memories of the time. She ran, not wanting to look back, not wanting to think at all. She just ran and ran until she realized the grade of the earth was changing, that it sloped downward toward the valley below. She ran into the rain and the wind and didn't find it at all refreshing. She ran, crying and stumbling until she recognized the distant pinprick light of a camp and realized she was almost there, almost home.

She ran toward the light. She let the light consume her.

"Sasha!"

At first, it was a dim echo of a cry that the wind quickly blew away. Then, as she neared the camp, and the sputtering fire the rain was quickly putting out, she heard John more clearly. He had stayed behind to tend to the fire. He stood near the copse of trees where the gate was located, signaling to her with his bow. Sasha sobbed and put everything she had left into it as she ran toward him.

"Sasha, did you find Quinn?" John asked. He was standing there impatiently, the pack on his back, practically leaping from foot to foot. He had his bow gripped securely in one hand, and a pterosaur lay crumpled nearby, the rain washing its blood away into the earth.

She ran right into him and sobbed. It was answer enough.

John steadied her. "I'm sorry, Sasha. I am *so* sorry."

"We have to go, John," she panted breathlessly. They had perhaps a half hour left, maybe less. "Did you get the gate open?"

He nodded. "And stabilized. But the wind is starting to change."

She grabbed the bow out of his hands, snatched at a quarrel in the pack on his back, turned, and fired blindly at the shadow looming close. The pterosaur that had been silently descending upon them was deflected when the quarrel struck its wing, wheeling off screaming into the night. "We have to go *now*, John." She grabbed him by the sleeve and together they crashed through the tall grasses just as more birds began to turn and head in their direction.

Ahead, she saw the spinning of the sails and the gloomy ghostlight of the gate. It shone in a brilliant blue cone over the dais, small insects buzzing all about it. At first, she thought they were the huge prehistoric insects she was no so familiar with; then she realized they were flies and other tiny insects that did not yet exist in this world. She never thought she would be so happy to see insects from earth flitting in and out of the light! John saw too and was elated. He pointed at the dim outline of the bustling daylit streets surrounding the Palace of Westminster. "I always wanted to visit London," he stated happily.

They raced between the sails and leaped to the top of the dais. At that point, Sasha pulled John up short. "Give me your quarrels."

"What?"

"Your quarrels!" she screamed into the wind and rain drenching them both. "Give them to me!"

John unhooked the pack of quarrels from his rucksack and Sasha took them, dumping them unceremoniously like pickup sticks at her feet. "What are you doing?" he demanded to know.

"I'm going to wait for She," she said. She turned to look at him, at the expression of disbelief on his handsome, sunburned face. "Goodbye, John," she said and forced a smile. Then she pushed him, hard.

John stumbled backward, weighed down by the pack on his back, a pack that no doubt held his notes, bits of bones, and plenty of other impractical things that he could not be parted from. Wonderful things that would change the face of paleontology forever. He stumbled and fell back, vanishing into the light.

Sasha was alone, except for Newton, who had leaped first to the dais, then to her shoulder. He put his cool nose to her ear.

She lifted John's bow and prepared a new quiver, eyeing the sky keenly for pterosaurs. If Quinn was alive, she knew he'd be headed this way, toward the light of the gate. And she would be ready.

| 75 |

She was coming.

Sasha heard her long before she sighted her fuzzy dark outline lumbering through the grey morning rain. She took a deep breath and stilled her thudding heartbeat. So far, the birds had left her alone, no doubt too afraid of the weird, unnatural light from the gate to approach, and dissuaded by the torrents of rain. But She was not afraid. Sasha sensed the rhythmic thumping of the earth as She lumbered toward her. She felt nothing. She was numbed, resolved. She raised the bow, sighted down her target, fully prepared to kill Quinn's killer…but suddenly something came out of the rain and grabbed her.

She screamed and fought, almost dropping the bow, then realized it was human, whatever it was, and familiar, and it was hugging her and holding her tight in a big, wet, squishy embrace.

"Quinn!" she screamed, for a moment so overwhelmed by his sudden appearance that she started to sob in pure, unadulterated joy. She clutched him and clutched him tighter, and without saying a word, he clutched her back, so hard she could not breathe for a moment.

"Sasha," he said in her ear. "My darling. You waited."

"You made it," she said, sobbing against his neck. "You made it…"

She was almost upon them. In all the excitement, Sasha had momentarily forgotten about her.

But Quinn had not. He let Sasha go, took the bow and quarrel from her, turned, and fired blindly as she had fired earlier at the pterosaur. He fired just as the great beast lunged at them, her acrid breath blowing over them both like a hot desert wind. The quarrel hit her nasal horn, bounced along the side of her face, and struck her good eye.

She roared in agony and stumbled to the ground just outside the circle of sails, kicking up a windstorm of dust and rocks.

"Bugger it," said Quinn, as if surprised he had hit her. He turned and smiled at Sasha...then pushed her right into the light.

| 76 |

Like in the beginning, there was darkness and a carnivorous wind that seemed to rip at her with giant teeth. Sasha felt herself tumble, felt the storm rip at her clothes and hair. She did not know which way was up, assuming there even was an up, and so all she could do was fold her arms about herself, squeeze her eyes shut, and hope for the best. Like in the beginning, the journey seemed to last forever. It seemed to last seconds. There was a bright light and a tremendous rush, and suddenly a cobblestoned street was rushing up to meet her. She hit it hard on her side and rolled until she hit the curb of a gutter. She sat up and immediately dodged to one side as a coach roared past her, spraying her with stagnant gutter water as the driver drove his horses on with a bullwhip.

In another life, she would have been enraged. Now she was only relieved.

She stood up and looked around in wonder at the familiarity of the narrow, cobbled streets twisting this way and that, the rearing brick buildings, the vendors hawking their wares in the streets, the coach-and-fours passing her on every side. The stink of close-packed humanity was enough to make one's hair curl. It was the most wonderful thing she had ever smelled!

She stepped down off the curb and into the street, and an old woman on the corner, holding a basket, offered her a small, half-rotten apple, thinking she was a beggar by the look of her clothes. Quinn was heading toward her, looking as bad as she, she imagined. The moment she spotted him, she raced toward him. He opened his arms and she jumped. He caught her expertly and swung her around, right there in the crowded street, while she laughed and cried and sobbed like some lunatic let loose from an asylum. Others looked at them in curiosity or pity, but she did not care. She had Quinn, and they were alive, and that was all that mattered.

"We made it," she told him. "We made it we made it we made it home!"

Seconds later, John raced up to them, still bearing his pack, and Sasha and Quinn welcomed him into their circle, and together they hugged and danced and kicked up mud while coaches veered off and people looked on in aghast horror at the fools dancing and whooping in the filthy street.

And then the gateway, which was not quite closed yet, spat out one more thing.

And that thing was She.

| 77 |

The creature landed firmly in the narrow street, scattering coaches and people wide. Blinded, confused, She struck out at the chaos surrounding her, snapping wildly at anything within biting distance. A large cart carrying produce down the street was the first thing she attacked. The horses reared and She leaped upon them, overturning the cart and sending it crashing into the street. A wheel spun off, missing Sasha by inches as it skipped down the road.

She snorted and spun about, scattering more people as she tried desperately to find a target.

Quinn pulled Sasha away, and the two of them darted down the crooked, narrow street with John close on their heels. "That creature *really* dislikes you two," John helpfully pointed out when they had reached the bottom of the hill, panting and wheezing from both terror and exertion.

Sasha spun about and grabbed John by the arm. "Can you get help? Get the police?"

John looked stricken, his eyes wild. "Yes, of course." Then he looked around, noting that She was presently entangled in some wash lines that had been strung between two buildings. "Um...eh, where are we?"

Sasha looked too. They seemed to be in Covent Garden, Quinn's old stomping ground, the seedy square full of night-houses, low taverns, and squalid, unbecoming slums.

"Don't bother. The police won't come here," Quinn said, resting wearily against a tall, iron gas lamp. His eyes swam in his head and he breathed only in broken gasps. Sasha was reminded that Quinn had been running almost nonstop all night and had to be close to collapse from exhaustion. "Believe me. Not unless there's a terrific row."

"There's a damned dinosaur in the middle of the streets!" John cried, gesturing wildly. "How can the police *not* come?"

"This is the East End. They'll think some drunks are hallucinating," Quinn gasped, sounding angry now. "At least until it's too late and the bloody thing has torn up half the slums. Trust me on that. If they couldn't catch Jolly Jack, do you think they'll have any luck with She?"

Sasha glanced around a corner. There was another calamity as She turned in the narrow streets, knocking aside more coaches and trampling vendors and newspaper carts in her clumsy search for them. People—scoundrels mostly, the homeless and prostitutes—raced wildly past their hiding place.

There had to be a way. Sasha pushed John toward what looked like a pub, probably brimming with criminals. "Go inside and make a row until the police come. But for heaven's sake, John, keep your wits about you!"

He looked at them, nodded, and started off.

It was only once he was gone that Quinn spoke. "You did that on purpose to spare John," he said. He reached up for a laundered shirt on a wash line, slipped his arms into it, and began to button it up over his terrible, bleeding back.

"Yes, of course," she admitted, breathing hard. "She isn't after John, Quinn. He has no business suffering for what we've done."

"What have we done, Sasha?" he asked, offering her a chemise.

"Something necessary," she said, sliding like a snake into it. It wasn't proper, but it was far better than the ragged shirt she'd been wearing. "But still, something a lot of innocent people may pay for." She shuddered as several people screamed on the street while She roared and stomped the ground in rage and frustration. She swallowed hard. "We can't let this continue, Quinn. She has to die."

He took her hand as they both huddled against the shelter of the wall. "Sasha, your altruistic intentions both amaze and frustrate me to no end. What do we do?"

Sasha nodded. "We kill She."

Quinn grunted and glanced past her down the street. "There's a butcher shop a block south from here."

"Is that relevant?"

"Do you trust me?"

Sasha smiled. "Yes, of course."

Quinn kissed her hand. Together, they hurried down the street.

The shop was full of hanks of flyspecked meat hanging from skews supported by long racks. The moment they entered, the proprietor tried to stop them. Quinn ignored him, moved to the racks, and unhooked one of the long, iron rods that supported several butchered pigs. The meat flopped to the floor in a bloody, insect-crawling pile. Behind the shop, the pigs that had not yet been dressed were squealing, already alerted to impending danger. Good, Sasha thought. Their distress would undoubtedly draw She on. Meanwhile, the shop owner threatened to fetch the local constable before racing off, which was just as well. The sooner the police got here the better. Sasha picked up several long butcher knives and secured them to her waist with the catgut the shop owner kept behind the service counter. She imagined the two of them looked like wild, primitive cave people.

Back in the street, Quinn had caught some horses pulling an abandoned coach. "Help me, Sasha," he said. Then he spotted her knives. "Find me catgut, as much as you can."

Sasha helped him walk the horses to the front of the butcher shop, then returned to the counter and the butcher's supply of catgut on an enormous spool. She kicked it onto the floor and rolled it out into the street. Quinn had set the horses free and was using the coach as a brace for the rod. Already Sasha could see what he was up to.

"Will She come?" she asked. "Do you think the pigs will be enough to attract her?"

"Let's hope." He took the catgut and the knife she had found and began winding the tough, fibrous material around the rod to hold it in place so it projected like a javelin from the floor of the coach up through one window.

"I should get more knives," she said, her heart racing. And then, for one moment, she stopped. "I love you, Quinn."

He looked up as she reached for one of the horses standing nearby, eating from a barrel of apples at the grocers next door, and it was only then that she realized her mistake. He knew what she was going to attempt. What she *had* to attempt. Quinn was finished, so feverish there was no way he could do more than he was doing right now. It was up to her. But that didn't mean Quinn was happy about it. "Sasha...don't."

"Don't worry about me," she told him. She pulled the broken reins of the horse around and slipped up onto the long, warm back of the animal. For one moment, she reveled in its familiarity, then she turned the animal's head to smile at Quinn. "I have every intention of returning so you have the opportunity to make a proper wife of me."

"Sasha, I absolutely forbid you from doing this thing!"

By that time, she was already halfway up the street, and Quinn's voice was a distant echo. She resolved to obey him *after* they were married. And, of course, if she lived long enough to do so.

On her shoulder, Newton chattered a warning seconds before She leaped out at her from a narrow side street, much swifter and more graceful than Sasha had anticipated. The horse reared and she screamed and held tight as the Ceratosaurus's fetid breath blew down at her. She jerked the horse's head to one side, and just in time as the enormous slavering jaws clacked shut inches away from her, spattering her with hot saliva and blood from her already numerous kills.

Sasha jerked the horse's head around, and for one scary moment, the horse's hooves slid on the cobblestones, then she righted herself and Sasha kicked her in the sides and they were off with Sasha shaking the reins. She could practically feel She's hot breath on her neck, feel her heat like a blast furnace as she followed. She snapped, and Sasha felt the tip of one braid break away. She resisted the urge to scream.

The cobblestoned streets trembled and cracked as Sasha drove the horse on, dodging the debris strewn across the abandoned street.

She roared, the sound nearly stumbling Sasha's horse with the force of it. Only her long experience in riding at her Aunt Margaret's farm allowed her to regain control of the panicked animal and direct her down the hill toward Quinn and his homemade trap. As Sasha closed it, she eased the horse to one side.

She, blinded, desperate, raging, never saw the trap. The rod sank deep into She's belly, carried along by her own momentum. The whole coach collapsed onto its side, but the damage was already done. She screamed as she fell upon the coach, the rod still embedded in her belly, her voice venting all of her rage and her pain, her voice amplified by her nasal horn to a near-deafening pitch so that Sasha toppled off her irate horse and found herself tumbling on the ground only a few yards away. She clapped her hands over her ears, and still, the sound filled her head until she felt tears spring to life in her eyes. Quinn appeared beside her and she reached up and clutched him about the neck, burying her face in his shirt, sobbing in victory and utter exhaustion. They clung to each other and waited, trembling, as She's cries faltered and the great beast collapsed, kicking and writhing in the street.

Lord Sirius Quinn and Sasha Strange stayed with her until it was over, until the last breath went out of her huge, tortured body, and her respiration slowed and finally stopped. The beast filled the narrow street with her blood and her chaos, but they stayed and watched over her death until the police finally arrived and led them away.

| 78 |

London, England

10 Years Later

Even though she had come to love Africa, Sasha found herself eagerly awaiting the sound of the *Britannia's* steam whistle. The moment she heard it, she excused herself from her family's dining table in a very ladylike manner, then raced like an overly exuberant child up the stairs to the starboard deck. From there, she rushed to the rails and peered out at sea at the Port of London. Distantly, little more than a dim line on the horizon, was the Customs House and Tower Bridge. She leaned out precariously far in the salty, foggy air, hoping to catch a better view of it. A stiff wind caught her unawares, and her best hat slid off the shiny reams of braids piled high on her head and blew down into the sea. "Oh bloody hell!" she cried, making a snatch at it even though she knew it was hopeless.

A steward standing nearby looked on her with great alarm.

"Sasha?" said a voice behind her, coming out of the fog. "Sasha, what are you up to, my dear?"

She continued to lean out. "Oh, bugger it all! I lost my hat!" she cried.

A pair of large powerful hands took her by the waist and hauled her back to safety. "Well, I don't need *you* going over the rail as well, my dear," Quinn said.

"Oh, Quinn, you worry so much," she told him, turning about and smiling demurely. Despite the years, he was still very fit and strong, despite his now silvery hair. He was very brown from the hard work of cultivating their fields. And very wealthy. They had done well in building their fortune together.

He raised his brows at that. "I always worry about you, my dear. I have to."

"What happened to Mama?" their son Isaac asked, creeping up to the rail to peer over, his little sister carefully in tow. Newton clung to Elizabeth's neck, chattering excitedly.

"Mama has hat problems. Nothing a trip to the hat shop wouldn't fix," Quinn told him, laying his big hand protectively on Isaac's shoulder before bending to scoop Elizabeth into his arms. He lifted the girl high until she pointed at Tower Bridge and said *Bridge* very carefully, drawing the letters out so they sounded a bit too much like *Breech*.

Isaac laughed at his sister. He was almost ten, but his sister was a dainty, shy five years old…and the complete and utter apple of her Papa's eye. As far as Quinn was concerned, she could do no wrong. He did anything she asked, gave her anything she requested—the greatest of things humbled by the smallest. Elizabeth did not like to socialize quite the way their precocious Isaac did, but she was talented in many other aspects. She loved shiny things, loved taking them apart to understand how they functioned. Quinn had not had a decent pocket watch in years.

"Dada, I want to see the Bridge," Isaac said, pulling very hard on Quinn's worsted striped suit coat.

Sasha put her hand on the back of the boy's neck. "You can see the Bridge from where you are."

"No, I want Dada to lift me up!"

Sasha eyed their son. "Isaac."

"It's perfectly all right, my dear." Quinn handed Elizabeth off to her and lifted the boy, wrinkling his suit coat terribly just so he could set the boy on his shoulders. Finally, Isaac, pleased, started pointing at landmarks and naming them one by one.

"Nanny taught us all of them," he stated imperiously, reminding Sasha very much of his father. His blue eyes, his red hair, his arrogant stance, and sometimes overbearing temperament were all Quinn through and through. The only thing that saved the boy from the switch at times was the fact that he was absolutely fearless and fiercely protective of his sister. "I know *all* of them. I'll *never* get lost in London."

"Don't be so sure of that, young man," Quinn told him. "London is a very dangerous place."

"Quinn, you worry far too much," Sasha told him, taking her husband by the arm while still juggling Elizabeth. "London is a perfectly wonderful place, Isaac," she said, managed to pull an altered pair of opera glasses from the case around her neck. They allowed her to see at a much greater distance and were one of her favorite inventions. With two precocious children filling their house, plus all her inventions, Sasha had become very good at multitasking.

"I have to worry every minute, Sasha," Quinn said. "He's your son."

In the beginning, Sasha had lived in fear that Quinn would lose his temper with their very trying boy. She'd even feared that something of Quinn's father would surface in him. But Quinn was a patient and loving father, a good husband, even if he *was* rather proud and arrogant at times. That had never changed. And though he'd certainly mellowed over the years, he was still capable of his infamous redheaded anger.

She and Quinn sometimes engaged in rows so powerful it drove their nanny and other staff members right out of their house in Africa. It always began the same way, with Sasha doing something Quinn regarded as dangerous. It ended the same way too, usually with one or both of them laughing as they quickly forgot what they were fighting about. By now, the staff was utterly convinced their master and mistress were mad with jungle fever.

The *Britannia* had finally docked and the gangway was being lowered. Sasha scanned the faces of those waiting on the receiving dock. It only took her seconds before she spotted her father and his coach. Holding Elizabeth tight, she raced down the plank to the sound of Quinn cautioning her not to trip.

Papa held his arms out to her. "Sasha, my darling!"

She hugged her Papa tight with Elizabeth caught between them as people made a steady stream around the two of them. This was their first visit in five years, and the first he was seeing his granddaughter. He was delighted by Elizabeth's huge brown eyes, so like her mother's, he said, and her curling ginger hair, which Quinn seemed doomed to grant all his offspring.

Quinn wandered over, piloting Isaac forward despite the boy's desire to run off in every direction, and shook his best friend's hand heartily. Albertus Strange, large and round and clutching his walking stick, smiled cheekily at his son-in-law. "You look fine, fine, my friend! How is she treating you?"

Quinn put a hand over his heart and mocked bowed. "Every day is a tribulation, sir."

Sasha twisted her face into a scowl.

"Now, see there, you've made her angry, Sirius."

"She never stays that way for long, I assure you." Quinn reached across the space between them and ran his hands over his wife's cornrows, a familiar gesture that Sasha had come to relish. "Albertus, she is a delight...except for her cooking, her housekeeping, and the fact that she will not obey her husband at all and contends everything I say. She told me only last week that she wants to hunt lions." He raised his brows at that. "We have a pair of rogues haunting one of our villages just outside Zimbabwe."

Albertus gave his daughter a disapproving look. "Lions, is it?"

"I've hunted worst," she told them, waving her homemade spyglasses around. Why did the men in her life insist she could not handle herself? Her history proved otherwise. With a javelin, she could hunt anything.

Isaac pulled on his father's hand. "I want to hunt lions, Dada!"

"You absolutely cannot hunt lions, Isaac," Sasha insisted. "Not unless I can."

Albertus smiled appreciably on his daughter and touched her braids. "I think, young lady, you'd best hunt a hat!"

Despite the rather deceptive way he'd brought her and Quinn together, she had long ago learned to forgive her father his meddling. After all, he'd been right. Quinn was the best thing that had ever happened to her. And he said the same of her.

He no longer drank or fought. He had long ago paid off his debtors, and together they had restored his big, rambling home in Rhodesia and built an incredibly rich life together. That did not mean they had a perfect marriage because they most certainly did not, but Quinn was faithful and loving. He was gentle with his children. Sasha could easily forgive him for his occasional bouts of stubbornness or high-handed arrogance. After all, in the end, he usually did what she wanted him to do.

She was about to retort her father's statement when a caddy of police pulled up in one of those new motorized coaches that were all the rage in London these days. The lead man jumped out and introduced himself as the Chief Inspector and asked to speak to Lord Sirius Quinn immediately. Frowning, Quinn moved to the fore of the group and said, "I'm Lord Quinn. What can I do for you gentleman today?"

"You are the man who slew the Ceratosaurus just ten years ago, yeah?" He spoke with a very broad Cockney accent.

"I am. Well, my wife and I did," he said, reaching for her hand and pulling her alongside him.

"Yes, well, the boys and I be wondering if you'd be willing to give us a hand. It seems a very strange creature was sighted circling the Bow Bells. A large creature, they say, at least as wide as four men together. My boys swear it were a dragon."

"A dragon?" Quinn said, impressed. Then he turned to Sasha. "My dear, when you were fine-tuning that Tuning Machine, could you have sent one of the pterosaurs through by accident?"

Sasha shrugged. "It's possible, of course. But we won't know until we see it."

Quinn turned back to the police. "Sir, take us to the Bells."

The Chief Inspector looked worried. "I dare say, it might still be roosting up there, sir."

"All the same, we absolutely *must* see it."

The man smiled grimly. "Come along, then, sir."

Quinn handed off his children to their grandfather and started toward the cab. Sasha kissed her father on the cheek and begged him to look after Isaac and Elizabeth while she was gone. "You be nothing but a gentleman for your grandfather," she warned Isaac, wagging her finger in his face. She cuddled Elizabeth close, who was trying very hard to say *Dragon*, before following her husband over to the police cab.

"We'll need javelins, of course," she insisted, linking her arm through his. "And a bow and a quiver of arrows."

"Yes, of course, my dear."

The Chief Inspector climbed up into the cab but looked bemused. "You are bringing your wife, sir?"

Quinn looked insulted as he climbed in after the man. "Yes, of course," he said, helping Sasha up into the cab after him. "Sir, I never hunt dragons without my wife!"

The End

ABOUT THE AUTHOR

K.H. Koehler is the author of various novels and novellas in the genres of horror, SF, dark fantasy, steampunk, and young and new adult. She is the owner of KH Koehler Books and KH Koehler Design, which specializes in graphic design and professional copyediting. Her books are widely available at all major online distributors and her covers have appeared on numerous books in many different genres. Her short work has appeared in various anthologies, and her novel series include *The Kaiju Hunter, A Clockwork Vampire, The Nick Englebrecht Mysteries,* and *The Archaeologists.* She is the author of multiple Amazon bestsellers and was one of the founders and chief editors of KHP Publishers, which published genre fiction from 2001 to 2015. She has over fifteen years of experience in the publishing industry as a writer, ghostwriter, copyeditor, commercial book cover designer, formatter, and marketer. Visit her website at https://khkoehler.net.

www.ingramcontent.com/pod-product-compliance
Lightning Source LLC
LaVergne TN
LVHW031609060526
838201LV00065B/4785